# THE ART OF FORGETTING

CAMILLE NOE PAGÁN

# the art
*of*
# forgetting

DUTTON

DUTTON
Published by Penguin Group (USA) Inc.
375 Hudson Street, New York, New York 10014, U.S.A.
Penguin Group (Canada), 90 Eglinton Avenue East, Suite 700, Toronto, Ontario M4P
2Y3, Canada (a division of Pearson Penguin Canada Inc.); Penguin Books Ltd, 80 Strand,
London WC2R 0RL, England; Penguin Ireland, 25 St Stephen's Green, Dublin 2, Ireland
(a division of Penguin Books Ltd); Penguin Group (Australia), 250 Camberwell Road,
Camberwell, Victoria 3124, Australia (a division of Pearson Australia Group Pty Ltd);
Penguin Books India Pvt Ltd, 11 Community Centre, Panchsheel Park, New Delhi—110
017, India; Penguin Group (NZ), 67 Apollo Drive, Rosedale, North Shore 0632, New Zealand (a division of Pearson New Zealand Ltd); Penguin Books (South Africa) (Pty) Ltd,
24 Sturdee Avenue, Rosebank, Johannesburg 2196, South Africa

Penguin Books Ltd, Registered Offices: 80 Strand, London WC2R 0RL, England

Published by Dutton, a member of Penguin Group (USA) Inc.

First printing, June 2011
1   3   5   7   9   10   8   6   4   2

REGISTERED TRADEMARK—MARCA REGISTRADA

LIBRARY OF CONGRESS CATALOGING-IN-PUBLICATION DATA
Noe Pagán, Camille.
The art of forgetting / Camille Noe Pagán.
p. cm.
ISBN 978-0-525-95219-0 (hardcover)
1. Women editors—Fiction.   2. Female friendship—Fiction.   3. Memory disorders—
Fiction.   4. New York (N.Y.)—Fiction.   5. Psychological fiction.   I. Title.
PS3616.A33665A89 2011
813'.6—dc22        2010042277

Printed in the United States of America
Set in Celeste
Designed by Amy Hill

PUBLISHER'S NOTE

*To JP and Indira—*
*for all of my best memories.*

*Forgiveness means giving up*
*all hope of a better past.*

—LILY TOMLIN

# THE ART OF FORGETTING

# One

There is only one way to boost your metabolism: exercise. I realize this in the middle of editing an article about how cayenne pepper, cinnamon extract, and massive amounts of coffee might, just *might,* trick your body into burning more calories (but probably not). I'm contemplating how to nicely tell my boss that the story is a load of unprintable crap when the phone rings.

Sigh. I hate the phone. Then again, I'm hating this story, so I pick up.

"Is this Marissa Rogers, the world-renowned weight-loss expert?"

"Hey, Jules," I say, relieved it's my best friend and not a publicist pitching me the latest fat-melting wonder drug. "You won't believe this drivel I'm working on."

"Let me guess: a recipe for vegan cardboard cookies?"

"That sounds like something you'd actually eat." I laugh, referring to Julia's endless quest to maintain her whippet-thin figure. "You're close, though. One more try."

"Um . . . one hundred forty-two ways to lose the last five pounds."

"Very close, but no dice," I tell her. "Metabolism makeovers."

Julia snorts. "I cannot believe you're doing that story *again*."

"I know. We've only covered it half a dozen times this year," I say, and it's not entirely untrue. *Svelte*, like many health magazines, essentially runs the same ten articles over and over, each one tweaked ever so slightly so it doesn't sound identical to the last. Metabolism stories, I have decided, hover near the top of our most-repeated topics: above colonics (explosive but effective) but below celebrity get-skinny secrets (diet and exercise, which is Hollywood parlance for Adderall and anorexia).

An e-mail alert pops up in the right corner of my computer screen. As soon as I click it closed, another appears, and then another. "Listen, I have to run if I'm going to get out the door in time for tonight," I tell Julia. "We're still on, right?"

"Definitely," she says. "That's actually why I'm calling. I can't *wait* to see you. But any chance you can do six thirty? I'm running the tiniest bit behind." Then she adds in her sweetest voice, "I just have to pick up a little something."

"No presents!" I scold her. "Tonight is my treat to you. You're the one who got promoted, remember?" I say, referring to her recent bump to senior publicist for the New York City Ballet.

"This isn't a present, nut job."

"Julia."

"*Marissa*," she mocks me. I can practically feel her smiling on the other side of the phone. "See you there. Don't be late!"

Two hours and half a glass of cabernet later, I'm sitting by a window at the restaurant and trying not to be irritated, although it's nearly seven and Julia is nowhere to be seen. If I were waiting for anyone else, I would have left fifteen minutes ago; having been raised by a mother who's perpetually behind schedule, I have no tolerance for tardiness. But in this instance, I have only myself to blame, because I know full well that the chances of Julia showing up when she says she will are on par with polar bears floating down the Hudson River.

I take another sip of my wine and poke at the chunk of cheese the waiter gave me to sample (not realizing that at nine grams of fat per minuscule serving, it isn't going anywhere near my mouth). Outside the window, Gramercy is buzzing with life. I love this area, with its low-hanging magnolia trees and crumbling brownstones. There's still a little daylight left, and like so many Septembers in New York, it is warm enough that people are still strolling about in shorts and sandals.

In the distance, I spot a familiar brunette striding down Irving Place and I'm struck with a fleeting pang of envy; unlike Julia, I will never be the woman who gets up-and-down looks from fellow pedestrians. It's not that she's the Victoria's Secret type— in a city full of models that would hardly be noteworthy. But her heart-shaped face and wide gray eyes are striking, and she carries herself with a confidence that invites staring. When we're out, people often stop her to ask her where she's from. Each time, she deadpans a new answer—*Honduras. Ukraine. Syria*—in her best Midwestern accent, then doubles over in laughter.

As Julia comes into focus, I see that she's holding an enormous bouquet of white peonies, undoubtedly for me. Out of season, the flowers must have cost a fortune, but it's unlikely she even asked about the price before passing her credit card to the florist. I once told her I felt guilty that she always seemed to be bringing me some small token. "My love language is gift giving; yours is quality time," she informed me matter-of-factly, and so I eventually stopped protesting when she showed up with a bag of coffee she picked up in San Juan, a blown-glass ornament she found at a sidewalk sale, or like today, flowers.

Julia makes her way down the street in record time, no doubt aware that I've been waiting. She reaches the corner, and seeing me through the window across the street, gives me an enormous smile. I lift my wineglass to wave at her and she waves back, then does a little skip toward me and steps into the street.

Before I even put my glass back on the table, a cab hits her.

The accident unfolds so quickly that I am barely able to process the streak of yellow metal that slams into Julia, tossing her off its hood and onto the pavement.

I don't scream. In fact, I do nothing until I realize my pants are wet; I've spilled wine all over them. I leap up and run out the door, pushing my way through the small crowd that has gathered. Everyone is talking at once, and I overhear one frightening snippet of conversation after another: "Definitely bloody," "Skull fracture," "Natasha Richardson," "*Dead.*"

Trying to shake off the shock I'm feeling, I steel myself for a gruesome scenario. When I finally reach Julia, though, she's not only conscious, but actually trying to push herself into a sitting position. Her hair is hanging in her face and her right knee, poking out from ripped tights, is bleeding. Otherwise, she looks no more flustered than if she'd just tripped.

She looks up at me, then glances wistfully at the white petals strewn around her. "Your flowers."

"Julia! Are you okay?" My mouth is dry, and there is a metallic taste on my tongue. "Don't worry about the flowers. Let's get you out of the street."

An older woman with a heavy New York accent wags her finger at Julia. "Young lady, you hit your head, and *good.* You'd best get yourself to a hospital."

"I called 911," the cabdriver says to no one in particular. The rims of his eyes are red, and I realize he has been crying.

"No hospital," Julia says, slowly rising to her feet. "I'm fine." She points at the cabbie weakly. "You could have killed me."

I obviously look worried, because Julia says, "I'm okay. Just wobbly."

"Of course. Why don't you go sit down?" I snatch her leather clutch off the street. "I'll get the driver's info for you."

"Thanks," she tells me, and allows a banker type, who is obviously smitten, to walk her over to a bench in front of the restaurant.

"That woman was right, hon. You need to get checked out," I call back, digging through my purse for a pen and paper—not an easy feat, as I can't stop shaking. I'm having a hard time processing the fact that my best friend was just nearly flattened by oncoming traffic. "You don't want to find out you fractured something when you show up to dance practice tomorrow."

The crowd quickly thins out, and I wait at the curb for the cabdriver to get his registration and insurance card. After triple-checking the info I scribbled down, I turn back to the restaurant.

Immediately, I know something is wrong. Julia is hunched over on the bench, her hands cupped around her ears. "I have a headache," she says. She sways slightly as she attempts to look up at me, and I spot a small trickle of blood under her right nostril. Then she groans. "I might be sick."

In spite of myself, I cringe—I can't stand the sight or smell of vomit. But instead of throwing up, Julia slumps over on the bench before the banker can grab her.

"Ambulance coming?" she manages to mumble.

Then she passes out.

# Two

At fourteen, I lobbied my mother to send me to the magnet high school in Ann Arbor. Middle school had been hell; I wanted a clean break from my few flaky friends and, more important, the bullies who'd tormented me incessantly. I also knew that the high school I was heading to in Ypsilanti, where we lived, was one of the worst in the state. I relayed this information to my mother, who promptly took the pen I was holding and signed the transfer request form I'd already taken the liberty of filling out.

The minute I stepped through the swinging double doors of Kennedy High, I regretted my decision. The kids in the hallway were practically *Beverly Hills, 90210* extras. The girls, whose faces were painted with just enough makeup to look alluringly trashy, wore ruffled blouses and stretch stirrup pants that I could not only not afford, but that would look ridiculous on my short, curvy figure. And unlike the guys from my neighborhood—whose idea of style involved Cross Colors T-shirts and jeans that hung around their knees—Kennedy seemed to be swarming with quarterback types in pastel polo sweaters and jeans that actually—gasp—fit. It was clearly not my scene.

This suspicion was confirmed in homeroom when not a single living soul spoke to me. I tried a smile and a cheery "Hi!" several times, but even the prepubescent dork to my left, clad in tight pants and a superfro, just stared back.

By lunch I was convinced I'd just made the biggest mistake of my teenage life. I tried to put on my best game face as I picked up my blue lunch tray and shuffled through the lunch line, but as I walked out into the crowded lunchroom and realized I had no one to sit with, I was fighting back tears.

Suddenly, I heard: "Over here!"

There was Julia, motioning me to her table. I was so surprised that I actually looked over my shoulder to make sure she wasn't talking to someone else. "No, you, silly." She laughed, and motioned to the seat next to her. "Marissa, right? I saw you in biology." I stared blankly. I'd certainly seen Julia, holding court among a crowd of perfectly coiffed Jennifers and Jills, but didn't think she'd so much as glanced my way.

She continued. "I was just telling Jen here"—the blonde next to her, I gathered—"that you have the best hair! What do you do to it?"

I smiled, simultaneously embarrassed and flattered. I had realized long before high school that I'm accurately described as average looking. The one thing notable about me is my hair: thick, wavy, and auburn-verging-on-red; it is by far my best feature, and I've always been more than a little vain about it.

"Oh my gosh. Thank you," I told her. "I don't do anything special. Really. Aussie shampoo and a little Aqua Net and I'm done."

"So fabulous! I'm jealous," she told me. That Julia, already stunning at fourteen, would be envious of *me* was laughable, although I certainly wasn't going to point this out. She put her arm around my shoulders. "Come sit down and I'll introduce you to everyone. I know the girls are just going to love you."

As I predicted, the Jennifers did not, in fact, love me. But to my astonishment, Julia did. "You're *hilarious.*" She giggled after I muttered some witticism, shooting Jen S., formerly known as "the funny one," a sharp look for daring to roll her eyes at the compliment. It soon became apparent that although gorgeous, charismatic Julia loved being surrounded by admirers, she lacked the one thing she really wanted: a confidant. She grew weary, she confessed to me, of her friends' utter lack of curiosity about anything outside of fashion and football players. "But you and I, Marissa," she told me conspiratorially, "now, *we* can talk about anything." And we did: We'd stay up until dawn discussing whether Emily Dickinson was happy being alone, if 7-Eleven Slurpees were worth the calories, and most often, how much better life would be when we finally became adults and we could flee Michigan for greener pastures—specifically, New York, where she would take the ballet world by storm and I would become the youngest editor-in-chief in magazine history.

It wasn't long before we were inseparable. Being Julia's best friend was like being granted a ticket into a fun, frantic, and extremely privileged world, and the first six months were nothing if not a crash course in keeping up. "You haven't heard of Pearl Jam?!" Julia squealed upon learning yet another of my inadequacies. No matter; she spent the next two days introducing me to grunge. When I revealed my utter lack of knowledge about the male anatomy, she filled me in on what sex ed class had left out. And although she never said a word about my pitiful wardrobe, we soon began embarking on regular Saturday shopping trips where she taught me to pick the best pieces from thrift shops and to dress so my ample hips became an asset.

Julia was a live wire, and everything she touched became electrified—including me. I felt like she had woken me up after years of deep sleep. How could I not have known that my life had been so boring? And yet we seemed to be in such different stratospheres that I couldn't shake the feeling that I was a charity case.

As the months wore on, I began to understand that Julia's shiny veneer hid a jagged, imperfect center. The only child of wealthy parents, she was used to getting her way and, unlike me, had zero qualms about making a scene if she didn't. Although she had more self-confidence than anyone I'd ever met, she was also extremely possessive. "You and Heather have been spending an awful lot of time together," she once pouted about my biology partner, and not wanting to rock the boat, I'd quietly requested that my teacher pair me with someone "less talkative," leaving poor Heather baffled. Mostly, though, I was the one to calm and comfort her, to help keep her sharp edges hidden from the rest of the world.

Late one night our freshman year, she called me crying. "Mar, come over now. I can't deal." Worried out of my mind, I snuck out, hopped on the bus, and then walked half a mile from the stop to the Ferrars' house, where I quietly let myself in.

Julia's room was empty, so I checked the library that her parents had transformed into a dance studio. There, I found her dressed in a T-shirt, tights, and pointe shoes, tears running down her face.

"God, what happened?" I asked. My heart was beating a mile a minute; I had never seen her like this before.

"It's my parents," she said, wiping her cheek with the back of her hands. "They don't understand me at all. Sometimes I feel like they hate me."

I draped my arm on her thin back as a makeshift hug. "Your parents adore you. You have no idea how lucky you are."

"No!" she wailed. "They're blind. Daddy says Harvard, not Juilliard. I don't want to go to Harvard. What dancer goes to *Harvard*? His lawyer brain is so obsessed with logic that he can't see my destiny." She began to cry again.

I wouldn't dream of saying it out loud, but I didn't understand why Julia was so upset with her parents. My mother—having assumed the role of sole parent when my sister, Sarah, and I were still in elementary school—worked long hours, and when she was around, her idea of parenting consisted of telling us what we were doing wrong. "Marissa, I don't think that skirt is doing you any favors," she'd say by way of a greeting when we ran into each other in the bathroom in the morning. Sometimes I'd try to get her attention by telling her something outrageous, like that I wouldn't be home until two a.m. and that they might be serving beer at the party I was going to, and she'd look at me from behind her romance novel and mutter, "You're a smart girl. Use your head and avoid any guy who reminds you of your father." As for college, she made it clear that if I chose to go, I was on my own, which made an Ivy League education out of the question.

Julia's parents, on the other hand, seemed to think that the sky was the limit—for both of us. "I bet you're the next Katharine Graham," Grace would tell me enthusiastically as I pored over my English notes in her living room after school. Unlike my mother— who seemed to know so little about me that she was genuinely shocked each time I told her that I didn't like mayonnaise—Grace knew that I loved science, even though I was miserable at it, and that I had a weakness for peanut butter chocolate bars. She even knew I had a crush on Adam Johnson, a junior who I suspected was in love with Julia. That was the thing: Grace and Jim sincerely seemed to *like* their daughter, and me, too. Grace would gab with us for hours if we let her. Jim pretended to be strict: "No dancing until you've finished your homework," he'd tell Julia. But he was always smiling as he scolded, giving you the impression he barely meant what he was saying. I loved the Ferrars so much that when I'd wake up after spending the night at Julia's, I'd pad into their enormous kitchen to pour myself coffee and pretend I was home.

"Jules, you have another three years to change his mind," I comforted her. "Besides, where you go to school isn't important. You're going to be a star, no matter what."

"You think so?" she said after a minute.

"You know I do," I said, gently pushing her hair out of her eyes. "And so does everyone else."

"Oh, Marissa. What would I do without you? Just when I think I'm going to jump, you're there to talk me off the ledge."

"That's what friends are for, right?" I soothed. "Besides, you'd do the same for me. Now, let's stop worrying about your parents and start worrying about you being the world's most amazing dancer. Why don't you show me that *Giselle* scene you've been rehearsing?"

"Okay," she said with a weak smile, tightening the ribbons on her toe shoes. "I'll start from the top."

It was that night that I realized I was far from a charity case. The truth was, Julia needed me as much as I needed her.

# Three

The human brain contains billions upon billions of neurons. Microscopic nerve cells that operate not unlike worker bees, they connect and communicate millions of times in the span of a single second. It is their conversations that allow us to move, see, think, breathe, live. But when the brain is shaken by a blunt force, its fragile neural fibers are stretched, rendering them brittle and inefficient. And if the force is strong enough—as it was, I learn, with Julia's accident—the ravaged neurons die, and with them, memories and abilities and countless other possibilities that may not become apparent for weeks and even months to come. This is why although Julia is alive, it is not clear whether or not she is okay.

In the waiting room, Dave and I are greeted by a suspiciously cheery Doogie Howser look-alike, who introduces himself as Julia's neurologist. Doogie tells us that Julia is awake, and that we can see her soon.

"Luckily, her skull wasn't fractured and the CAT scan didn't show any major clotting. That would have been much worse than what we're dealing with here," says Doogie emphatically. "Blood clots put pressure on the brain, cutting off oxygen and potentially causing severe damage. We're talking persistent vegetative state–type damage." I must look horrified, because he leans in and says, "What I'm trying to say is, your friend is extremely fortunate. Many people who are in an accident of this nature don't survive."

"Thanks, Doc. We got it," Dave says curtly, letting him know that there's no need to delve into worst-case scenarios. He is standing with his hands in the pockets of his jeans, so calm that we might as well be waiting to be seated at a restaurant. I always thought it was cheesy when people referred to their significant other as their "rock." But over the three years we've been dating, I've come to see Dave that way (not that I'd ever say it out loud). He's the steadiest, most in-control person I've ever met—and I say this as someone who is invariably described as "extremely dependable" on her performance review. I suspect he is the sole reason I'm not catatonic right now.

Doogie, who is actually named Dr. Bauer, tells us that Julia's brain shows some signs of bruising and swelling. "When she hit the pavement, her brain lagged behind the speed at which her skull moved," he explains. "That made it drag on the skull's rough edges, causing what we refer to as a brain contusion." I wince and Dave puts his hand firmly on my back, as if to brace me from the impact of the doctor's words.

"It's not great," Dr. Bauer acknowledges. "The tricky part is, it's difficult to tell on a CAT scan exactly how much neural tissue was affected."

He rubs his forehead, suddenly looking less like a preppy collegiate and more like a weary physician. "I don't know what your friend was like before her accident. But traumatic brain injury can play out in many ways. She may seem okay tomorrow, then show signs of serious memory loss a week from now. She might be a wreck next week, and then recover over the course of several months, or even years. We won't know until we get there."

I wonder how many times a year he must have to give some version of this speech. It occurs to me that neither his prestigious position nor his enormous salary spares him from the business of delivering bad news. It's like my mom bluntly informing anyone who seems impressed that I'm an editor at a glossy magazine: "When it comes down to it, every job involves shoveling crap."

"When is Julia's family coming?" Dr. Bauer asks me.

"Her parents are on a plane on their way here."

"That's good." He nods. "Husband? Boyfriend?"

I shake my head. As far as I can recall, Julia's ex is somewhere in France, choreographing a modern dance production, and they haven't spoken in more than a year anyway.

"Well, it's good that you're here. Julia is going to need a lot of support throughout her recovery," Dr. Bauer says. "The one thing I must stress is that she may not be the same person you knew two days ago. She might forget things—things you've done together, but also people, and even simple words. It's too soon to tell, but her mobility could be impaired, and her mood may be off, too. What you should remember is that we're just at the beginning of a very long road."

I'm not sure if he means this is a good thing, or bad.

I'm too afraid to ask.

When Julia calls to me, I immediately think of Dr. Bauer's warning: *She may not be the same person you knew two days ago.*

"Hi," she says with a faint smile, seeming to recognize me. She looks around as though she's just noticing her surroundings for the first time. "Is this the hospital?" she asks.

Her sentence is complete; her words more coherent than I'm expecting. But they're also all wrong. Julia's voice is not the rich, gravelly voice of the friend I have grown up with. Instead, it is high and light, like a middle school girl talking to the boy she has a crush on.

Dave glances at me sideways, just as shocked as I am.

"Yes, hon. You've been here since yesterday. Remember, a taxi hit you?" I ask, approaching the hospital bed. Instead of hugging her, I grab her hand and squeeze it, afraid to come too close to her head, even though it's unbandaged.

Julia blinks at me blankly, and I decide now's not the time to quiz her on what happened yesterday. "I'm so happy to see you," I tell her. "You don't know what a scare you gave me."

"I'm sorry," she says, almost playfully, like a child apologizing because she's been instructed to. Then her eyes dart around suspiciously. "Who are you? Where is my mother?"

"Your mom will be here tomorrow," I respond, trying not to let my voice betray the panic quickly wrapping its tentacles around my heart. "I'm Marissa. Don't you recognize me?"

"Mom," she says, sighing, her voice a little lower this time. It's not obvious if she's saying this to calm herself or is simply incorrectly addressing me. "I'm tired. I want to sleep, but these silly women keep waking me to make sure I'm okay." It occurs to me that by "these silly women," she must mean her nurses. It sounds juvenile and syrupy, and not like something my quick-witted friend would normally say.

She turns back to me and gives me a small smile. "Doctor says I'm lucky."

"I think we're the lucky ones," I tell her, blinking back tears. Sitting in the waiting room last night, I had let my pessimism take over. As I paced the stark blue lobby, my mind spiraled further and further into worst-case scenarios. I imagined being told that Julia had died. I wondered what her funeral would be like, and who would be there, and even whether she would prefer lilies or orchids for the service. I dreaded calling friends of ours to tell them she was dead, and tried to wrap my mind around life without my best friend.

I squeeze Julia's hand again, confirming that she really is sitting here in front of me. Alive.

But as my fingers close around her palm, she jerks away, nearly pulling the IV out of her arm. Her eyes dart from my face to the hospital door, and for a second I expect her to make a run for it.

"What is it, Jules?" I ask her.

"Nothing," she snaps. "It's nothing, Jenny. Don't worry about me."

"Jenny?" I ask. "Jules, it's me. *Marissa.*"

"Oh, I *know* who you are," she says haughtily, instantly reminding me of my grandfather after he developed Alzheimer's. The comparison sends a chill straight down my spine. "Now leave me alone. Do you hear me, Jenny? LEAVE ME ALONE!" she yells, and on instinct, I back away from her bed.

Oblivious to my alarm, Julia yawns, suddenly calm again. She looks at me, her eyelids heavy. "I'm really tired . . . you and Nathan don't mind if I lie down?"

"Of course not," I say, stomach lurching at the mention of my college ex, who looks nothing like Dave. I look over at my boyfriend, who is staring at Julia quizzically but is not nearly as fazed as I by her inability to identify him.

Julia falls asleep right away, but Dave and I stay for another hour. Every few minutes I glance at her chest to make sure she's still breathing, the way I did with my niece when she was an infant. Eventually, a nurse pops her head in the door to Julia's room. "We'll be doing more tests shortly," she says, implying that it's time for us to get going. Sensing my anxiety, she smiles kindly. "Don't you worry. I've been working in neurology for years now, and most patients get better every day. You'll see."

The next morning, I oversleep—tuning out not one but three alarms—and arrive at the hospital long after visiting hours have started. Julia's parents are already in her room, sitting in plastic chairs against the wall. They stand to greet me and try to muster smiles, which come out more like grimaces.

"Where's Julia?" I ask, looking at the crumpled sheets in her empty bed.

"Getting some more tests," says Grace, and dissolves into tears. "I'm sorry," she says, pinching the bridge of her nose to try to stop crying. "I've been holding it together all morning. It's too much."

"Grace, it's just me. Don't apologize," I tell her, and pass her a tissue from the table next to Julia's bed. "I was just as bad yesterday. If Dave hadn't been here . . ."

"Well, if you hadn't been here with Julia," says Jim, "God only knows what *we* would have done. We were in agony on the plane ride over, but we knew you'd at least be taking care of our baby."

"You know she would do the same for me."

"I certainly hope so," he says gravely.

Grace and Jim update me on what they discussed with Julia's team of specialists that morning. I'm surprised to learn that unless anything changes dramatically, Julia won't spend more than a week in the hospital. "There's not much they can do here, other than observe her and give her medication to keep the brain swelling down," Grace tells me. "Dr. Bauer said that although she'll need to go through a lot of therapy, it'll be on an outpatient basis."

"But yesterday she seemed like such a . . ." I want to say "wreck," but it seems inappropriate, if not a little Freudian. Before I have a chance to finish, a nurse rolls Julia back in the room in a wheel-chair. To my delight, her face lights up when she sees me. "Hello!" she says in the same awful, high-pitched voice.

"Hi, Jules," I say. "Do you remember who I am?" I ask, then instantly want to kick myself.

"Of course I remember. Why would I?"

"You mean 'Why *wouldn't* I,'" Grace says gently.

"That's what I said, stupid," says Julia, showing a flash of the same anger she had yesterday, and this time, Grace doesn't correct her.

"Jules, how are you doing today?" I inquire gently, not pushing the name issue. "Are you sore? Does your head hurt?"

The question prompts her to touch the side of her scalp, and Grace quickly reaches out to stop her. "It's f . . . fine," Julia says slowly, and feebly bats her mother's hand away. Then she turns to me. "I have a . . ." She struggles to find the word, and I say nothing, not wanting to irritate her by filling in the gap. The four of us sit in uncomfortable silence as Julia furrows her brow. After what seems to be an eternity, she lies back on the angled mattress and closes her eyes. "Headache," she finally says. "I have a big headache, so they gave me some pills." She opens one eye and starts to sing. *"One pill makes you larger . . . and one pill makes you small . . ."*

Jim and Grace stare, their mouths agape. I decide it's a good sign. If Julia can remember the lyrics to a Jefferson Airplane song written more than a decade before she was born, then all hope isn't lost.

·  ·  ·

The next day, I'm feeling less Pollyanna and a whole lot more Chicken Little. I'll never have my best friend back; I just know it.

"I hate everything," Julia growls when she sees me. "Including you. *Especially* you." I look at her with my mouth open, not sure what to say. She has yet to correctly identify me, and yet somehow she knows she hates me. "They're assholes, too," she says, pointing at her parents. Julia's never been big on swearing, and with her falsetto she sounds slightly ridiculous. This doesn't stop me from being completely terrified of her.

"Uh . . . why, Jules?" I ask her. I glance at Jim and Grace with pleading eyes, completely at a loss for how to respond, but they offer no direction.

"*Because you all fucking suck!*" she screams at the top of her lungs. Then her face crumples and she starts to wail. "I feel horrible. I wish I would have died," she says, writhing in her sheets. "You should have left me there. Why didn't you leave me there, Jenny?!"

Jenny. Three days in the hospital and I am still Jenny. I want to grab her by the shoulders and yell, "Can't you see? It's me. Marissa! Your best friend of sixteen years!" But instead, I smile weakly, not convincing myself or anyone else that I'm okay.

"Now now," says the same nurse I saw the other day. She walks through the door briskly, no-nonsense, and sits on the edge of Julia's bed. "You're just feeling bad because of your brain injury. You don't mean that at all," she says, patting her arm, and for whatever reason, Julia stops hollering.

*Why couldn't I calm her down?* I think, irritated at myself. That's what I do. And yet now, when it really counts, I'm standing here like I'm the one who just took a blow to the head.

When it's clear that Julia isn't going to erupt again, the nurse checks her chart and darts off. She returns and adds a clear liquid to Julia's IV. "This will make you feel better," she soothes. As the medication sets in, Julia's face starts to droop, and within moments, she's passed out.

By the time Dave meets me at the hospital early that evening, Julia is awake, and to my relief, no longer seems hell-bent on ripping out my hair and using it as dental floss. In fact, she practically glows when Dave deposits a stack of tabloids on her lap. "Thank you, Don!" she squeals, and I breathe a sigh of relief: Don is a big step up from Nathan.

Around seven, Grace announces that Julia should probably get some rest. Exhausted from the emotional roller coaster I've been riding all day, I agree, and explain to Julia that although I have to work the next day, I'll be back in the evening.

"Okay," she says nonchalantly, as though I just informed her tonight's Jell-O would be lime flavored. I remind myself not to take it personally.

Grace follows us into the hallway. "I know this isn't easy, and I really appreciate everything you've done," she says, embracing me. "Jim's right; I would have gone out of my mind if I didn't know that you were here." She sighs, looking even older than yesterday under the unyielding glare of the fluorescent hospital lights. "You have my cell if you need to get ahold of me. We're staying at Julia's apartment for now. I don't imagine that we'll be there much over the next few days, but at some point we're going to have to get some of her things together so we can take her back to Ann Arbor."

"What?" Grace's words throw me: Of all the things that I've considered over the last few days, Julia leaving New York was not one of them. Her entire social circle is here, not to mention her job. Julia may not have made it as a professional dancer, but she revels in her publicist position at the Ballet, and lives to dance with her recreational corps. Ann Arbor may be her first home, but it's miles from her passion, and I have to think that there's no way that can be good for her recovery.

Sensing my anxiety, Grace tells me, "Sweetheart, the doctor says that some people with traumatic brain injury are never able to return to their normal lives." I can't help but notice that she sounds like she barely believes what she's saying. "Obviously, we hope Julia is not one of them. She's a fighter, and that makes me optimistic, maybe more than I should be. But you saw her back there. She's going to need at least a year of rehab, and constant monitoring for at least the first two months. Jim and I can't just pick up and leave Michigan."

"But—" Logically, I know she is going to need help. Lots of it. Help that I can't give her. Emotionally, I cannot bear the thought of my best friend halfway across the country when I just came so close to losing her.

Dave interjects. "Marissa, it's been a long day. Let's have this conversation tomorrow."

I nod, although what I really want is to behave like Julia did earlier; I want to scream and throw a fit and tell Grace that I hate her, even though I know she doesn't deserve it. But as raw as I feel right now, I don't have it in me to make a scene. And so I say good night and walk away.

Back at my apartment, Dave and I order takeout and eat silently in front of the TV. When we get in bed, he wraps his arms tightly around me and presses his face into the nape of my neck. "I love you," he whispers to me. "It's going to be okay."

I don't respond. Because the only thing I can think is, *I am all alone.*

# Four

I should be working; the final copy for my stories is due at the end of the week. Instead, I'm browsing Wikipedia entries on traumatic brain injury.

"A subdural hematoma occurs between the dura and the brain membrane . . ."

*Wrong!* I hit "edit" at the right side of the page.

". . . actually occurs within the dura, rather than beneath it as the name implies," I type in, adding a link to the National Institutes of Health site I pinched the info from.

I've been at this for an hour and have corrected three errors already. Each one makes me feel a little less stressed.

"Marissa?"

My boss's voice startles me so much that I jump a few inches out of my Aeron chair.

"Hey, Naomi," I say, trying to look nonchalant as I quickly click the Wikipedia page closed and spin around to face her.

"Can I?" she asks, gesturing to a stool next to my desk. She sits down before I have a chance to answer. Damn. This means she's not just swinging by to gossip about the last episode of *Lost*.

"I wanted to see how you're doing," she says.

"Great," I respond, looking her straight in the eye as if to say, *See? I'm fine.*

"Are you sure?" she asks. Her brown eyes crinkle at the corners, making her look as gentle and motherly as she is. "Because you know it's okay if you're not, right? You can be honest with me."

Damn. I should have known that Naomi—who has volunteered for every charity organization known to man and, as a result, speaks empathy as a second language—would see right through me. The truth is, I am so not okay. It's been three weeks since the accident, and although Julia is now correctly identifying me and no longer seems to want me dead, she's still undeniably touch-and-go.

Then there's the fact that I'm exhausted. I've spent every non-work second with Julia. Going with her whenever I can to round-the-clock appointments with neurologists, neuropsychologists, speech therapists, physical therapists, and occupational therapists (and those are just the ones I can remember). Quizzing her on vocabulary. Catching her up on all of the trivial things going on with our friends and fielding calls from her coworkers, who are anxious to hear about her progress and who are still hoping in vain that she'll return to the office. Waiting for some sign that Julia's going to start acting like herself again.

But I'm not ready to admit this out loud. I have been gunning for a promotion to deputy editor all year and I am not about to let the tiniest crack in my armor jeopardize my chances.

"I'm fine. Promise," I say, cocking my head to the side and smiling like a pageant contestant—a gesture, I realize as I'm doing it, that I've snatched straight from Julia's playbook. "I've already finished the last round of edits for the metabolism article and have almost wrapped up the wacky diet secrets story." It's true. I haven't fallen behind as much as you'd expect from someone who spends half the day doing research on something completely unrelated to her job, because when it comes down to it, I care too much about what other people think to visibly fall apart.

"Of course you have," Naomi says with a grin. Unlike the rest of my coworkers, who have been whittled by years of low-carb diets and triathlon training, she is neither thin nor particularly athletic, and has zero qualms about eating a Big Mac and fries in the middle of an edit meeting. In spite of this, or maybe because of it, she is the most well-liked person in our office. We've gotten on famously since she interviewed me five years ago, and I'd be lying if I said that she wasn't a big part of the reason that I moved up the ladder so quickly at *Svelte*.

"Marissa, you know I think the world of you, and Lynne"—our editor-in-chief—"does, too."

"Thank you," I say sincerely.

"The thing is, you haven't taken a real vacation in close to two years. And taking three days off to be at the hospital with your friend does not count."

"But—"

"*Two years*," Naomi says again, making it sound much worse than it really is.

"I've been busy. You know Claire quit and my pages doubled and—"

"Honey, no offense, but we're a pretty well-oiled ship. I think we can manage without you for a little bit. In fact, that's why Lynne and I want you to take at least a week off before December."

"That soon? But I'm—"

Naomi wags her finger at me. "No excuses. You need a break. Go do something fun."

. . .

At three o'clock, I make a Starbucks run for what will be my second venti cappuccino since this morning. Yes, I have a bit of a caffeine problem. But coffee seems so low on the totem pole of addiction that I can't be bothered to do anything about it, and at this point, I'm not sure how else to get through my day.

A week off. No excuses. What the heck am I going to do with myself? After all, Julia is going home to Ann Arbor with Grace and Jim in a week. Dave is working around the clock like usual, and although it's tempting, I'm not the type to jump on a flight to Kauai by myself.

"Anything else?" the heavily tattooed barista asks after I order my drink.

I eye the pastry case. As someone who has gained and shed the same fifteen pounds more times than I care to count (and who is currently on the losing side of that battle), I don't really do sweets. And since I've been working at a health magazine, I've been especially cautious; my coworkers may give Naomi a pass, but I have little doubt that my days as a diet editor would be numbered if I let myself turn into the heifer my stubborn DNA mandates.

But I suddenly feel ravenous, like I've been doing the Master Cleanse for a month.

"I'll take a chocolate cupcake," I say. I open my wallet to see how much cash I have. "Actually, I'll take a vanilla one, too."


When I arrive at Julia's apartment that evening, she is wearing a new purple robe.

"Do you like it?" she asks, searching my face for a sign that I do.

"Of course," I assure her, although the bulky, nearly fluorescent frock makes her look like she's auditioning to be Barney. Moreover, it's yet another reminder of how things have changed. Before her accident, Julia was on a first-name basis with the salesgirls at the city's chicest boutiques, thanks to the fact that her parents heavily subsidized her moderate salary. But over the past few weeks, Julia has been requesting purple. *Lots* of purple. When she went through her closet—full of dark denim and thin-knit cashmere sweaters—she slammed the door closed with a disgusted look on her face. "These look like they belong to an old lady."

"She insisted on purple, and it was the only thing I could find on short notice," Grace whispers to me. According to one of Julia's neurologists, fixations such as her newfound love of all things lavender are a common side effect of brain injury. "She might grow out of it," the doctor informed Grace and me. But her completely unconvincing tone leveled the hope I'd been feeling that day after Julia, a Scrabble champion, used the word "collude."

"So, Jules, what's been going on?" I ask her, hanging my bag on the door hook and plopping down on the end of her bed.

"Oh, you know. A little of this, a little of that," she says, sounding weirdly secretive, her voice still several octaves too high.

"What do you mean?"

She leans toward me and whispers, "I don't want to say too much. Mom's here."

I glance over at Grace, who is sitting in an armchair in the corner of the room. Of course I feel bad for her, maybe even worse than I feel for myself—which is saying a lot, given the vat of self-pity I've been wallowing in lately. At the same time, I am a little irritated with the woman who mothered me all these years. She has become a permanent fixture in Julia's one-room apartment, and while I can't fault her for her devotion, I also can't help but think that she's monitoring my every interaction with her daughter.

"Just stick to simple conversations," she instructed me the first day Julia was home, as though I hadn't just spent the past week with her in the hospital.

"But the doctor said it was good for me to talk to her like I used to," I told her.

"I don't want anyone to make it worse by bringing up people or things she can't remember," Grace fretted, and too exhausted to argue, I'd agreed.

But I longed to talk to Julia about something—anything—substantial. Although I knew it was ridiculous, I couldn't shake the feeling that if I could just have a solid conversation with her, if I could just remind her of old times, she would start to come back.

"I can go for a walk if you girls want," Grace says, sounding like she doesn't mean it.

"That would be good," I tell her. I am not exactly known for my ability to be direct. But over the past few weeks, I've made a conscious effort to stop beating around the bush. Life being short and whatnot.

"So what's on your mind?" I ask, after Grace leaves.

"Welllll," she says. "I think I'm ready to see people again."

"Oh, hon. That's fantastic! I can set something up with the girls," I tell her, referring to Nina and Sophie, our closest friends. At Grace's request, they've kept their visits to a minimum, but have been anxious to spend time with Julia before she leaves for Michigan.

"Sure," she says ambiguously.

She pauses to blow her bangs out of her eyes, a new habit. "And I want to see Nathan."

I feel like I've been sucker punched. "Excuse me?"

"I miss him. Don't you?" she asks, as though it's not a loaded question.

"I haven't thought about him in years." This is a lie. When Julia said his name in the hospital, it unleashed waves of memories that I've since been trying to surface from. The one thing I had not considered, however, was that her mentioning him may have been more than a fluke.

"That's too bad. He's doing good. Has a new dog," she informs me in a singsong voice.

"How do you know that?" My mind is reeling. This doesn't seem like something you could find out via Google, and I know that he and Julia are not Facebook friends. She must have talked to him recently. The realization is like a second blow to my gut.

"You know," she says, blowing at those damn bangs again.

"Not really."

She holds up her hands, examining her cuticles carefully. I have always thought that people's hands match their personalities. Mine are those of a worker: small and nimble, with straight fingers and square nails. Julia's are slender and beautiful, with long, oval nails that could slice paper.

After a minute, she looks in my direction without meeting my eyes.

"Did I tell you I think Dr. Bauer is in love with me?" It's not obvious if she is deliberately changing the subject, or if she has lost her train of thought, which happens frequently these days. I tell myself to give her the benefit of the doubt.

But I can't help but wonder if she has really broken the pact we made over a decade ago. Or if she's simply forgotten about it.

# Five

Julia and her father never did have a showdown about college; as it turned out, she wasn't accepted to Juilliard or Harvard. Instead, she received a full ride to study dance at Oberlin. Against my better judgment, I stayed in Ann Arbor and went to the University of Michigan, because they gave me more financial aid than any other school I'd applied to.

"We'll see each other at least once a month," Julia assured me the night before she was set to drive to Ohio with her parents. We were sitting in her kitchen, sipping celebratory champagne that her father had supplied. "Of course," I said, clinking my glass with hers, although I had a sinking feeling the next time we'd be face-to-face was winter break. I was, frankly, terrified of being alone. Bolstered by the confidence I gained from my friendship with Julia, high school had been far from the tortured experience I'd expected that first morning at Kennedy. Instead, I'd spread my wings, successfully running for student council, becoming captain of the ecology club, and rising to fourth in my class (two spots behind Julia, who would graduate as salutatorian). And yet in spite of my success, college felt like the great, lonely unknown.

In what I realize now was a self-fulfilling prophecy, I didn't even make an effort to meet people my first two years. *And why should I?* I thought to myself. College was just a holding pattern before I touched down in real life. In what I hoped would be four very short years, Julia and I would reunite in New York and begin our careers in dance and publishing.

With this grand plan in mind, I kept my nose buried in a book my freshman and sophomore years and ignored the über-rich East Coast students in my dorm, who were more than happy to return the favor. When I wanted company, I hit the library with Liza, a hilarious but (as Julia dubbed her) "unfortunate-looking" girl from Portland who had befriended me in journalism class. And although Julia was so wrapped up in dance practice and classes that she rarely made it back to Ann Arbor, we called and e-mailed several times a week, which was better than nothing, I decided. Besides, we had the summers to hang out.

My junior year, Ramen noodle dinners ceased to be a cliché when my scholarship was abruptly slashed by 50 percent because of a budget crisis. I found myself utterly, depressingly broke. Liza encouraged me to apply at the cafeteria where she worked, but I couldn't bear the thought of scooping mashed potatoes onto the plates of snobby New York girls who would likely throw them up an hour later. Instead, I landed a job at a coffee shop downtown called World Cup. At the very least, I figured I would get free coffee.

It was there I started patching together some semblance of a life again. After two years of near-monastic solitude, I thrived on the buzz and commotion of the busy café. And with the exception of

Charlene, my irritable manager, I liked my coworkers: Taryn, who despite seeming perpetually stoned, seemed to know everything about everyone; Ray, a good-natured jock on the six-year plan; and Leila, a Lebanese-American student with razor-sharp wit.

Then there was Nathan. Whose very presence made my knees lock. Whose name I couldn't say aloud without blushing. Who made the crushes I'd had in high school seem entirely laughable.

"Hey," he greeted me, saying it as though we'd known each other for years. He wiped his coffee-covered hands on his apron, but instead of shaking my hand, he just looked at me long and hard.

"Uh, hi," I responded, totally flustered. *Pull it together*, I scolded myself as I proceeded to fumble through the rest of my shift. *He's not even your type.*

But he was. He was exactly my type—I just hadn't known what that was until he was standing in front of me. Nathan wasn't remarkable: average height, solid build, hazel eyes. But there was something about the way he cocked one eyebrow when he was listening carefully, the way he smiled with his whole face, the way he seemed to stare straight into my soul, leaving me simultaneously unnerved and filled with longing. He was, I quickly realized, not unlike Julia: the type of person who could charm anyone. But for whatever reason, he seemed hell-bent on charming me. This reawakened my old suspicion that I gave off a distinct *"rescue me!"* vibe that somehow attracted people like Julia—and Nathan.

I was a mess around him, so I did the only thing I could think to do: act completely and utterly disinterested. My chilly reserve was no match for his warmth. He responded by teasing me, asking me whose hearts I'd been breaking, and nicknaming me "Tiny" (normally annoyed at references to my diminutive stature, this somehow made me dissolve into fits of giggles). It wasn't long before we were swapping Charlene horror stories and having epic literature debates (agreeing that *Ulysses* was James Joyce's elaborate practical joke, but almost coming to blows after he insisted Jane Austen was a repressed romance novelist). It did not go unnoticed that he treated me differently than he did our coworkers. With them, he was jovial, light. But with me, he spoke low, moving close as though he were telling me a secret. And that voice. Even with his flat Midwestern vowels, he had a hint of a drawl, the remnant of a Georgia childhood. All he had to do was say "Marissa" and my heart was ready to drop out of my chest and onto the floor.

One afternoon, he grabbed my black apron and pulled me into the supply closet before our coworkers could see us. I laughed, trying to hide my jitters. Was he going to kiss me? Tell me he knew I was totally obsessed with him?

But he just put his hands on his hips and said, "I think I'm going to murder Charlene if she doesn't knock it off. A guy at Shaman Drum offered me a job the other day when I was there buying books. What do you think, Tiny? Should I take it?"

*What do I think?! I think you shouldn't have pulled me in here to ask me career advice. I think you're standing so close to me that I might die if I can't touch you.*

But I just smiled and said, "You can't get free java at a bookstore, you know."

He frowned. "You know, you're right. I guess I can put up with Charlene if you're here to help me." Then he patted me on the arm like I was a teammate on his intramural soccer team, turning my frustration into raw fury. Was that all I was to him? Was this some kind of game? I was so angry I couldn't see straight, and spent the rest of the afternoon turning cappuccinos into lava-hot lattes, breaking mugs, and muttering near-obscenities at customers.

But the very next day, Nathan asked me to hang out outside

of work. Two days later, he did it again. We started going on long walks through the seedier parts of the city, browsing the shelves at my favorite used bookstore and drinking too many gin and tonics to count at the shacklike house he shared with four other guys. I was both elated and utterly unhinged. Every interaction felt so charged that I thought I might explode from the tension, yet he made no attempt to move things out of the realm of friendship.

But I refused to be the girl who asks "So what are we?" I figured if he wanted something more than friendship, he would go for it. The ball was in his court.

That winter, Julia developed chronic Achilles tendonitis. When she refused to take time off from dancing ("And let the understudy take my place? *Never,*" she scoffed), it became severe. Ignoring pleas from her instructors, it was only after a doctor told her that her tendon was one practice away from rupturing that she agreed to a two-month time-out. Which meant that she finally had time to visit me at school.

I hadn't told her about Nathan. I had never kept a secret from her before; our policy was to tell each other everything, even when it wasn't pretty. Sure, that had resulted in a few arguments, like the time I admitted that I hated her hanging out with two football players who had alcohol-induced rage issues ("But they're so funny most of the time!" she protested, only truly getting angry when I pointed out that what she liked best about them was that they worshipped her).

This time, though, I didn't feel like explaining the quandary that was my relationship with Nathan, nor listening to Julia lecture me on how to take the reins and make it happen. There was another reason, though.

Nathan was so magnetic that I knew there was no way Julia wouldn't be drawn to him. And I didn't want to share him.

I made the mistake of telling Nathan about Julia, however, and he insisted on meeting her when she came to town. "If you don't introduce me, I'm going to have to believe this friend of yours is in the same category as unicorns and fairies," he mock-chided, and reluctantly, I agreed.

I figured World Cup was as good of a place as any to bring the two of them together. Plus, I could take Julia there under the guise of showing her where I worked, rather than for the specific purpose of meeting Nathan. I settled on a Saturday afternoon when the café would be bustling and Nathan would likely be too swamped to chat.

Sadly, this was not the case; World Cup was almost empty when we arrived. "So this is the famous Julia." Nathan grinned, extending a hand to her over the counter. "Let me guess: Americano with a shot of sugar-free vanilla syrup."

"Hello, psychic friend," Julia purred, perching herself on the rattan stool at the bar and somehow managing to look sexy in spite of the cumbersome walking cast on her right foot. "How did you know?"

*Because that's what I drink,* I thought.

"Lucky guess," Nathan responded with a shrug and a smile.

The minute he walked away, Julia turned to me, her eyes open wide. "*Cuuuute.*"

"Yeah, he has a lot of fans."

"Anyone I know?" she asked sneakily.

Julia often joked that she could read me like an open book in large print, and I wondered if she could tell that I was bluffing.

But I'd had practice perfecting my poker face lately, and decided to chance it.

"Nope."

"Huh. You're nuts."

Nathan came back with a mug for each of us. "On the house," he said, grinning at Julia. "But one more thing." He ran back to the kitchen, giving us a shot of his perfect backside in the process and prompting Julia to pretend to swoon. *Hands off,* I thought with irritation, but just smiled benignly at her.

When he returned a minute later, Nathan held two white ramekins, which he presented with a flourish on the bar, then handed us each a tiny silver spoon. "Chocolate lava cakes," he announced. Then, more sheepishly, "It's just a little recipe I'm trying out. I thought you beautiful ladies might make good guinea pigs."

Crusty on the outside but soft in the center, the mini cake was better than the best thing I had ever eaten. "Wow," I almost whispered, savoring the sharp, sweet cocoa that lingered on my tongue. "This is heaven."

"As good as my chocolate madeleines?" Julia asked, the faintest pout detectable in her voice.

"Of course not," I fibbed, reminding myself of what my mother always said: White lies existed for the sole purpose of protecting other people's feelings (not that she was one to worry about inflicting wounds).

"Well, I really *shouldn't* have any. The doctor said I'm not to put on a single pound while my tendon is healing. But in the name of research, I'll have a smidge," Julia said, scooping out a nano-bite of chocolate with her spoon. She sighed and declared it delicious, although I was skeptical about her ability to taste such a small amount.

Nathan was visibly disappointed that Julia didn't make a dent in the cake, but he quickly recovered. "So you bake?"

"I do!" she said, as though he'd just asked her if she wanted to save the planet. "Marissa didn't tell you? I'm legendary in certain circles." She turned to me. "Tell Nathan about my pear tart!"

And so it went for the better part of the afternoon: Nathan would bring something up and Julia would have me explain, at length, how it related back to her or our friendship. For the life of me, I couldn't figure out what her motivation was. Was it a sudden strike of modesty that left her unable to toot her own horn? Was she trying to impress Nathan by showing him what a great friend she was to me? I was baffled, but more alarmed about a growing hunch that Julia was interested in Nathan—and that the feeling might be mutual. After all, he seemed more than happy to slough off to spend the afternoon with her.

When Nathan's shift ended, Julia enthusiastically agreed to his suggestion that the three of us do dinner, so he and I helped her hobble over to Red Rock Grill for burgers. From there, we moved on to Benno's, a dive bar that didn't bother carding even the most obviously underage patrons. I wasn't thrilled about our all-day date, but with the two of them getting on like a house on fire, I didn't feel like I could end the outing without being obvious.

At one point, Nathan ran off to grab more drinks, leaving us at the booth where we were seated at Benno's. "Oh, I missss you," Julia shouted over the bar buzz, throwing her arms around my neck.

"That's just the alcohol talking," I told her, although I was secretly pleased, if only because Julia wasn't telling me how great Nathan was like she had every other time he turned around.

"You and Nathan have probably spent more time together this semester than you and I have in the past two and a half years," she added, changing moods as though she was shifting from one ballet position to another. "It's not fair."

I knew this routine well—but this time, there was a lot more at stake than a new biology partner. "You mean at work? No, our shifts barely overlap," I responded somewhat shakily.

"Oh, come on, Marissa. You guys obviously see a ton of each other outside of work. You can't blame me for wanting to switch places." With whom, she didn't say. I knew that either way, it wasn't good.

As the next hour wore on, my unease only deepened. *Look at him, all dimples from across the booth. And look at her, coyly making sure he knows she's just as smart as she is beautiful.* The two people I cared about most in life were falling in love right in front of me—I just knew it.

After one last round, Nathan walked us back to my dorm. "Tiny," he said to me, making a show of leaning down to give me a kiss on the cheek, even though he had all of six inches on my five-two frame. "See you mañana."

"And tiny dancer," he joked, giving Julia a big hug. I grimaced at him using my nickname for her, although that was easier to swallow than the sight of them embracing. "You stay in touch, okay?" Nathan told her. "Marissa will give you my e-mail address."

Lying on a cot that night as Julia slept in my bed next to me, I tried to convince myself that I was fine; it was just one weekend, it meant nothing. But when Julia left for her parents' house Sunday morning, I had never been so happy to say good-bye. By the time I went to work that night, I had worked myself into such a lather that I could barely look at Nathan. All I could think about was how *close* I'd been to getting him to like me and how Julia weaved her enchanting spell once more, making him forget about me.

"What the hell is going on?" he asked me after saying good night to Taryn, who had closed down the café with us. We were standing on State Street, which was blanketed in snow, and I was shivering, although I couldn't tell if it was from the cold or my nerves. I crossed my arms in front of me for warmth, realizing that it made me look especially defensive but unwilling to change position.

"Nothing."

"Really, Marissa? Because I think failing to utter a single syllable to me all night is something."

The dim light of the streetlamp lit his face, and I could see that he was seething.

*Oh well*, I thought. *It's over now anyway. Might as well.*

"What do you expect me to say, Nathan? That I'm paralyzed with fear that you'll fall for my best friend, like everyone always does? That I feel like an idiot for thinking, for once, that I'd be the lucky one?"

The minute the words escaped my mouth, I wanted to crawl into a snowdrift and die. I was that girl after all.

But when I finally looked at him, he wasn't looking at me with anger, or even pity.

"Marissa," he said softly. "I wanted to hang out with her because she's your friend. I thought it would be a good way to get to know more about *you*, not her. That's it."

He gently unfolded my arms, and pulled me so close that I couldn't tell if the steam rising in front of my eyes was from my breath or his. Tilting my chin up, he ran a finger over my bottom lip, and then my top, warming my entire body.

"How can you not know that I'm crazy about you?" he asked.

That night, there was no question about where I stood or what we were. But the next morning, as I lay on his futon watching the sun slowly melt the crystals on his windowpane, I had a small but unshakable premonition that my happiness would not, could not, last.

Two days later, I got a one-line e-mail from Julia: "I think I'm in love with your friend Nathan."

# Six

I can't believe the sheer amount of stuff that Julia has crammed into her 450-square-foot studio: ancient VHS tapes of her dance recitals, framed photographs of what seems like everyone she has ever met, clothing with the tags still on, college textbooks, three different sets of dishes that are, for all intents and purposes, unused. And I have volunteered to spend my Saturday boxing all of it up so it can be shipped to the Ferrars' house in Ann Arbor, where, barely a month after her accident, Julia has moved.

"You're a saint for doing this, you know," Dave tells me, trying to figure out the best way to wrap a porcelain dog figurine that had flanked Julia's fireplace.

"Then that makes you a saint for helping me," I respond. Although he regularly vows he's going to work less, Dave inevitably spends Saturday—and often Sunday—at the office, so this favor does not go unnoticed. Especially when I'm not sure I could have physically or emotionally handled packing up Julia's place on my own.

I look around the apartment. In any other city, it might be considered a closet, but for Manhattan, it's a great space. Located high in a converted old factory, its southern wall is made entirely of small rectangular glass panes looking out over the Lower East Side. And though cluttered, the white wood floorboards, Tiffany-blue walls, and a claw-foot tub in the bathroom are undeniably charming, making it seem like a tiny jewel box perched in the sky.

"I love it here."

"I don't think you should do it," Dave responds, referring to the fact that Grace and Jim, who technically own Julia's apartment, have offered to rent it to me for next to nothing.

"Why not?"

"I don't know," he says, sealing up a box. I cringe as the clear packing tape makes a squeaking noise. "It just feels wrong."

"How so?" As logical as you'd expect a tax attorney to be, Dave is not one to go on instinct.

Even as I ask, I'm not sure I want the answer. I've been thinking about moving out of my dingy apartment in Park Slope—land of La Leche League and Pee Wee Soccer, where I, a nonbreeder, stand out like a sore thumb—for ages. But because I've lived there for so long, the rent is half that of the going rate in Brooklyn, allowing me to enjoy little pleasures like Pottery Barn throw pillows and non-boxed wine without going into debt. That is to say, I feel stuck. Moving into Julia's place could be the opportunity I've been waiting for.

"I mean, for starters, do you really want to be paying rent to Julia's parents? I know it's a steal, but still," Dave says, scribbling something illegible across the cardboard.

"It's like the deal of a lifetime," I tell him.

"Yeah, but this place has Julia written all over it. Every time you turn around, you're going to be reminded that your best friend is halfway across the country because she can no longer take care of herself."

I know he is right. Even after we have taken down the photos and stripped the bed of its fluffy white duvet and packed up all of the trinkets, I still see Julia everywhere. That, I suspect, is precisely why I want to live here.

Finally, the only thing left to box up is Julia's computer. I hadn't seen her use it more than one or two times since her accident, so I'm surprised to find that the sleek silver laptop has been left on. As I flip it open so I can turn the power off, the monitor lights up, and Julia's e-mail flashes in the middle of the screen.

*I won't read it,* I tell myself, as much a command as a confirmation. It's true that I have just sorted through my friend's underwear drawer and emptied her medicine cabinet, but reading her e-mail is different, more invasive somehow.

And yet her Outlook folder is right there, taking up the better part of the screen, making it impossible not to see the contents of her inbox. And that two of the e-mails she has received over the past three weeks are from nbell79@gmail.com.

Nathan.


I am in a most foul mood. Luckily, Dave assumes it's because I miss Julia, and insists that margaritas and Mexican are just what I need. On the latter point, he's not wrong. The minute we walk into Mary Ann's, with its low-lit star lanterns and cheerful Spanish music, I feel more relaxed.

"Ready to order?" asks our server, whom I recognize from the many times we've dined here.

"Chicken taco salad, no shell, no cheese, dressing on the side," I say.

"Pollo Yucatán," says Dave. "No cheese enchiladas?" he asks after the waiter leaves, referring to my usual order. He playfully nudges me. "It wouldn't kill you to have something more substantial."

"I think eating carbs may actually decrease my odds of longevity," I tell him, and take another sip of my margarita. There are some women who deal with stress by not eating; I am not one of them. Consequently, since Julia's accident, I have put on enough weight that my favorite 7s look less bootcut and more sausage casing. That this even bothers me makes me deeply ashamed: I am a decent person with a good life and, unlike my best friend, I have a healthy, undamaged brain. This should be enough. But it isn't, and so I order a salad and pray it will help get me back into my skinny jeans.

"Marissa, you're gorgeous," says Dave, lacing his fingers through mine, and I know that he means it.

"And you, my love, are delusional." I smile, half serious. When I met Dave three years ago at Nina's annual Derby party, the very first thing I thought was, *Too good-looking for me.* Tall, with dark hair and eyes and the straightest, whitest teeth I'd ever seen on a real person, he looked like he belonged on a sitcom instead of in Nina's living room. But he went out of his way to talk to me, took my number and, to my surprise, called the next morning to see if I had plans that night. Within two weeks, we were dating exclusively.

"I took one look at you and knew you were the one," he confessed to me six months later. By then, his ever-so-slightly hairy back and propensity to talk at length about tax code had dispelled my initial belief that he was perfect. But he acted like he had just won the lottery when he found me standing next to a pitcher of mint juleps, and he was, and is, the best man I have ever met.

Which is why I feel horrible that while Dave is animatedly telling me about the latest saga with his lazy boss, I find myself thinking about Nathan.

# Seven

I didn't respond to Julia's e-mail for a full week. Nathan and I were in bliss mode, and I wasn't ready for reality to crash our party. We spent our days meeting between classes and staring at each other over books while pretending to study in the library stacks; nights were filled with frantic attempts to make up for all the time we'd lost being just friends. Dating Nathan was a dramatic shift from what I'd experienced with my wishy-washy high school boyfriends, who practically ignored me in public only to be aggressively affectionate in private, and who seemed to revel in feeding me a steady stream of half-truths. With Nathan, there were no mind games. He immediately told all of his friends as well as our coworkers that we were dating and paraded me around town like I was Julia Roberts, rather than a chunky, frazzled-looking collegiate. He spent hours cooking me elaborate meals that, while not always culinary masterpieces, often left me in tears simply because they were so generous.

"I love you, Marissa," Nathan told me on our fourth night together. "You are absolutely perfect."

"No, you don't. It's too early for you to know that," I scoffed, even though I was completely in love with him myself.

"I've never been so sure of anything in my life," he said so sincerely that I couldn't help but believe him.

Blissed out as I may have been, I could only ignore the blinking message light of my phone for so long. After finally listening to some of Julia's frantic voice mails—"Where are you? Have you been abducted? I'm worried!"—I realized I had to get in touch with her before she started pasting my face on milk cartons. So, at long last, I picked up the phone and called her.

"Finally!" she scolded.

"Yeah, sorry I haven't been in touch," I mumbled. "I've been completely swamped with that lit paper I was telling you about."

"That's okay. I'm just glad you're not facedown in a gutter somewhere. It's not like you to be incommunicado for so long."

"I'm not lying in a gutter," I reassured her. "But can we catch up next week? I really have to put my nose to the grindstone if I'm going to get this assignment finished in time."

"Not a problem!" she responded. "But listen, before you go, I have a teeny, tiny favor to ask."

*Of course you do,* I thought. *And the answer is no.*

"I'm going to be in town in two weeks. Will you set up a get-together with that hottie from your work?"

*Hottie from my work? That's what you say about the guy you're supposedly in love with?* "You mean Nathan? I think he's dating someone, Jules," I told her, unable to disguise the wariness in my voice.

She pressed on. "I don't think so, Mar. He really seemed like he was into me. Of course, it could have been the vodka messing with me!" She giggled. "Anyway, guess we'll find out soon enough!"

"Jules—" I began.

"You'll be there, right? And I can crash with you?"

"Y—"

"Perfect! Can't wait to see you—and Nathan!" And with that, she hung up.

Even though Nathan had sworn up and down that he had no interest in Julia, I couldn't bring myself to tell him about our conversation and the fact that she thought she was interested in him. At the same time, I didn't ask Julia not to come to Ann Arbor, nor did I tell her that Nathan and I had started dating. As if ignoring the situation could somehow change what had already been set in motion.

"So when are we going to go by your work?" Julia asked. She was splayed out on my bed, moving her leg—newly free of the walking cast—in small circles, which, she explained, would help rebuild her muscle tone.

"I'm not sure if Nathan's working this weekend."

"Then why don't we call him? Here, tell me his number, I'll call," she said, swinging her legs to the ground and grabbing the phone off my nightstand.

"I don't know it."

She looked me with a cocked eyebrow. "Are you deliberately trying to torture me?"

"No!" I said, too loudly.

"Seriously, Mar, what's the deal? I asked you about this weeks ago! Plenty of warning. And you know I don't ask for much," she said, giving me her best sad-sack face.

"Nothing," I responded, this time more evenly. "We'll go to the café. Let's just have dinner first, okay? I feel like I haven't seen you in ages and I want to catch up."

"Okay," she said, pouting. Then, quick as a light switch, she gave me an enormous smile. "I know you miss me. I don't want you to feel neglected!"

After dinner, Julia and I walked over to World Cup, where I knew Nathan was indeed working that night. I was relieved to see that unlike the last time I brought Julia there, it was bustling, giving me a good excuse to get in and out as quickly as possible.

"Hey! Look what the cat dragged in!" Nathan called out to us from behind the industrial-size espresso maker.

"Hi," I said meekly.

"Hey, you," Julia said to Nathan. Spotting two empty stools at the bar, she plopped down on one and patted the seat of the other so that I would come sit next to her.

By this point, my stomach was doing somersaults. I wanted to tell Julia at dinner, but the words sat in the back of my throat so long that I eventually gave up and swallowed them. Besides, I could barely get a word in edgewise, with her yammering on about what a perfect match she and Nathan were. ("We both love baking, exercise, and *you!*" she said, having no way of knowing how ironic this statement really was.)

"Hi, sweetie," Nathan said, walking toward us.

Assuming he was talking to her, Julia's face lit up. At that split second, I saw what an enormous mistake I'd made.

Nathan barely glanced at her as he leaned over the bar and kissed me firmly on the lips. Then he grinned and, finally, turned to Julia. "I'm guessing Tiny told you the good news?"

"Good news?" she asked sharply, drawing the stares of the customers seated closest to us.

"Marissa?" Nathan asked, looking at me quizzically. "You didn't tell Julia about us?"

"Oh," said Julia, quickly recovering. She smoothed an invisible wrinkle in the front of her cream cashmere V-neck. "Of *course* she told me. I was just confused, because you made it sound like she was knocked up or something."

I had a feeling that I'd thrown myself in a very deep hole, and it had yet to be determined if Julia was going to hoist me out or shovel dirt on me. I looked at her, my eyes pleading for mercy, but she just shook her head as if to say, *Not now.*

The two of us tried to act normal, but the minute Nathan stepped away to help a customer, she grabbed my arm, hard.

"When were you planning on telling me?" she hissed. "And how could you let me keep talking about him like that? You made me look like a total fool. Which," she said, grabbing her bag, "may have been the point." She hopped down off the stool. "I'm going back to the dorm."

"Of course," I said, my face burning. I watched her strut toward the door, head held high.

"Julia's not feeling well," I called to Nathan from over the bar, and to my relief, he didn't seem to notice that anything was amiss. "I'll call you later."

Julia barely acknowledged me when I joined her outside, and we walked home in silence.

"I'm sorry," I said quietly as I slid my keycard through the slot to get into the dorm.

"It's fine," she muttered, then said it again, making it sound like she was trying to convince herself, rather than me.

I assumed she'd call her parents from my room to pick her up. Instead, she announced that she wanted to go to bed, and quickly changed and lay facedown on my bed. I put my pajamas on, got on the flimsy cot on the other side of the room, and pretended to doze off. But it was hours before I finally fell asleep.

The next morning, Julia was gone, although I was relieved to see that her bag was still in my room. I went down the hall to shower, and when I came back, she was sitting at my small table with coffee and bagels.

"A peace offering," she said, holding a Styrofoam cup out to me.

"Thanks."

"I was thinking . . ."

"I'm really sorry," I said, cutting her off.

"I know. Me, too. I realize that was really self-centered of me to not even think that Nathan might go for you." Her words stung, but I let the pain sink in because I knew I deserved it. "I mean, I obviously get why you couldn't resist him," she told me, picking a speck of lint off her spandex workout pants. "I knew the minute I saw him that he was amazing, and here you get to spend every day with him."

"I know," I admitted. Then, unable to help myself, I added, "But, Julia, you can have *anyone*. Why Nathan? Why can't you just be happy for me? You know I've never been in love before."

"Mar, I think you need to look at the situation from a different angle," she told me earnestly. "When I was thinking about it this morning, I realized that no man is as amazing as our friendship. That's what's important." She walked over to me and put her hands on my shoulders, bringing her face so close to mine that I could smell the coffee on her breath. "That's why I think we should both forget about Nathan. It's not fair to either of us, and it's not fair to him, if you think about it."

"Okay," I said, not really getting what she was saying.

"I mean, first of all, this guy has driven a wedge between us. You *never* kept a secret from me before he came on the scene," she said gravely. "Second, what are the chances of the two of you being together forever? Nil! But you and I—we're going to be friends until the end. Just think about it. What will happen after we move to New York? You heard what Nathan said when we all had dinner last time I was in town. He wants to stay here after graduation." She made a face as though he had informed us he wanted to live in a junkyard, rather than Ann Arbor.

She paused, then added, "In the interest of full disclosure, I will say that I don't trust myself to not be jealous if the two of you are together. Who knows what that could do to our relationship."

The picture, out of focus for the past two weeks, was suddenly crisp and clear. It didn't matter if Julia was *actually* in love with him—which I highly doubted, given her history of commitment issues. What mattered was the fact that Julia couldn't stand the thought of being left behind. Or worse: being ignored.

She gave me a kiss on the forehead.

"You understand, don't you, Marissa?"

"Of course," I said.

But I didn't. Not at all.

# Eight

The odds of dying in a plane crash are roughly one in ten million—practically nonexistent compared with the odds of dying in a car accident (one in seven thousand in any given year)—and yet people get in their vehicles every day without so much as blinking. I remind myself of this factoid each time I fly. Sadly, it's never as reassuring as I'd like. After all, I don't have a car, and while I'm no mathematician, I can't help but believe that this pushes my plane crash odds in the wrong direction. Plus, Julia never drove, and look what happened to her.

*Relax, relax, relax,* I chant in my head, breathing slowly like I learned in the yoga class I was forced to attend during *Svelte's* team-building week last year. As the 757 rises slowly over the city, I try to concentrate on the vast gray and brown expanse of Queens, the sun's silver reflection on the Chrysler Building—anything but the fact that sitting in a massive piece of metal that will soon be

35,000 feet in the air, I have absolutely no control over the next two hours of my life.

Making good on my promise to Naomi, I am taking time off. Only instead of going somewhere that actually qualifies as vacation, I am heading to Michigan, where I will spend Thanksgiving and the following week visiting my family and the Ferrars.

It is the first time I'll see Julia since she left New York in early October, and frankly, I'm dreading it. Despite my best efforts, I haven't been able to douse the anger that's been simmering on low since I came across Julia's e-mails from Nathan. Why, I keep asking myself, would they be speaking after all this time? After stumbling across Julia's messages to Nathan, I felt so sneaky and horrible that I couldn't bring myself to search the rest of her e-mail. And yet a tiny part of me wishes I'd dug deeper before boxing up the computer so I could find out exactly why she'd reached out to Nathan—and when. I want to believe that her interest in him is "just her brain injury talking," as Dr. Bauer describes the odd behaviors that she's exhibited since the accident. But I can't shake the feeling that this is something she has been contemplating for a while. At this point, I wouldn't be surprised to find out that they'd been in touch long before her accident.

As my mind wanders in this direction for the hundredth time since I packed up Julia's apartment, I feel a familiar pang of guilt. In the face of the biggest crisis that's ever happened to either of us, shouldn't I just let it go?

Statistics save the day, and the plane touches down without incident. I make my way through the Detroit Metro Airport—so sleek and modern and removed from the crumbling city it serves—and to the baggage claim. After a few minutes, I spot the hideous red duffel I've been meaning to replace since college. The overpacked bag, which causes me to huff and puff as I navigate my way through the crowd, is a cruel reminder that it wouldn't be the worst idea for me to set foot inside a gym sometime this century.

Sarah's waiting at the curb in the Death Star, as I have nicknamed her enormous black Suburban. Though her hair is highlighted blond and she is far closer to her fighting weight than I am, we are clearly sisters: Like our father, we have deep-set brown eyes and noses that are a little bit too long; like our mother, we are proof that careful grooming can take a woman from plain to passably pretty.

"Gosh, it is so good to see you," she says, leaning over the armrest to give me a big, lingering hug.

"Hey, sis," I say, patting her back awkwardly. We spent twenty-some-odd years doing our best to avoid each other, but since my sister got involved with an evangelical mega church a few years ago, she's become very touchy-feely, and I'm not always sure how to respond.

"How *are* you?" she asks, in that way people do when they've spent more than a little time telling others they're worried about you. I wonder how many of her fellow Bible studiers have prayed for me this week.

"Fine. Happy to be here." Seeing Sarah glance at me out of the corner of her eye as she weaves through traffic, I feel compelled to add, "Really," which only serves to make me feel like a big fat liar. I spend the next twenty minutes babbling about how busy work has been in order to save face.

We arrive at Sarah's Craftsman bungalow, which is nestled in the cozy, inconspicuously upscale Ann Arbor neighborhood of Burns Park. As her SUV's name implies, my sister is living the dream: perfect house, great figure, nuclear family. Staying at her place is not unlike one of those occupation vacations, where you spend a week apprenticing with a wine maker or carpenter or pastry chef to find out if you really want that job. I always come away a little envious, but with a renewed appreciation for how much work goes into the whole deal.

"Auntie M!" yells Ella, flying out the front door and down the stairs. "I've been waiting for you all day!"

"Hey, sweetheart," I say, scooping her up in my arms. "How is my favorite niece in the whole world?" I would do anything for this kid. On top of being ridiculously adorable, she has been something of a living, breathing olive branch between Sarah and me since she was born six years ago. The more time I spend around Ella, the more I look forward to becoming a mother one day, even though I am on record as having negligible interest in spawning.

She looks up at me. "Auntie M, Mommy says Auntie Julia is very sick. Are you sad?"

"Yes, cutie. I'm sad sometimes," I tell her. "But the good news is, Auntie Julia is getting better every day. In fact, you might even get a chance to see her soon."

"Yay! I'll draw her a picture!" yells Ella, jumping up and down. "Of a ballerina! Like Auntie Julia!"

"Ella, I guarantee that she would love that."


"So, I'm kind of afraid to ask, but how's Mom?"

Sarah and I are sitting in her kitchen after dinner drinking wine, and as per usual, we are discussing our mother. She's a favorite topic of conversation because one of the few things Sarah and I agree on entirely is that Mom is off-the-reservation nuts.

"Worse than usual," says Sarah. "She called two days ago to tell me that she's thinking of divorcing Phil because she can't stand his snoring." Phil is my mother's husband; they married the year after I graduated from college. He considers watching golf a hobby and finds weather to be a fascinating topic of conversation, but is, for all intents and purposes, a nice guy. Truth be told, neither Sarah nor I can figure out what he's doing with our mother.

"I give it a week."

"If not less," retorts Sarah. "She'll be at Target with two hundred dollars worth of stuff in her cart and realize that her days of carefree shopping for underarm wrinkle cream and lawn gnomes are numbered without Phil. Suddenly his snoring will sound like angels singing."

We both laugh. Phil makes a good living as a mechanical engineer, and my mother's marriage to him is nothing if not a well-calculated business relationship. Although she does seem to love him, he also provided a meal ticket that allowed her to quit both of her jobs and live a cushy life that she'd previously only read about in her beloved romance novels. After the way my father left her without so much as a second thought, let alone money to raise his children, I can't exactly blame her.

"How are things with you and Marcus?" I ask Sarah, referring to her husband, who's out shooting hoops with his friends.

"Eh." She drains the last of her wine. I am not expecting her to elaborate, but she continues. "We're not you and Dave, that's for sure."

"But you guys seem so happy," I say, secretly pleased that my sister thinks of my relationship as ideal.

"We *did*," she corrects me. "Lately he's been weird. Distant. I'm afraid he's got something going with this woman at church."

"Seriously?"

"Yep." She nods, and makes a disgusted face. "It's the assistant pastor's wife. How gross is that? I doubt they're sleeping together—something tells me Marcus is too afraid of God to drop his pants—but I've caught them making nice one too many times after service."

She looks at me wearily. "The thing that kills me is that this woman is *frump-yyy.* I mean, if she were gorgeous, I'd be jealous, but I'd understand. But if he's in love with someone who can't be bothered to pluck her eyebrows, it's so much worse. That means it's more than run-of-the-mill male lust."

"Ugh," I say, because that is worse. Still, I have a hard time picturing my benign brother-in-law, who has worshipped Sarah since the day they met, so much as thinking about cheating, and I tell her as much.

We end up chatting for another hour before turning in for the night. As I wash my face and pop my contact lenses out, I think about the fact that Sarah and I talked more this evening than we have in ages. Obviously, I'm not glad she's having a hard time with Marcus. He's a good dad, and having grown up without a father myself, I wouldn't wish it on anyone, especially not Ella. But my sister confiding in me—and in the process, actually admitting that her life's not flawless—is a refreshing change. And, I realize as I drift off to sleep, our conversation was one of the very, very few I've had over the past couple of months that wasn't about Julia.

The next day, I borrow Sarah's car and drive to the Ferrars', which is just a few miles away. Unlike my sister's neighborhood, where houses are within striking distance, the Ferrars' place is nestled in woods along the Huron River, and the houses are hidden from passing cars and each other. Even so, I know the area like the back of my hand, and I don't have to check the street numbers on the roadside posts to know which driveway to pull into.

I press the shiny bronze button on the door's molding and hear a chime. It feels strange to ring the doorbell after letting myself in through the side entrance for so many years. Through the window, I see Jim padding over to the door.

He greets me warmly. "Marissa, come on in. Julia is excited to see you."

"Thanks, Jim. I'm excited to see her, too," I say, and mean it. In spite of my conflicted emotions about her e-mails to Nathan, I miss my friend terribly, and can't wait to see if she's doing as well as her parents have told me.

"Grace here?"

"Nope. She ran to Whole Foods to get a few things. Should be back soon," Jim tells me, and motions for me to follow him into the living room.

I am nervous. I sit on the Ferrars' white Ultrasuede sofa, but as soon as I do, I wonder if the indigo dye from my jeans will rub off on the upholstery. I decide to switch to a smudge-proof leather Barcelona chair.

"Well, now that you're no longer on the white couch, I'll offer you something to drink," Jim jokes.

I laugh, grateful for the diversion, and tell him I'm fine.

"Okay. I'll go get Julia."

"Marissa! *Hiiii!!*" Julia says with delight when she sees me.

"Jules, you look great," I say, walking over to her. And she does. Her hair is longer than it has been in years, and it flatters her. Her face no longer looks puffy, like it was after the accident, and I see that she's even wearing a little lip gloss.

I give her a hug, and she hugs me back. Then she holds me at arm's length and looks at me as though she hasn't seen me in years. She touches my hair softly. "Still so pretty," she says.

"Still such bad eyesight," I joke, but immediately regret trying to make light of the situation. Plus, I don't even know if she gets humor or not. There are so many things I'm unsure about.

To my relief, Julia laughs. "My eyesight is fine, thank you very much. The doctor says that I'm almost as good as new. My limp is even gone!" she says, referring to a hip problem she developed after the accident. Her specialists couldn't seem to tie it to an actual injury, and concluded that it was a result of her brain trauma. "Think of the brain as the body's control panel," one of her specialists explained. "Even if your hip is just fine, something in your brain isn't getting the message that that's the case, so it's affecting the way you walk. It might be permanent, but it might go away as quickly as it came."

"Come on," Julia says, tugging on my arm the way that Ella does when she's trying to get my attention. "Let's go to my room. I want to show you something."

I am more than a little surprised to find Julia's childhood bedroom redecorated. "Wow, Jules," I say, looking around. The walls, last a pale shade of gray, have been painted lavender, and her bed is covered with a violet quilt that would be sort of cute if it weren't surrounded by nearly a dozen matching pillows and a lavender throw. It is completely and utterly un-Julia, who'd always had an unwavering devotion to neutral colors.

"It's really . . . purple."

"I know. It's a little overkill, isn't it?" she says, raising an eyebrow and surveying the room as though she, too, is taken aback by it.

"A little," I admit.

"The doctor told me that I might get hung up on stuff. Colors, certain foods, words. Nothing I can do about it. At least this makes me happy." She starts singing Sheryl Crow, *"If it makes you haaaappy, it can't be that baaaaad"* . . . which makes me smile, because breaking into song is such a Julia thing to do. *See, there are good signs all around,* I tell myself. *You just have to look for them.*

But my optimism is quickly squashed by the presence of a small wad of fur emerging from under her bed.

"Snowball!" Julia squeals, spotting the white kitten. She grabs the animal and hugs it. "This is what I wanted you to see. My new cat!"

Julia hates cats. Correction: hated. "Snowball?" I ask, warily eyeing the mass of fur that's clawing at her as though he intends to open a vein. "You named it Snowball?"

"Well, yeah," she says, as though I'm dense, and I realize that the cat's name is not meant to be funny. "Just look at him. What else could I call him? Isn't he *adorable*?"

Now, I am the first to admit that I'm not a cat person, but I've seen cute-enough cats before. This creature does not make the cut. Although fluffy and soft, he has a flat, wrinkly face and mean yellow eyes that make me suspect that a small alien has decided to use him as its host. Snowball hisses and launches off Julia's frail-looking arm, but she just giggles as he runs back under the duvet edge.

"So do you miss work?" I ask Julia, surveying the dozens of get-well cards scattered around the room, many of which are undoubtedly from her colleagues.

She looks at me quizzically. "Work?"

*Come on, Julia. You love your job. You can remember this,* I silently plead.

"At the Ballet?" I say gently.

She doesn't take the bait, and my optimism instantly evaporates. "No ballet. The doctor says I can't dance anytime soon. Maybe even never," she responds in a singsong voice. Suddenly, she sits on the edge of her bed and her voice drops. "Ohhh. Ow. I think I feel a migraine coming on."

"Crap. Should I get your parents?" Julia has been suffering from headaches since the accident, and instead of getting less intense, they've been escalating; last week, she told me she had one so severe that she passed out. This terrifies me far more than I let on, because based on an article in one of many medical journals I've permanently checked out of *Svelte*'s research library, I recently learned that migraine sufferers are at an increased risk for "silent brain damage." Normally, this type of damage doesn't cause any symptoms—but given how sensitive and addled Julia's neural tissue already is, I have to wonder if the migraines will make it even worse. *Increased risk doesn't mean it has to happen,* I remind myself. *And most people with brain injury suffer from headaches and still manage to recover.*

"No, it's okay," Julia tells me. She gingerly leans back and squeezes her eyes closed. "I'm going to lie down for a bit. Will you just close the shades before you leave?"

"Of course."

"Thank you," she whispers. "Come back tomorrow?"

"You know I will."

I find Grace in the kitchen, putting groceries away.

"Julia's got a migraine," I tell her. "Should I bring her some medicine?"

"Oh goodness." Grace sighs. "No. The migraine meds aren't doing a thing. I'm going to start her on acupuncture this week to see if it won't help a little." She puts a tub of berries in the fridge. She closes the door, then puts her hand on my arm. "It's wonderful of you to be here, Marissa. You know the doctor said it's really good for her to be around familiar faces. People she trusts." Grace looks at me. "Are you sure you won't take her apartment?"

"I'm sure I'll regret saying this later on, but I really think I should stay put for now," I tell her. "Plus, Julia might be ready to move back at some point. Her boss did say that they'd hold her position open, after all. I think it will be easier if I don't take over her space."

"Marissa, we need to be straight with you," says Jim, walking into the room. "You should know that we've spoken with Julia's new neurology team at length about this, and as much as I hate to be the bearer of bad news, they think it's highly unlikely that Julia's going to be on her own anytime soon. The headaches aren't a great sign." He rubs his temples. "And let's face it. The elephant in the room is that she's not the same person she was before. The mood swings, the memory loss . . . there's no telling what she is and isn't capable of." His words bring all of the fears I'd just suppressed flooding back.

"Jim, don't say that," Grace says sharply.

"It's true," says Jim quietly. "I hope as much as you do that she doesn't live here forever. That she'll be able to go out and make a life for herself again at some point. I mean, I love her, but she's a grown woman and returning to the nest is not what you wish for your daughter."

"No," says Grace with resignation. She dabs at her eyes with the dish towel she's holding. "It certainly isn't."

"Well, at the very least, she seems happier now," I tell them, because, well, *someone* has to try to look on the bright side. "Not so depressed and hopeless like after the accident."

"I suppose that is progress," admits Jim.

"Julia's happiness is a nice surprise," agrees Grace. "She was so unpleasant there for a while that I was truly concerned that she'd stay that way."

On my drive home, I wonder if there's any truth to my theory, or if it's just something I've concocted to make the Ferrars—and myself—feel better. Julia *said* she was happy. But I know that three months ago, if my fiercely independent friend saw herself now, living in a purple bedroom in her childhood home with a cat named Snowball, she would be horrified. And that makes me deeply, exhaustingly sad.

At the same time, it makes me furious. I want to shake my fist at the universe and say, "Why not pick someone else?" Julia has made mistakes, just like anyone else. She's not perfect. But she's a good person, and she doesn't deserve the hand she's been dealt.

I grip the steering wheel tight and let the feelings of rage wash over me. Because the angrier I get about the accident, the easier it is to let go of the resentment I've been harboring against my best friend for going back on our promise.

# Nine

After my dad left, we stopped celebrating Thanksgiving. Instead, my mom would take us to the local IHOP for a late pancake breakfast, and then we'd spend the afternoon seeing a double feature at the discount cinema. Some years, if Sarah and I begged enough, my mother would let my grandmother drive out to pick us up so we could spend the holiday with her and my grandfather in Grand Rapids. Most of the time, though, we were too worried about leaving Mom alone. She refused to go to Grand Rapids, so it was the three of us, stuck in Ypsilanti, pretending like it was any other day of the year.

This is why Sarah and I find my mother's elaborate Thanksgiving spread, which looks straight from the pages of *Martha Stewart Living*, to be so bizarre. "After seven years of Mom channeling her inner domestic holiday goddess, you'd think I'd get used to this, but it still seems so . . . freaky," Sarah whispers to me as I stare incredulously at the fifteen-pound turkey, seven side dishes, pumpkin, pecan, and apple pies, assortment of cookies, and buffet table covered with bottles upon bottles of wine and sparkling cider. Clearly, my mother has our family confused with Overeaters Anonymous members who've fallen off the wagon and decided to stay there. The irony of the situation is that I don't dare help myself to seconds because I'll hear about it from her for the next month.

"I can't tell you how thrilled I am to have my girls here!" my mother says, emerging from the kitchen with a lace apron tied around her waist. She is even more done up than usual: Her short blond bob is freshly dyed, her burgundy dress fits her like a glove, and she is wearing new Fendi rhinestone-embellished eyeglasses. "Hi, Mom," I say, kissing her cheek. "I like the glasses. Very hip."

"Thank you, my love. You look nice, too," she says unconvincingly, giving my red turtleneck sweater and jeans a once-over. "I hope you know that I really appreciate you sacrificing your holiday with Dave to be with Phil and me."

*My mother the martyr*, I think, but say, "I told you I'd spend this year with you guys. And it gives me a chance to see Julia."

"Oh, I am so broken up about that," she says, frowning into her pinot grigio. "She was such a lovely young lady. Such a nice figure."

"Mom, she's still alive, you know," I balk. "And not that it's important, but she looks the exact same."

"*I* know that. Don't be morbid, Marissa," she scoffs. "Let's just thank God her face wasn't smashed in. Beauty like that doesn't grow on trees." I nod, and slowly turn to roll my eyes at Sarah, who tries not to spit her drink out. Although my mother barely paid attention to Julia and me in high school, she's since come to "adore" Julia so much that I suspect she'd replace Sarah and me with her in a heartbeat. As for Julia, she's so familiar with my mother's many quirks that she refers to her as "Susan the somatic narcissist"—yet she still feels compelled to win her over at every turn. Put the two of them in a room and it turns into one big nauseating love fest ("You look amazing!" "No, *you* do!" "But I love your shoes!" And so on).

"How is your friend doing?" asks Phil, shaking my hand hello— even after all this time, we're still essentially acquaintances.

I don't mind giving him an update, though, because I know he'll only chat with me as long as the commercial break lasts; then he'll be right back to the sofa to catch the rest of his PGA tournament. "She's so-so," I tell him. "Physically, she has no broken bones or anything like that. But she has some memory loss and she gets really bad headaches. She never talks about her job or her dance group anymore, either."

"No ballet?" my mother asks, aghast.

"Well, she hasn't brought it up once without being asked, not even when her dance friends came to see her in the hospital," I tell her. "It's kind of weird. And she just seems . . . different," I say, unsure about how to explain how odd Julia has been behaving lately, or whether it's even worth the effort.

"Man, tough break," Phil says, shaking his head. "Let her know we're thinking of her, and if there's anything we can do . . ." He gestures with his beer bottle instead of finishing his sentence, and walks back to the TV.

"Near-death experiences do have that effect on people," my mother tells me after he leaves. "I saw it on *Dr. Phil.*"

"That's the thing, Mom. I don't even think she realizes she could have died. She doesn't really remember the accident, and although she can recite what her doctors tell her about the changes she's been through, she doesn't seem to realize that she's different at all. Like, she's obsessed with purple and is bringing up people from our past that we haven't talked about in a decade."

"Wow," says Sarah. "That's got to be hard on you."

"It is," I say, and feel a surge of gratitude toward my sister for acknowledging this.

"That happened to a buddy of mine," says Marcus. Sarah gives him a quizzical look, so he elaborates. "In college, my friend Trevor was out drinking one night and decided it would be funny to climb over this fence that was blocking off a construction site. It was dark, so he couldn't see that there was a huge ten-foot hole on the other side of the fence. He fell in it and hit his head really bad."

"Marcus! That is so not okay! It's just like people telling me horrible labor stories when I was pregnant with Ella," Sarah scolds.

"No, it's all right. I want to hear this," I say. "So what happened?"

"He was fine. I mean, he went to the hospital and everything, and he acted weird for almost a month after that. He did have seizures every once in a while, too—that was scary," Marcus says. "But for the most part, he went back to being the same Trevor as always. I haven't talked to him in at least a decade, though," he adds sheepishly. Blond and clean-shaven with rosy cheeks, Marcus reminds me of a golden retriever. He looks relieved that I'm not upset, and for a second, I have an urge to command him to lie down so I can scratch his belly. Instead, I suppress a smile and excuse myself to the bathroom.

At four o'clock, my mother ushers us into the dining room. Before we sit down to eat, she asks us to hold hands around the table, and requests that Sarah bless our food. I look around, expecting Sarah, at least, to be as surprised as I am—after all, my mother is neither sentimental nor religious—but all the others, including Ella, have already bowed their heads.

I reluctantly close my eyes as Sarah starts to speak. "Dear God, thank you for this wonderful meal, and for bringing us together here today. Please continue to bless us, and to allow us to support each other through trying times. We especially pray for Marissa today as she stands by Julia during her recovery. Watch over her and give her strength. We are humbled and give special thanks for the great blessing that you have given us: one another."

Sarah, who is sitting next to me, squeezes my hand before adding, "Amen." I squeeze back, and when I open my eyes, I am surprised to find that I am just the tiniest bit teary.

# Ten

W e're almost there," says Julia, dragging me by the hand. All week, she has been begging to take me to a new restaurant in downtown Ann Arbor. I look anxiously down the street, which is aglow from holiday lights and colorful window displays, and try to pass my furrowed brow off as curiosity. Clearly, I won't be leaving *Svelte* to star on *All My Children* anytime soon; Julia immediately senses my unease. "Don't worry so much. I know where I'm going," she informs me. What she doesn't pick up on is that it's not her navigational skills that are stressing me out.

The truth is, I'm nervous to be out in public with her.

I've seen Julia almost every day since I've been in Michigan. Things had been going, as my mother would say, "swimmingly"; we've had longer and more involved conversations, and she's even brought up things from high school that I hadn't remembered until she mentioned them. There are other good signs. She has started wearing some of her old clothing, and although she hasn't been dancing, she's been walking on the Ferrars' treadmill, which her neuropsychologist deemed "a significant step forward." Granted, she seemed a little confused when I talked about a few mutual friends of ours in New York, making me wonder if she was only pretending to remember them. But on the whole, she seemed to be on the mend.

Then, two days ago, she had a meltdown.

We were in the Ferrars' kitchen making scones. Despite the fact that she barely ate baked goods herself, Julia could always turn a stick of butter and some flour into a heavenly concoction. This time, though, the dough had morphed into something more appropriate for a kindergarten art class than for consumption.

"It's not supposed to be this pastelike, is it?" I asked, trying—rather unsuccessfully—to prevent the mixture from sticking to my flour-coated hands. "Any suggestions?"

Julia whipped around and looked at me as though I had just asked her if she wanted to put her head in the oven. Her eyes filled with a look of rage that I had never, in our sixteen years of knowing each other, seen—not even the day she threw a fit in the hospital.

"If you don't like it, then figure out how to fix it, genius!" she screamed at me. "Isn't that what you love to do? *Make everything better?!*"

I stared at her, initially more shocked than offended. She stared back so fiercely that I thought she might be trying to telekinetically throw me against the wall.

"Jules, you don't mean that," I finally said quietly. But deep down, I knew that at least a little part of her did. While Julia was still in the hospital, Dr. Bauer told Grace, Jim, and me that one of the more common side effects of frontal lobe damage was unflinching honesty. "That's not to say that you should believe everything she says; some of it will be complete gibberish," he informed us. "But don't be surprised if Julia seems to lack the internal filter that keeps people from speaking their minds—and hurting others in the process." Of course, Julia was right: I *am* too eager to step in and try to make things okay. But it was painful to think that she'd probably held this opinion long before her accident, and simply kept it to herself in order to shield me.

"Of course she doesn't mean it," I heard Grace say from behind me. "Come on, honey," she said as she walked over to Julia and put her arms around her. "I know you're having a bad day, but there's no need to scream at Marissa. She's your best friend, remember?"

"Yes," Julia said meekly, and started to cry.

"I didn't mean to upset you," I told Julia.

"I know," she said between sobs. "I don't know what got into me."

"Let's go lie down for a little bit, okay?" Grace said softly to her daughter, leading her out of the kitchen.

By the time Grace came back, I had kneaded the dough so many times that it had become dozens of little balls that refused to adhere to one another.

"You can't take it personally, Marissa," she said, looking at me sympathetically.

"I know."

"That's what I say, too," Grace said. She sat down on a chair and crossed her long legs under her like a pretzel. "It still hurts. She's lost it on me a few times. Several times, actually. Her neurologist says that it's to be expected, even now. Those frontal lobe issues." She touched her hairline, as if to remind herself. "She told me I looked old the other day, and didn't really seem to understand why I was upset about it."

"Yikes." It's true that Grace has let her hair grow gray and hasn't succumbed to the Botox craze, but it's precisely her silver streaks and the smiling creases at the corners of her eyes that make her beautiful. Still, there was a shred of truth hidden in the statement, however cruel.

Grace went on. "Her new neurologist says the area of her brain that acts as the mental 'brakes,' so to speak, isn't working correctly. So instead of heeding red lights, she flies through them full speed."

"That's an eerie analogy."

"Isn't it?" she said, laughing a little and making me feel better in the process.

But it's that very analogy that has me worried as Julia steers me through the crowds on Main Street. We veer off the bustling thoroughfare and onto West Liberty, which is calmer and reminds me of some of the best parts of Brooklyn, with its cozy brick buildings and low-arching vintage streetlights. After a block, we stop in front of a small, sleek-looking café. Above the door hangs a sign: BEBER. *Clever*, I think, recognizing the word for "drink" from the Latin American phrase book that became my bible when Dave and I were in Chile two years ago.

"Okay! This is it!" she tells me, clapping her hands with delight.

"Cute," I say. "Let's go inside."

"Okay! But I have something to confess." She looks positively giddy as she tells me this, and I almost expect her to start jumping up and down.

"Spill it."

"Um—" she starts, but before she has a chance to finish, I see something through the glass. Even though I only catch the smallest glimpse of the person at the bar, it is enough that I recognize him, and at that instant, I realize why Julia has brought me here.

"Jules, why would you do this to me?" I say, drawing in my breath sharply. I pull her away from the window and toward the cobblestone parking lot so that we are out of sight.

Too late.

"Oh my God," drawls Nathan, grinning at me as he walks through the door onto the sidewalk. "The two amigas, together again. I had to come outside to see if I was hallucinating." He wipes his hands on his jeans and I see that he is leaner, more muscular than he was in college, and slightly gray around the temples. If it is possible, he looks twice as good as he did a decade ago.

I don't want to meet his eye, but I don't want to be rude. As we survey each other, I feel mildly light-headed. *This cannot be happening*, I tell myself. But it is.

"Surprise!" says Julia, giving Nathan a big hug.

He doesn't seem even the slightest bit alarmed that Julia sounds like a prepubescent version of herself, leading me to believe that he not only knows about Julia's accident, but has actually seen her since, rather than just corresponding via e-mail.

"I'm glad you were right—it's so great to see you both," he says, but he is looking straight at me.


A memory, it turns out, is not just a memory, or so I discovered during one of my marathon Google sessions on brain health. Studies show that the more times a person recollects something, the less accurately she is able to do so; her memory becomes affected by other factors, like how she feels about the incident and what other people say about it. The brain, in turn, responds by lumping fact and influencing factors together, making it difficult and often impossible for the rememberer to decipher what's real and what's imagined. This is why people who witness crimes often testify about what they read during a news report instead of what they actually saw. This is also why, although I vividly recall the last time Nathan and I spoke—March 18, 1998, to be exact—I cannot be certain about the fidelity of my recollection. Because I have thought about it dozens, hundreds, maybe thousands of times at this point.

I didn't break things off right away. After all, I reasoned, I only promised Julia that I would let him go, not that I would do it immediately. She must have suspected my hesitancy, because she repeatedly e-mailed and called me to find out how Nathan took the news. I never hated her more than I did then. And yet I could not bring myself to stand up to her, even though every cell in my body was screaming, *I take it back!*

Nathan didn't know that each conversation, each touch over those few winter weeks was a long good-bye. I wasn't about to tell him about my conversation with Julia, and so I acted like nothing was wrong. If anything, we were more in love every day. We stayed up until dawn, studied together, moved in concert, became Nathan-and-Marissa. He was the first thing I thought about when I woke up, the last person I spoke to at the end of each day. I could not imagine life without him.

I couldn't imagine life without my best friend, either. And eventually, Julia's check-ins, which I had been ignoring, loomed too large. It was time.

I decided the only way to handle the situation was to get bombed out of my mind and unceremoniously dump Nathan. Like many best-laid plans, it did not go accordingly.

We went to a local pub for dinner. I soon discovered that getting drunk wasn't going to happen: I didn't have the stomach to so much as sip at my gin and tonic. I was so tense that it wasn't hard to pick a fight, though, and so I began to complain that we would never work out, given that he wanted to stay in Ann Arbor after he graduated the following year, whereas I was determined to move to New York.

"It makes zero sense for us to keep this up, when we're just going to end up in a long-distance romance," I informed him, trying to look bold even though my legs were shaking underneath the wooden booth we were seated at.

"M, we'll make it work," he told me, kissing the inside of my wrist. "If I have to live in New York for a few years, so be it. I'll do what it takes to be with you."

"A few years?" I said testily, whipping my hand back to my side of the table. "It will take me at least a decade to become an editor-in-chief. And I'm certainly not planning on leaving after that happens."

"Fine, we'll figure it out when we get there. No reason to ruin what we have based on pessimistic speculation," he said, popping a fry in his mouth nonchalantly.

"You're just saying that to shut me up. And the point is, this is a college romance. There's no way that it can last," I said, repeating what Julia had said to me in my dorm room.

"My parents met in college and they've been married twenty-nine years."

"That was the seventies," I said with disdain. "And my parents met in high school and managed to wreck each other before divorcing fourteen years later."

"Okay, Marissa, I honestly don't know what's going on with you." Nathan sighed. "Why don't we talk about this tomorrow, after we've both had a good night's sleep?"

"I don't want to sleep," I said, feeling as though my chest had been hollowed out and the remaining cavity was filled with rocks. "I want to break up. I want to see other people. There's no point in being committed when it can't last."

"Marissa, you don't mean that," Nathan said, leaning forward.

"I do," I said, looking down at my silverware so he wouldn't see that my eyes were filled with tears.

Nathan grabbed my hand. "Marissa Rogers, I will marry you tomorrow, if that's what it takes to show you that I'm committed. You say the word and we will go to city hall at nine a.m. and tie the knot with a couple of bums looking on."

"You can't be serious," I said, but as I looked up at him—his golden-green eyes peering intently into mine and trying to understand what was making me say these horrible things—I saw that he was.

"I'm sorry," I said, again, pulling away from him. I grabbed my coat and turned to leave, but halfway to the door, I turned around and walked back to the table. Then I leaned over Nathan's stunned face and kissed him, trying to memorize the feeling of my lips on his.

"I love you," I said. "But this will never work." *Because I love my best friend more than you.*

And with that, I ran out the door and onto the street.

Never once turning back.


Since that night, I have imagined reuniting with Nathan so many times. In my mind, he was The One That Got Away—never mind that I was The One That Ran Away—although over the years, I eventually stopped pining for him and simply missed him. I had told him things that I had never told anyone, not even Dave or Julia—like the fact that as a child, I used to dream of luring my father back to my house and duct-taping him to a chair until he agreed to stay. Or the fact that although I didn't mind being five-two, I was scarred by my mother telling me at age thirteen that a girl of my height couldn't afford to gain even five pounds and I would have to spend the rest of my life on a diet.

But seeing Nathan standing here in front of me is not the blissful reunion I envisioned. In fact, I am not happy to see him. Not under these circumstances. And particularly not hugging my best friend.

"I thought you said you couldn't convince Marissa to come visit?" he asks Julia.

"She *definitely* never asked me," I say, my mind spinning with questions. Why would Julia tell Nathan that? Did she not want me to see him before now? And if so, why?

Julia ignores me. "Did I?" she asks Nathan, a puzzled look on her face. "I don't remember."

I look at him, and then her, and a familiar bubble of anger rises in me. *Don't make a scene,* I chide myself. But another voice in me says, *Marissa Rogers, it's time to grow a pair,* and this is the voice I heed.

"So I've been a favorite topic of conversation for the two of you for some time now?" I ask. "I figured out a while ago that you were e-mailing back and forth, but I certainly didn't think it was about me." Even as I say this, my curiosity bubbles up again; I'm dying to ask them, *Why? Why are you talking about me?* But the festering anger inside of me wins this round.

"Really? How did you know we were talking?" Julia says.

I ignore her and turn to Nathan. "Obviously, you're aware that Jules is a little messed up in the head."

He raises an eyebrow at me, but doesn't look angry. "The accident? Yes, I know."

"Then you know all about her memory issues. Conveniently, Nathan, she neglected to tell me that you two had become so *close.*"

I spit out the last word as though it's a curse. I'm fully aware that I'm causing a scene, but the floodgates have opened and I see no reason not to drag everyone under the current with me.

"I was only—" Julia starts.

"I'm not really interested in what you were doing," I say indignantly, even though this is a bold-faced lie. "I decided a decade ago that what's done is done, and if you want to revisit the past, then you can do it on your own."

"Marissa, I'm sorry," Julia whines. "Please don't be mad."

I want to storm away, to be the one to leave Julia behind for the first time in our long and sordid history. At the same time, I know that I cannot strand her without a ride. Especially when I'm not even sure she understands why I am upset.

"Fine," I say. "I forgive you. Now let's get the hell out of here."


"Auntie Marissa, are you crankypants?" asks Ella as I move my little yellow man three squares on the Candy Land board.

My niece is peering at me with a concerned look on her face. This makes me laugh, which makes Ella giggle, making me laugh even harder. Before I know it the two of us are doubled over.

"Crankypants? Is that what Mommy says when you're having a bad day?" I ask, wiping my eyes with the back of my hands.

"Yes!" she giggles, bouncing up and down on her knees, which are folded under her.

"Then yes, sweetie, I think I am."

"You need some ice cream!" Ella declares. "That's the only thing that makes me feel better on crankypants days."

"Ice cream makes me better, too, Ella," I tell her. "Let's see if Mommy wants to go get some with us."

Sarah agrees that ice cream is just what we need—never mind

that it's twenty degrees out—so the three of us bundle up and head to Stucchi's, which, in a survey of one particularly picky diet editor, was voted the best ice cream on the planet.

"So, I hate to bring it up, but are you okay? What happened earlier?" Sarah whispers after Ella walks over to the freezer case to pick a flavor.

I give her the rundown.

"Wow. I haven't thought about Nathan in years. I guess I didn't know you still had a thing for him," she tells me.

"I don't," I say, which is true, even if I can't get his face out of my mind. "But I guess I never really dealt with our breakup and what happened with Julia. And when I saw those e-mails, it was like an old wound had been ripped open. I don't want it to bother me. I mean, it was more than a decade ago, and I love Dave. It's not like I'm going to leave him to go be with Nathan."

"Are you sure?" Sarah asks, but she doesn't sound judgmental.

"I'm positive," I tell her, and hearing myself say it out loud makes me even more resolute. "I guess what really bugs me is that Nathan and Julia could be having a relationship. I mean, God forbid they're actually dating, which would just be totally wrong—but them even striking up a friendship is a blatant betrayal to what she and I agreed to."

We get our ice cream—double truffle and mint chocolate chip for me, vanilla chip and cherry cheesecake for her—and sit down at one of the small tables against the wall.

"I think this isn't about Nathan," Sarah says after a few minutes. "I think this about is Julia." She takes another bite, then says, "It reminds me of this sermon I heard recently."

"*Sarah*," I groan. I should have known she was trying to convert me.

"No, hear me out," she says, looking over her shoulder quickly to check on Ella, who is sitting with a little boy she's befriended.

"Our pastor—"

"The one with the loose wife?"

"No, the main pastor," she says, swatting at me. "Last Sunday he was talking about loving others. He said that most people get the whole idea of love totally wrong. They think that love is about being the smaller person—putting aside your own needs and wishes to serve someone else. But the truth is, when we do that, we become resentful. It isn't until we acknowledge our own needs and let ourselves shine just as brightly as the people around us that we can truly love them."

"So you're saying I'm afraid to let myself shine?" I ask, trying not to be offended.

"Don't get me wrong, Marissa. I think you shine plenty bright. I mean, I tell my friends here what you do for a living and they act like you're a celebrity."

"Thanks," I say, the compliment softening the blow of her earlier comment.

"It's just that I've always gotten the impression that when it comes to you and Julia, you take the backseat. And this whole Nathan situation is a prime example of that."

"I don't know, Sar," I say, but as I scrape the last of my ice cream out of the cup, it occurs to me that my sister—and yes, her pastor—may just be on to something.

# Eleven

My phone beeps.

Ten seconds later, it beeps again. Then again.

Exasperated, I grab it off the dresser to turn the alert off and see that I have three new messages.

Ugh. I want to drop the $250 wireless ball and chain in the toilet and call it a day, but I realize that it's probably in my best interest to check my voice mail in case Lynne—who, despite running the tenth most profitable magazine in the United States, somehow finds the time in her day to leave multiple vague-but-urgent messages for her staff—is trying to get in touch with me. I hit the "play" icon and lift the phone to my ear.

The first message is from Naomi. To my relief, she's not calling with an edict from Lynne, but to give me a heads-up that I have finally, after two years of begging, been given an assistant, and that said assistant has started. This is a welcome diversion and makes the prospect of going back to my job on Monday infinitely less anxiety-inducing.

The second is from Sophie, who says she has a favor to ask and asks me to call her when I get a chance.

The third is from an Ann Arbor number that I don't recognize. "Marissa Rogers? This is John from West Side Book Shop on West Liberty. Someone purchased a book for you, and unfortunately, we don't deliver, so I'm calling to see if you're able to come pick it up sometime today or tomorrow. We're open till seven. Call with questions."

*Julia,* I think as I press the pound key and beam the message up to the digital garbage in the sky. She probably felt bad about what happened with Nathan the other day and—evidence that her personality hasn't done a complete 180—got me a present to make up for it.

I know West Side Book Shop well; I spent endless hours there when I was in high school and college. But the thought of returning doesn't give me the warm fuzzies. Because, unfortunately, it happens to be just a few doors down from Beber.

*Please don't let this be another one of Julia's crazy set-ups,* I pray. I'm dying to see what's waiting for me, but I can't chance running into Nathan—not after the other day. In order to appear as incognito as possible, I borrow a big wooly hat and thick down coat from my sister and park a few blocks from the bookstore. Then I hustle down busy Main Street, where I'm least likely to be spotted by Nathan, and duck into West Side. The minute I get inside, I let out a long sigh; not only did I make it without being seen, there's only one other customer there, and his hunched-over figure and threadbare coat confirm that it's definitely not Nathan, or Julia, for that matter. Mission accomplished.

An aging hipster with a beard that should have been trimmed a month ago greets me from behind the counter.

"I'm Marissa Rogers. Someone left a book here for me?" I ask.

"Oh, yes," he says, disappearing behind the wooden shelves that separate us. I hear rustling, and after a minute, he reemerges with what looks to be an ancient copy of Jane Austen's *Pride and Prejudice.*

"Handle with care," warns the clerk, and I almost expect him not to pass the book to me.

"Of course," I tell him, fingering the fraying cloth cover. I've read *Pride and Prejudice* countless times, but that doesn't dim my excitement at the thought of adding this copy to my (admittedly tiny) collection of old books.

"I have to say, that's quite a find," says the clerk. "Although it's not one of the first editions, it's a rare printing from the early 1900s. Not something we come across too often." He smiles. "I'm sure you want to know who it's from. Your book fairy left a note inside."

I gingerly open the book cover and a small piece of paper tumbles to the ground. I pick it up and see that the note has been scribbled on the back of a receipt.

*Marissa:*

*I feel horrible about how the other day went. I had no idea Julia didn't warn you. I'm really hoping this book will soften that blow.*

*Anyway, in spite of it all, it was great to see you—it's really been too long. Call me if you're so inclined, or even better, stop by the restaurant. I'm there until close most days.*

*—Nathan*

*P.S. It took me a long time to come around, but you're right: Austen was hardly a romance novelist. I've had my eye on this copy for a year. Now it will have a happy home.*

I swallow hard. I'd been so certain the book would be from Julia that I never even considered Nathan might be the sender—even though West Side had been one of our favorite bookshops, and now his restaurant was practically its next-door neighbor.

I thank the clerk and walk out of the store in a daze, this time not looking around to see who I might bump into. Before I can even think about what I'm doing, I wander down the street. And once again, I find myself standing in front of Beber.

My usual indecision and internal fidgeting are suddenly over-taken by a bolder, more confident voice. *Sarah's right; I need to stop taking the backseat in my own life. I might as well face Nathan on my terms this time.*

I fling open the restaurant door, striding as though I aim to take no prisoners. Sadly, my bravado is wasted; instead of Nathan, a pretty redhead in a black button-down and apron is manning the mahogany bar.

"Is Nathan here?" I ask, looking around. At eleven a.m., I expect to find the restaurant empty, but a few customers are lingering over cappuccinos and newspapers at the small café tables against a mirrored wall.

"Yes, although if you're applying for the waitressing posi-tion, you should start by filling out an application," the redhead responds, wiping down the marble counter with a rag.

"No, no, I'm a friend," I tell her, although it occurs to me that this isn't entirely true.

"Oh. Okay, give me a minute." She picks up the phone. "Nathan? Someone here to see you. Says she's a friend."

As quickly as my confidence appeared, nervousness sets in, and I feel my palms growing clammy. Before I can contemplate whether this was a spectacularly stupid idea, Nathan emerges from the kitchen.

"Hey," he says, immediately giving me a big bear hug. I stand there limply, my arms plastered to my side; I'm unable to reciprocate his affection, yet somehow unwilling to stop him. All I can think about is how good he smells, even though I can't seem to detect a particular scent. Must be pheromones, I realize, recalling the story *Svelte* recently did on the chemical responses people unknowingly give off. Most of the time, they don't make a difference—but match the right two people and they trigger a powerful sexual response. Which explains why every illicit encounter he and I shared during college is being played out like a grainy home movie in my head right now.

He releases me and the spell breaks.

"I can't stay," I practically mumble. "I just wanted to say thank you for the book. That was really—"

"Oh, it was nothing." He grins. He motions for me to join him at the bar. "Come on. Let me at least get you a coffee."

"Uh . . ." I say dumbly.

"Brooke? Two coffees with steamed milk, please," he tells the redhead.

"No problem, boss," she says with a wink. It occurs to me that she's probably got a thing for Nathan, and his flirty, friendly demeanor probably does little to dissuade her. But why should I care? I ask myself, trying to ignore the tiny tug of jealousy I'm feeling. After all, Nathan's probably in a serious relationship, or even married, although a quick glance at his hand reveals that his ring finger is bare.

"So . . ." I say.

"So . . ." he responds with a smile, "How's things?"

My command of the English language fails me as I stare at his grinning face. "Good," I manage.

"Well, that's excellent. Me, too. As you can see, I finally followed through on all that crazy talk about opening a restaurant and bar," he says, gesturing to the restaurant with obvious pride.

"I'm impressed," I tell him, and take a sip of the coffee that Brooke stealthily slid in front of me when I wasn't looking. "You know, you honestly didn't have to do that," I finally add, referring to the book. I think of the little things he used to do for me when we were dating: fresh-baked cookies slipped into my pocket on cold days, copies of my favorite poems tucked into my textbooks. Come to think of it, he and Julia weren't that dissimilar when it came to gift giving.

"I know, but that whole scene two days ago went so bad that I just wanted to do *something*," he says, looking uncomfortable for the first time. "I guess it still hasn't sunk in how bad her head injury really is. I mean, her mom told me—"

"You talk to Grace?" I say, a tiny spark of anger flaring inside me.

"Marissa, Julia and I have been in touch for a while now," Nathan informs me matter-of-factly. "She e-mailed me in October, and we started chatting back and forth. Then she came by the restaurant with her mom a few weeks ago, and that's when I got a better picture of what was really going on."

I swirl my coffee and watch frothy white foam coat the sides of the cup. "Well, I had no idea that the two of you had become so tight."

"We're not, really," Nathan responds, shaking his head.

I'm about to ask him to elaborate when my phone starts buzzing in my pocket. I instinctively grab it to check who's calling. Dave's name and photo flash across the sleek glass screen and send a jolt of reality through my system. Now is not the time for answers, no matter how much I'm itching to know about Nathan and Julia. Now is the time to get back to my life before I plummet down some rabbit hole of memory that will leave me small and vulnerable.

"Listen, I really have to get going," I tell Nathan, gulping down the last of the coffee. "I appreciate the drink, and the book. Really. But I've got to run."

"Okay, if you must," he says, smiling. "It's been terrific seeing you, Marissa. I'd wondered about you over the years, so it's nice to actually be face-to-face again. I'm guessing you don't make it back to Michigan often, but I'm always here if you ever want to get together." Apparently some things don't change, I think. In college, Nathan was always available on a moment's notice, even if it meant dropping some major project just to hang out with me. It suddenly strikes me how different this is from Dave and me. We plan nearly every date, and even which nights we're staying at each other's apartments, in order to make our crazy schedules work. But we're adults with busy lives—not college students who can drop anything with few consequences—and so it has to be that way, I remind myself.

"Okay," I tell Nathan noncommittally. I catch a glint of amber in his deep-set eyes and suddenly it's as though every ounce of adrenaline in my body has been released. *Fight or flight,* I realize; I know the feeling well. *Time to fly.* "Well, bye," I tell him hurriedly as I grab my coat. "Thanks again."

"No prob—" Nathan starts to say, but I'm already out the door.

Dave doesn't usually have time to call in the middle of the day, let alone e-mail, so I call him back the minute I get home to see what's up.

"No, no, nothing's wrong," he says, shooing away my concerns. "I was just thinking about you and wanted to see how it's going."

"Oh," I say, surprised. I'd been complaining to him that his workaholism seemed especially bad lately (although admittedly,

Julia not being around made it seem worse). I just didn't expect my nagging to have an impact. "It's going . . . okay," I tell him.

"Just okay? Julia didn't pull another screaming fit on you, did she?" he asks with concern.

"No," I say. I know I should, but I haven't told him the second part of the story—the part about Nathan. *Later,* I decide. After I've processed it and can figure out how to explain the situation in a way that makes some sense.

"Well, that's a relief. Just remember, your goal is to make it through the next day. You'll be home before you know it."

After we hang up, I stash *Pride and Prejudice* in a dresser drawer in my sister's guest bedroom. Then I sit and stare at the wall for a while, doing my own little version of meditating. Except rather than repeat something Zen, like "I am at peace," I am thinking, *Thing of the past, thing of the past, thing of the past.* By the time I finally hoist myself out of the armchair I've been parked in, I've vacated my mind of thoughts of Nathan. Almost.

The next day, I wake early, shower, then pack my bags. I have decided to see Julia again before I leave; I'm still shocked about what she did, but I don't want to end my visit on bad terms, knowing that we may not be face-to-face again for months. Plus, as I have reminded myself half a dozen times this morning, she is not herself. *Frontal lobe damage,* I tell myself. *If she doesn't deserve a break, then who does?*

"Hi-hi-hi!" Julia says cheerily, flinging the front door open. Dressed in an oversized V-neck white T-shirt, black leggings, and purple ballet flats, she looks terrific, never mind that there are only about three other people on the planet who could pull off this outfit. If she remembers how we left things yesterday—with me peeling out of her driveway without so much as glancing back to see if she got in her house safely—she does not let on. Instead, she smiles and says, "Come on in! I've been waiting for you."

Grace and Jim aren't around, so we go straight to her bedroom. I notice that Julia's set up a small table near her window, and there's a notebook, some pens, and folded newspapers scattered across it.

"My makeshift desk," she tells me. "I'm looking for apartments."

"Really? That's a big step, no?" I ask, thinking of what her parents said about her not being ready to live on her own.

"It is. But Mom watches me like a hawk, and it makes me crazy; I feel like I forget more things than usual when she's around. I could really use my own space. Something small, of course— maybe a little one bedroom with a nice kitchen. A yard, if I'm lucky, for Snowball."

"When would you move out?"

"Well, the doctors say not for a while. But I want to be ready when the time comes." She plops down on her bed next to Snowball, who opens one alien eye to see what the fuss is about and promptly goes back to sleep.

"That's a good plan," I say. Noticing that the circled classified ads are from the local paper, I add, "In Ann Arbor?"

She nods yes. "Dr. Gopal"—her neuropsychologist—"says that it's good for me to be relatively close to Mom and Dad. Just in case. The headaches are getting better, but sometimes they come out of nowhere. And there's still the risk of me having a seizure or stroke. Especially this year."

It is surprising to hear Julia speak so frankly about her health. "I know, everyone acts like I don't know what's going on," she says, as though she just heard my thoughts. "I've been doing my research.

At first I felt like I was stoned out of my mind, everything was so foggy. But every day, I feel a little more like myself. I figure I might as well find out what's happening to me."

This is heartening. "Best thing I've heard all week, Jules."

"I knew you'd be happy for me," she says, putting her hand on mine. "Which reminds me, I wanted to talk to you about the other day."

*So she does remember.* "Shoot," I say, trying to sound amicable.

"I don't understand why you got so upset," she says. Even with her high pitch, there's a slight air of authority in her voice, a throwback to the old Julia.

"Are you serious?" I ask, trying to keep my temper from flaring even as I feel the vein in my forehead start to bulge the way it does when I'm about to blow a fuse. "Your memory may not be one hundred percent, but there's no way that you could have forgotten that I haven't seen Nathan in a decade because *you made me promise not to.* And now you've decided that I can talk to him again? Because the two of you are suddenly as thick as thieves? I'm sorry, but there's obviously something going on there, and you cannot possibly expect me to be comfortable with it."

"Marissa, you know I would never do anything to hurt you," she says, looking wounded. "It's just that if this accident has taught me anything, it's to let bygones be bygones. I don't see why I shouldn't be in contact with Nathan. And he's been so helpful to me since I moved back . . ."

"What do you mean? How often do you guys see each other, anyway? And when did you start e-mailing?" I sound paranoid but I can't help myself. I want to know why he and Julia are in touch—and, yes, if it's more than a friendship. It occurs to me that I should have asked him yesterday when I saw him, given that he doesn't have a brain injury and is therefore in a much better position to give me the straight story. If only I hadn't freaked out and ran like that, I lament.

"Ugh, can we please talk about it some other time?" she asks. "This is really giving me a headache, and the last thing I need right now is another migraine."

"But you brought it up—"

"Marissa, *please*." Julia sits gingerly on the edge of the over-stuffed chair. She squeezes her eyes tight and rubs her forehead.

Unlike Julia's last attack, this one seems staged. But having never suffered a migraine in my life, I instantly doubt my hunch. *She was hit by a car, for Pete's sake. Headaches are her daily life.*

"Okay, sorry," I concede. "I better go. It just sucks to leave things like this when I'm flying back tonight."

"Oh," she says, getting up from the chair to sit next to me on the bed. "I forgot about that. Are you sure you have to go?"

"If I want to keep my job, then yes," I tell her, although Naomi would probably be immensely proud of me if I called in to say I was taking more time off. The truth is, I'm itching to get back to the rhythm of regular life, where ex-boyfriends don't magically surface and the people I love don't scream at me for not knowing my way around the kitchen.

Yet in spite of all that's transpired over the past week, I have an inescapable urge to patch things up before I go.

"So are we going to be okay?" I ask Julia quietly.

"We're okay," she says and hooks pinkies with me—something we haven't done since high school. "Don't worry, I'll call you later this week and we can talk more about this. And the minute I get the go-ahead from my doctor, you know I'll be on a plane to see you." All signs of her headache gone, she squeezes me so hard I'm worried she might fracture my collarbone.

For that split second, I'm willing to forget everything that's happened and simply be grateful to feel my friend's arms around me.

# Twelve

*I*t's seven a.m., Monday, December sixth, and it's seventeen degrees in Central Park. It's going to be a sunny day today, but brisk, only getting up to a high of twenty-four . . ."

I groan and hit the snooze button on my alarm clock without opening my eyes. Flipping onto my back, I stick my hand out and feel the right half of my bed. There is a dent, but no Dave.

"Morning!" he says, as if on cue, walking through the bedroom door. He sits next to me, his weight yanking down the few inches of duvet I have covered my face with. "I brought you a muffin and some coffee."

I mumble thank you and reach for the mug of just-barely-milky coffee that he's holding. No doubt Dave, who is freshly showered and dressed, has already run several miles, had breakfast, and fired off a dozen e-mails before my alarm went off. Unlike me, he is a morning person, and if he weren't so cute, I'd find him ridiculously annoying.

"What's on the agenda for today?" he asks.

"Ugh. Major brainstorming meeting this morning, followed by a frantic afternoon of playing catch-up, then a post-work press event at some hotel bar." I sigh and add, "Where I'm going to do shots until my stomach bleeds."

"Very funny."

"Who said I'm trying to be funny?" I ask, and Dave takes the coffee out of my hands, sets it on the table, then tackles me. "You are so rotten," he says, tickling my sides as I squeal. He kisses me lightly, and then again, harder. "I missed you."

"I missed you, too," I say, and pull him on top of me to show him exactly how much. But as Dave and I tangle between the sheets, I'm disturbed to find that I can't fully get into it.

Because in the back of my mind, all I can see is Nathan's face.


Determined not to let my quickie with Dave prevent me from getting to the office early, I take a super-fast shower, throw on a chocolate-colored wrap dress that somehow makes me look both thinner and more businesslike, slap a little makeup on, and head out the door. The crowded subway platform reminds me of why I usually wait until after nine to leave for work, and I end up letting a packed train go by. When I finally squeeze onto the next one, I make the mistake of turning my head one centimeter to the left, and my blush is wiped off by the ample bosom of the Amazonian woman standing next to me. *This is why people move to North Carolina and Atlanta,* I think, recalling a *New York* magazine story on the recent recession-induced mass exodus from the city.

Miraculously, I am the first person at work—or so I think. When I reach my office at the end of the hall (further evidence, as I've told Naomi a million times, that the minuscule, windowless space was once a broom closet), there is a blonde sitting in my chair, typing away on my keyboard.

"Um, hello?" I say tentatively, although I can feel my blood beginning to boil. *I leave for a week and they move someone into my office?*

I look around, and to my relief, my books and Annie Leibovitz Lavazza calendar and the Smurf figurines Dave got me for my last birthday are all exactly where I left them. So I haven't been replaced. Then what, exactly, is this person doing at my desk?

The blonde spins around, a huge smile on her face. She stands up, and I see that she is immaculately dressed in a crisp white shirt, marble-size pink pearl earrings, and a black wool pencil skirt that shows off her long, tan legs. Suddenly my brown dress seems clingy and outdated, and I wish to God I would have slathered on some self-tanner after my shower.

"I'm Ashley! Your new assistant!" says the blonde, extending a manicured hand. Her unlined face leads me to believe that she is not a day over twenty-five.

What can I say? I hate her instantly.

"Hi, Ashley," I say, trying to regain my composure. "Naomi told me you started, and I'm really happy that you'll be working with us. But I didn't think we'd be sharing my office?"

"Oh!" She laughs blithely. "We're not sharing an office. Naomi told me to check on the status of the 'weird weight loss' story. I figured it wouldn't be an issue."

She adds, "I had to leave by nine last night so I thought I'd just come in early this morning to pick up where I left off."

Ah, the old "last to leave, first to arrive" line. I said it many a time myself when I was an assistant, and while I would normally welcome a fellow workaholic with open arms, I can't believe that she had the gall to use my computer without permission.

But when I open my mouth, it sounds like *I'm* working for

Ashley, instead of the other way around. "Um, well, from now on, you can access that info from your own computer. I can show you how, if you need?" I say almost apologetically.

"Oh no," Ashley says, and I swear I detect the tiniest bit of sarcasm in her voice. "I've got it under control."

*This chick may not be my replacement, but she'd like to be,* I realize. I'm about to tell her not to use my computer again when she says, "Well, I've got a busy day in front of me, so I'd better jet," and pivots on her heels to leave. When she reaches the door, she turns around, tilts her head to the side, and looks at me with what can only be described as pity. "I heard about your friend, by the way. *So* sad. If you ever need to talk, I'm just down the hall."

"*Seriously?*" I say, closing Naomi's door behind me. It's five o'clock and things have just now slowed down enough that I have a chance to talk to her.

Naomi takes her glasses off the bridge of her nose and rests them in her hair, which is fastened on top of her head with a pencil. "What?" she asks blankly.

"*Ashley,*" I hiss. "If it wasn't bad enough that she logged on to my computer this morning and somehow managed to move every folder on my desktop to the wrong place, she has managed to convince three of my writers that she's taking over for me!"

I add huffily, "And she's too damn pretty!"

Naomi bursts out laughing, and for the first time all day, I laugh, too, realizing how ridiculous I sound. "Marissa, she's twenty-three years old and has never worked in magazines before. She may be smart, but she has a *lot* to learn. Why does she intimidate you?" she asks, hitting the nail on the head.

"She doesn't intimidate me," I lie.

"Sure she doesn't," Naomi teases. "I bet if she fetched coffee, you'd love her."

"You're not wrong on that count."

"Go get your coat," Naomi says. "You've had a long day. Let's make a super-quick stop at the press event, and then we're going out for a drink."

One drink is Naomi's code for half a dozen. After downing a couple slim-tinis (which were so potent yet sweet that we decided the sole ingredients had to be diesel fuel and Splenda) in the ballroom where the press event is being held, we moved downstairs to the hotel's lounge. There, Naomi overtipped the bartender for our chichi drinks, landing us a free second round in the process. "One more for the road," she insisted, and though the room was already starting to spin a little, I didn't put up a fight. It felt good to be out of focus.

"So what should I do about the Julia and Nathan debacle?" I ask, having spilled the whole saga to Naomi two cocktails ago. I'd already asked her what she thought several times, but I pressed on, convinced in my drunken haze that clarity was just one question away. "Don't you think I should find out what the heck is going on between them?"

"If it's going to keep eating away at you, then definitely," she says, looking impressively sober. "I maintain that you should move on by whatever means possible. Even if that means going out of your comfort zone and contacting Nathan in order to get closure. I don't think you're going to be able to just ignore the situation and wait for it to magically resolve itself in your head."

"I just can't stop wondering what would have happened if I'd just stood up to her a decade ago," I confess. "Would Nathan and I have ever worked out?"

Naomi gives me her best *puhlease* face. "Marissa, you know I love you, but your biggest problem is that you really have no idea how good your life is. I mean, you're a star at work—"

"Am not."

"As your boss, I'm telling you that you are," Naomi says. "And Dave—well, let's just say if the two of you broke up and he wanted to date me, I wouldn't say no. Even if it meant it was the end of my marriage."

"You love Brian, you lunatic," I tell her, and look down at my dress to see if I have, as I suspect, spit on myself while talking. Affirmative. Note to self: No more hard liquor. "Besides, he's a workaholic. You'd hate that."

"Eh, Brian is no Dave," she says, pursing her lips for emphasis. Then she laughs. "You know what I mean, though. He's a catch, and you could do a lot worse than a guy with a little too much enthusiasm for work. And as for you and those damn ten pounds you're always complaining about? I think you should just stop obsessing and start living. Not everyone is meant to look like Lynne," she says, referring to the fact that our editor-in-chief, who is one of those annoying naturally thin types, could pass for the president of a pro-anorexia organization.

"It's about twenty pounds at this point," I say glumly, draining the last of my vodka orange.

"Whatever. I'm just saying: Own it."

"What the hell does that mean?"

"What do you think it means?"

"I'm thinking it means you sound so much like the therapist I dumped last year that I expect you to bill me a hundred fifty dollars for this session."

"You know what?" Naomi says suddenly, looking excited.

"What?"

"I just had the greatest idea. I need a third coach for Take the Lead."

"The running organization?" I ask warily. Even in my precarious state, I know that I am not interested in anything that involves me gasping for air and sweating buckets while my breasts, which defy all sports bras, repeatedly slap me in the face.

"Yes, the running organization," she says with mock exasperation.

"But I don't run."

"Honey, I barely qualify as a runner myself. But it doesn't matter! Take the Lead is amazing. We teach underprivileged elementary school girls self-esteem and discipline while training them to run a five-K race. I think it would be really good for you. It would give you some perspective," she adds.

"What's that supposed to mean?" I demand.

"You know my answer to that question," Naomi laughs. "Just think about it. I need to get someone on board by the end of next week. You'd only have to do it one afternoon a week for about an hour and a half."

"Okay. I'll think about it," I assure her, although as soon as the words leave my mouth my mind has already wandered to the French silk ice cream in my freezer and the three-hundred-thread-count sheets that I am going to slip between when I get home, possibly with said ice cream in tow.

Despite my newfound fear of cabdrivers, I am too drunk to protest when Naomi puts me in the back of a taxi. She takes one look at me swaying in the backseat and makes me promise to swallow three Advil the minute I walk in my apartment. "Best hangover prevention in the book. Trust me," she says, then instructs the driver to take the Brooklyn Bridge. I remark out loud that alcohol only seems to make her sharper, if it is possible, and she laughs and tells me to go to bed as soon as humanly possible.

That's exactly what I would like to do. But I told Dave I would call him to let him know I got in okay, so I flop down on the sofa—my bed and its sleek sheets just fifty feet away, yet too ambitious a target—and grope around in my purse for my phone.

"Marissa? What are you doing calling me at this hour?"

*Crap.* I realize, too late, that I accidentally hit my mother's number, which is next to Dave's on my favorites list. Damn the iPhone and its tiny, tricky buttons.

"What's wrong with your iPhone?" my mother asks. *Oops. Must have said that out loud.*

"Hi, Mom," I say, although it sounds more like "Hamma."

"Marissa Marie Rogers, are you drunk?" she demands.

"Nah," I slur. "Why would you think thah?"

"Because it's eleven o'clock at night and you're calling me sounding like you just had major dental surgery."

"I did have major dental surgery," I tell her, slurring some more. "Just a few hours ago, in fact." Then I start laughing hysterically, because this strikes me as the funniest thing I have ever said.

"Marissa," my mother scolds me after I've finally caught my breath. "You know I've told you a million times that the fastest way to get fat is to overdo it on the sauce." She pauses, and I hear her whispering something to Phil, something that involves the words "drunk" and "weight gain."

"Really, Ma?" I say to her. I have never once called her Ma but it seems more manageable, somehow, than Mom. And given her remark, I am not even sure she deserves the full three letters. "What if I was calling you to tell you I'd just been attacked? Or that Dave and I just broke up? The first thing you can think of is how many calories I've just consumed?"

"What do you want from me, Marissa?" she asks shrilly.

I sigh, and suddenly feel like sleeping for the next week.

"Nothing. Nothing at all," I say, and hang up.

# Thirteen

After nearly thirty-one years on the same planet with my mother, I should know it will be a very cold day in hell before she calls to apologize. Yet somehow, when my home phone rings the next morning, I assume it is her.

"Mom?" I ask, cradling the phone with both hands as though it will anchor me against the spinning room. Having spent the night on the sofa and woken up with a blood-alcohol level still borderline toxic, the day is not off to a stellar start.

"If that's what you want to call me, that's fine," says Dave, instantly deflating the small balloon of hope I'd been holding on to.

"Oh. Hi."

"Don't sound so excited."

"Sorry. I'm hung over."

"I kind of figured you were having a crazy night when you didn't call," he says.

"Ugh. Sorry. I passed out when I got home. But, you'll be happy to know, not before I managed to drunk dial my mother."

"Ah, Susan." Dave sighs. Although he is nothing less than a gentleman to her, he is far from my mother's biggest fan. "How'd that go?"

"As well as can be expected," I say, taking a quick peek in the mirror and immediately wishing I hadn't. No amount of Laura Mercier spackle will be able to conceal these purple circles.

"So, not good, but not so bad that you didn't think she'd call you this morning." Dave laughs.

"Well, if the definition of insanity is doing something again and again and expecting a different result, let's just say I'm ready to be committed."

I catch him up on the rest of the night, and tell him briefly about Ashley and the computer incident. Before we hang up, he asks me if I'm free that evening.

"Yeah, of course," I say. "Although I can't promise I'm going to be in great shape."

"That's okay," he says. "How about I swing by your work around six?"

"That's great for me, but can you actually get out that early?"

"I can get out of work, worrywart," he tells me. "See you then. Love you."

"Love you, too." *Now if only that was enough to keep me from thinking about my frickin' ex-boyfriend.*


I must look worse than I realized, because when I run into Naomi in the office kitchen, she asks me if there's any chance that I might be pregnant.

"You're kidding, right?" I say to her, popping off the tab to my soda. Naomi may swear by ibuprofen, but Coke is my hangover helper of choice. "Would I be drinking like that last night if I was pregnant? The kid would come out looking like a bottle of vodka."

"Don't joke. I was a wreck my entire pregnancy with Isla because I'd been drinking for almost a month before I realized I was knocked up," she tells me, eyes wide.

"Well, thank God, there are no Rogers-Bergman babies on the way anytime soon," I assure her.

"Whew," she says. "Because I seriously don't know what I'd do if you had to go on maternity leave."

"That makes two of us," I say, and drain the rest of my Coke.

The rest of the day, frankly, is a loss; it's all I can do to try not to fall asleep in the middle of a meeting with the sales department, and I spend almost an hour trying to edit a story only to realize that I have made a total of one change and can barely articulate what the piece is about. When Ashley corners me at four o'clock to find out if she can help me, I am actually relieved to see her.

"Yes, yes, and yes," I tell her. "I have tons of stuff for you to do."

"Fantastic," she says so perkily that I am tempted to ask her if she snorted an upper before knocking on my door. "Call me crazy, but I had a feeling you were a little swamped."

"No, I'm on top of things," I say, but as Ashley's eyes dart up and down, I realize that I, slumped over in my chair, wearing ancient pants and a sweater in nonmatching shades of black, do not exactly look like the picture of control. "It's just that I've been waiting to get an assistant for ages and there's a lot of back-end stuff that I'd love to have you take care of." Once again, I sound apologetic as I say this.

"Great!" Ashley says, smoothing the front of her red knit dress. "I'm here to help."

"Excellent." I grab a stack of files from the bookshelf. "There are instructions stapled to each file, including the phone numbers you'll need and where to put each file after you're finished with it."

Ashley looks surprised, and I am tempted to say, *See? I told you I was on top of things.* Instead, I say, "If you can wrap this up by the end of the week, that would be great. Oh, and if anything's unclear? Please just ask. I swear I won't mind."

"Thanks, Marissa," she says, and gives me what I recognize to be an actual smile, which is a welcome change from the chimpanzee-esque teeth baring she'd been doing.

"Thank *you*, Ashley."

The next two hours feel like twenty. Finally, when I feel like I cannot stare at my computer one more second, Gladys, our receptionist, buzzes me. "There's a very nice-looking young man here to see you," she teases.

"Now, Gladys," I hear Dave say in the background. "The good-looking guy took off five minutes ago. Tell Marissa it's me. I don't want her to be disappointed."

Here's the thing about Dave: Women *love* him. And not just in an "I wanna get you in bed" way (although he gets that from time to time, too). I don't know if it's because he's completely nonthreatening or because he grew up so close to his mom and sister, or all of the above. But the fact is, he rarely meets an XX chromosome carrier who doesn't instantly befriend him, be it Gladys or my sister or his boss, who chronicles her trials and tribulations as a mother to him daily.

"Well, Gladys, if the good-looking guy is gone, you might as well let the ugly one in," I tell her. Not a minute later, Dave is standing in my doorway. He's smiling, but looks ever so slightly concerned. "How are you feeling?"

"I've been better," I confess.

"Are you sure you're up for an outing?" he asks.

"Yeah, fresh air might do me good. Where to?"

"I'll show you when we get there," he says secretively.

I switch off my monitor and grab my coat and bag, determined to be a good sport, even though I'm having flashbacks of Julia's wild-goose chase through Ann Arbor last week. I still haven't told Dave about Nathan, because I don't trust myself to explain it in a way that doesn't make me sound like I haven't spent every second of the past decade obsessing about him. As far as Dave is concerned, Nathan is nothing more than a short-lived relationship from the very distant past, and I am determined to keep it that way.

We walk to the subway and hop on the southbound F train. After fifteen minutes or so, my ears pop, and I realize that we've just gone under the river.

"Brooklyn, huh?" I ask suspiciously. Dave has lived in the West Village since I've known him, and when he plans outings, that's inevitably where we end up. In fact, if I didn't convince him to stay at my place at least once a week, he'd happily be one of those New Yorkers who never leaves the island of Manhattan.

"Yep," he says and leaves it at that.

We get out at the Bergen Street subway stop, in the heart of Cobble Hill. Dave leads me a few blocks over to Clinton Street, which in spite of the wet sidewalks and barren trees, looks like a movie set. "You seem to know your way around pretty well for someone who doesn't do Brooklyn," I tell Dave, but he just smiles.

Finally, we reach a brownstone with a slate blue door. Dave starts up the stairs, and motions for me to follow him. He pulls a set of keys out of his pocket and opens the front door.

"What?" Still fuzzy from last night, I'm confused.

"One sec," he says, and grabs my hand, guiding me through the hallway to a door at the back of the first floor. He throws the door open. "Welcome to my new place!"

"Really?" I ask as I walk into the living room.

"Really. Let me show you around."

The apartment isn't big, but it's gorgeous, with dark, polished hardwood floors, marble fireplaces in the living room and main bedroom, butcher-block kitchen counters, and a small, light-filled second bedroom that will make a nice office space. Or, I realize, baby's room. The best part, though, is the small yard off the back of the kitchen, which, Dave informs me, is his alone.

"I love it," I tell him. "Can you imagine the barbecues you can have back here? The dinner parties?"

"No, Marissa. *We* can have here," he says, putting his arms around my waist. "What I wanted to say earlier is, welcome to *our* new apartment." He looks at me long and hard, his warm brown eyes reminding me why I fell in love with him in the first place. "I want us to move in together. But you haven't mentioned it, and I don't want to pressure you. So I'm just going to let you know that whenever you're ready—if you're ever ready—this is your home, too." He reaches into his pocket and pulls out another set of keys, which he puts in my hand.

"How long is the lease?" I ask, trying to do the math in my head. It is mid-December, so if he already has the keys, he must have signed the contract earlier this month and hasn't moved his stuff in yet.

"It's not a rental. I bought it," he says. "I've been saving for ages, and the market is so good right now . . ."

"You *what*?"

"Yeah," he admits sheepishly. "A coworker of mine told me about it a couple months ago, and I liked it so much that I barely looked at anything else. I knew you would, too. But it was just after Julia's accident, and you had so much on your mind . . . I thought

I'd just wait to see if the deal went through. I closed while you were in Michigan."

"Isn't it really expensive?" I ask incredulously. I can't even afford to rent in this neighborhood, let alone live here.

"Nope. I've been saving for a while, and my parents gave me a little money, so the mortgage is less than half of the sale price. So if you want to chip in—which I'd prefer you didn't—it would be less than half of what you're paying on your rental."

"Wow. I don't even know what to say." The apartment is, truly, perfect. Dave is perfect. Everything is perfect. And yet, somehow, the prospect of making such a huge decision right now makes me want to run back to my own apartment and hide under the covers until next summer. Because moving in with Dave is not the same thing as moving into Julia's apartment. This is giving up my own space—my security—to live with Dave. What if it turns out to be a disaster? What if he decides that I'm not the one because I can't be bothered to fully screw the cap on the toothpaste or I eat the last of his blue corn chips? What if I feel guilty because he's footing most of the mortgage?

*What if,* I think as panic rises from my gut and wraps its tentacles around my lungs and throat, *Dave isn't the one I'm supposed to be with?*

My mind is spinning from the possibilities, but none of them are things I can say aloud.

Besides, it's not Dave I want to talk to; it's Julia. The old Julia.

"Don't worry," Dave says, and kisses me on my forehead. "I know it's a lot to think about. Why don't we go to dinner and talk more about it later?"

"Okay," I agree. "But how about you give me the tour one more time?"

"Right this way."

# Fourteen

Normally, I ignore the advice that I dish out in *Svelte*, including but not limited to: avoid apple fritters (which contain so much trans fat they may as well be laced with cyanide); get eight hours of sleep a night (which would mean not watching *The Daily Show*); avoid consuming copious amounts of alcohol (why bother, when I already face certain death from liver disease?); and my personal favorite, start the day right by taking the stairs (which would require me to scale twenty-four flights in order to reach my office).

But I am forced to admit the article I'm in the middle of editing may actually be worth my attention.

What are friends for? Longevity, for starters—as well as better brain health, a slimmer physique, and sunnier outlook, according to recent research. A major Australian study of more than ten thousand people found that women with large circles of friends were nearly 25 percent less likely to die early than women with few social ties. Another study from Harvard showed that people with large social circles had better cognitive functioning and were less likely to be depressed than their wallflower peers. As if that wasn't enough, a similar study revealed that women who befriended those with healthy habits—like eating well, exercising regularly, and not smoking—were a whopping 60 percent less likely to be overweight than women with few friends or friends who had unhealthy ways. "It's proof that there really is power in numbers," says Stephen Jones, PhD, a psychologist at Montefiore Medical Center in New York City. "Good friends encourage you to do your best and to make smart choices, both personally and professionally," he explains. "Even highly motivated people experience peaks and valleys. Having a network can keep you going during low periods."

*Wow,* I think, tossing the manuscript on my desk. *I'm screwed.* Lately I've been feeling incredibly lonely. I may never have traveled in a large circle—that was always more Julia's style—but suddenly I'm feeling like I'm the sole inhabitant marooned on Marissa island. After all, Julia's in Ann Arbor for the foreseeable future, and Dave's tackling a major brief, which means he's working even more than his usual twelve-hour days in order to make sure his clients mind their Ps and Qs and cross their Ts and dot their Is and whatever else corporate tax attorneys do to keep mega-million-dollar corporations from getting caught swindling the government. (At least this is my interpretation of what he does for a living.) When I confronted him about how much he'd been at the office lately, I expected a fight—his workaholism is one of the few things we argue about—but he just sighed and said, "I know, Marissa. It sucks, and there's nothing I can do about it," which transformed my anger into pity for both of us: me for the constant nights alone, Dave for turning into a shadow of a person who used to have a life outside of his law office.

To make matters worse, I've seen Sophie and Nina all of two times since Julia's accident. Which, I realize, is my own fault: I've pulled out the old I'm-so-busy card every time they try to get together. But unless I want to die a research-proven untimely death thanks to obesity, stupidity, and depression, I need to start getting out there and being social again.

In a fit of inspiration, I dial Sophie's work number. "You have lunch plans?"

"Thought you'd never ask," she responds.

"Remind me, *why* aren't you doing anything for your birthday?" Sophie asks me an hour later, holding up a bright orange blouse to examine. We've decided to forego a proper lunch in favor of a falafel cart on Fifth and a quick trip to Anthropologie, which is in the middle of a huge preholiday sale.

"Well, I don't think thirty-one sounds all that fun, do you?" I ask, pushing one hanger after the other aside as I sort through a half-price rack. "Besides, it doesn't feel like a good time to be celebrating." Even as I say this, I realize that it goes against my new goal of being a more social person.

"Please tell me you're not talking about the Julia situation." Sophie is a dead ringer for Lucy Liu, and when she makes the don't-mess-with-me face she's making right now, I can't help but think of Lucy battling it out with Uma Thurman in *Kill Bill*. Needless to say, I am more than a little afraid of her.

"Um . . ." I sputter, not quick enough to come up with something to deflect her attention.

"Marissa!" she admonishes me. "That was three months ago. I know you're totally devastated and sad that she's not in New York anymore—I mean, we all are—but you've got to start living again."

"I'm living."

"Really?" says Sophie, peering at me skeptically over her black-rimmed glasses. "Examples, please."

"Request to adjourn until after lunch, may it please the court," I joke. Sophie is an employment litigator and although she despises her job, she is extremely good at it. A few months ago, she took the lead on a bogus sexual harassment suit and saved the company she was defending several million dollars. Arguing against her is pointless.

Sophie glances at her BlackBerry. "Uh-oh—gotta run. Jeff needs me on something," she says, referring to her supervising partner.

"Whew! Case dismissed." I laugh, although I am truly relieved.

"You're not off the hook just yet," she tells me, and kisses me on the cheek. "I want to see you Saturday. Let's do something fun."

"Define fun," I joke, but seeing her expression, I wave the white flag. "Name the place and I'll be there."


"Cut it. *Short.*"

Rubia looks at me as though I've just asked her to lop my ears off.

I press a picture of Anne Hathaway's wavy bob, which I have torn from *People,* into her hand. "This is what I'm going for."

I've never been the type to signal change through a haircut, not even after a bad breakup. In fact, after Nathan and I parted ways, I let my hair grow past my bra strap, as though, like Samson, its length would give me strength. But after such a tumultuous couple of months, I'm certain that a new look is exactly the fresh start I need—and the day before my birthday seems like the right day to make a drastic change.

Rubia does not take my request well. "But, Marissa," she protests in her thick Polish accent, gesticulating wildly with her comb. "Your hair. So beautiful."

"Don't worry," I reassure her as she massages my scalp, working my hair into a stiff shampoo lather. "I'm going to mail the ponytail to Wigs for Kids the minute I walk out of the salon."

"I worry you will not look like Marissa with short hair!" she warns, but after I convince her that I'm serious—and no, I won't hate her if I hate the results—she slowly begins taking off my locks. She slices and chops and razors my ends, then does the whole sequence again and again until she has taken off more than a foot. When she's finally satisfied, she puts me under the blow dryer, coats my head with a fine mist of hair spray, then spins me around in the chair so I can see the results.

"Wow." Rubia is right—I don't look like myself anymore. But I like what I see in the mirror: a woman who looks sharper, smarter somehow, and markedly more chic than the one who sat down in the chair forty minutes ago.

"Marissa 2.0." Rubia giggles, visibly relieved that I am not in tears. "You look like movie star." I blush. She is exaggerating, but I am surprised at how much my eyes stand out, and that for the first time, I look like I actually have cheekbones.

"Rubia, you're a genius," I tell her, and leave her an enormous tip.


Behold the magical mood-lifting powers of a good haircut, I think, spinning in front of the mirror that evening. I had woken up in a wretched mood. "Thirty-one is so much worse than thirty," I moaned to Dave over breakfast at our favorite diner. "Tomorrow

I'll be *officially* in my thirties, as opposed to just on the other side of my twenties."

"Personally, I like my thirties," he said, biting into a piece of toast. "I wouldn't go back to my twenties, or God forbid, my teens, if you paid me."

"Easy for you to say, old man," I told him. "You've had almost four years to try your thirties on for size."

"Touché," he said, and pretended to call to the waiter. "No more coffee for the young whippersnapper over here. She's very irritable and any more caffeine would set her over the edge."

"Har-har."

"I decided a long time ago that life goes by fast, and it's in my best interest to enjoy it as it comes rather than worrying about how old I am," he said matter-of-factly, only making me feel more irritated, despite the fact that I knew he was right.

But after my trip to the salon, my grumpy fog has lifted. In fact, I'm feeling downright cheerful as I get ready to go out. I'm meeting Sophie and Nina for a celebratory pre-birthday dinner at the Half King, a publishing hotspot where Nina likes to network and where I like the fish and chips.

"New year, new you!" crows Sophie from the booth where she and Nina are waiting for me.

"Seriously, you look hot," says Nina, whistling her approval.

"All right, ladies, no need to flatter me just because you didn't get me a gift," I tell them. We all laugh, then catch up on what's been going on over the past few months. Sophie tells us how her boss, who oversaw her sexual harassment case, has been making near-harassment-level advances at her. Nina pulls out pictures of her new dog, Max, a French bulldog with a flatulence problem that seems to be exacerbated by his penchant for houseplants. In turn, I catch them up on my adventures with Ashley and tell them about Dave's new apartment, which makes them swoon. "You'd be a fool not to take him up on it," Nina practically screeches. "I mean, I think you just won the housing and husband lotteries!"

"He's not even *close* to being my husband," I correct her.

"Ha! We'll see how long that lasts," she says knowingly. "Pete only waited four months to pop the question after we got our place together." Although Nina is an avowed career girl—she's the head of publicity at a major publishing house—she's also the homebody of our group, and is planning on having a baby "any second now," as she puts it.

Sophie and Nina are both eager for updates on Julia, but I have barely spoken with her since I got back from Michigan. I've repeatedly tried to get in touch with her, but she hasn't returned any of my dozen phone calls or e-mails, no doubt aware that I'm determined to get some answers about what's going on between her and Nathan.

"Well, I'm sure her not calling doesn't mean anything," Sophie tells me, unaware of what transpired during my week in Ann Arbor. I haven't told her and Nina because it doesn't seem right for my anger to influence their friendships with Julia, too.

"Besides, even if it does, she's not herself these days," she adds. She recounts how Julia recently called her at work and ended up babbling about her period to Sophie's legal secretary. "Nancy's hard to fluster, but I think fifteen minutes of tampon talk almost put her over the edge," Sophie says. "Julia's always been chatty, but she was never the type to be *that* personal, especially with strangers. You have to admit that she's a bit of a wild card these days."

"I miss Julia," says Nina sadly. "I wish things were how they used to be." We all nod glumly and Sophie waves our waiter down to order another round.

The conversation eventually turns to other subjects, and we

spend the next several hours talking over drinks and far too many French fries. Although it's frigid when we say good night in front of the pub, I feel warm and tingly inside. Maybe the studies are right and friendship really is healthy, I think. I resolve to see more of the two of them instead of trying to play catch-up every month or two.

Still, as I wave good-bye, I can't help but feel the tiniest bit lonely. Sophie and Nina may be great, but they're not Julia.

# Fifteen

Julia never called to wish me a happy birthday. In fact, despite my repeated attempts to get ahold of her, I don't hear from her until a few days before Christmas.

"Are you there?" she says on the other line. Her voice sounds strained.

"Jules? I'm here. What's up?" I ask, cradling the phone between my head and shoulder as I secure a wrapping paper corner with a piece of tape.

"Oh, nothing. You know. A little of this, a little of that . . ."

"Well, I'm happy to hear from you," I tell her. "I was a little concerned when you didn't return any of my calls."

"I was embarrassed," she says in a quiet voice.

"Huh? Why?"

"I got arrested," she practically whispers.

"You got what?" I sit up straight, not sure I've just heard her correctly.

"I was caught shoplifting. I wasn't going to tell you, but Dr. Gopal said I shouldn't be ashamed about this. That I should be honest about it."

I toss the gift I've just finished wrapping on the coffee table and head to the kitchen, because clearly this conversation is going to require chocolate.

"What happened?" I ask gently, determined not to sound judgmental.

"Well, I was at T.J. Maxx . . ."

"Really?" Despite her recent fashion 180, I still have a hard time picturing my luxury department store–frequenting friend in the discount megachain.

"Yeah. I like it there. One-stop shopping," she says. *More like five-finger shopping,* I am tempted to say, but recognize that now is not the time for snark. "Anyway, it was just a pair of sunglasses," she tells me defensively. "I mean, I tried them on and then left them on the top of my head, and apparently I walked out of the store that way without realizing it."

"So it was a mix-up?" I prod, and swallow the piece of bittersweet chocolate I've been savoring.

"I don't know," she says. "I'm pretty sure it was. The whole thing was so horrible that I've tried to block it out of my mind."

"Yikes. I'm sorry, Jules. That sounds terrible," I tell her.

"It was!" She sniffs. "They searched me to see if I stole anything else. It was humiliating. They let me off the hook in the end, because Mom explained about my accident and they felt bad for me or something."

"Thank God. What did your neurologist say about the memory issue? That doesn't sound great."

"He says I should explore it with my shrink." Then she says sadly, "Marissa, I wish you were here. I'm so lonely. And I feel so confused and hazy half the time."

I don't point out that this is a direct contradiction to what she told me when I saw her in Michigan last month. Instead, I say, "Hon, I wish I was there, too. I really want to come home for Christmas, but I promised Dave I would spend the holidays with his parents."

"But Dave's Jewish. He won't care if you're not there for Christmas." She doesn't say it unkindly, and yet the comment stings.

"We'll be celebrating Hanukkah with his parents, and Christmas at his new apartment," I tell her, then quickly correct myself. "*Our* new apartment." Despite my reservations, I accepted Dave's offer earlier this week, and have slowly started the process of moving my things there.

"What do you mean, *our* apartment? You're not moving in together, are you?"

"We are." I smile, thinking of how Dave practically jumped up and down when I told him yes. "I've been trying to tell you for weeks now. It's a big step, but we're both really excited."

"Do you honestly think that's a good idea?" she asks. "Because I don't. I just don't think Dave is going to be all that great to live with. You might as well be on your own. You know he'll never be home."

"What?" I ask, surprised; before her accident, she was constantly encouraging me to "take the plunge" and move in with Dave, and I'd expected her to show at least a little enthusiasm. In fact, I was kind of counting on her to help me get past the lingering doubt I've been feeling. "I don't get it, Jules. I mean, you're entitled to your opinion— but this is such a terrific step for us, and Dave's trying to cut back on how much he works. Plus, I *know* you know he treats me well," I tell her. Then, before I can stop myself, "Unless you don't remember?"

"Well, that was rude," she says. "Maybe I should go."

"Don't go. I didn't mean it." *What's wrong with me?* I think. Julia may not be filtering things, but suddenly neither am I. It's not how I want things to be between us, but I don't know how to respond to this new oversharing version of my friend. "I just wish you wouldn't disparage my decision. What am I supposed to do, suddenly inform Dave that I've changed my mind?"

"I guess not," she concedes. "Sorry."

"Me, too," I say, although what I really want to tell her is to put the cap back on her honesty valve. She'd always been gracious about my relationship with him, and I hate the thought that she may have been faking it all these years.

"I think I'm in love," I remember confessing to her one night over Chinese takeout at her apartment. Dave and I had been dating for four months at that point, and he'd already used the L word several times. I hadn't yet, but I had fallen for him, and hard; it was only a matter of time before I'd say it back.

"Oh my God, M," Julia squealed. "I'm *sooo* happy for you! You guys are going to have some ridiculously beautiful babies."

"Really?" I asked her, surprised by her gushing. Usually Julia was the first one to tell me to be careful, that New York men were too quick to trade up the minute they found someone better. And when she, Dave, and I were out together, I could tell that the two of them struggled to come up with things to talk about.

"Of course," she said, stabbing the air with her chopsticks for emphasis. "I can tell that he really loves you. Just watch: beautiful babies, I tell you. Beautiful babies who are going to *adore* their godmother. Hint, hint."

But today, all traces of Julia's graciousness have evaporated like so much of her memory.

"I'm just thinking about what's good for you," she says, indicating that we're not done with this subject after all. "Once you move in with someone, that's it. You end up married by default."

"Jules, that doesn't sound like a negative consequence to living together."

"Are you sure?" she squeaks. "Like really really sure? Because I just have a hunch that it's not going to work out."

I take a deep breath. It's clear that for whatever reason, she's no longer on Team Dave, and she's going to harp on about it as long as I let her. "Okay, can we change the topic?" I'm still anxious to bring up the things that were left unsaid last month. "Because there's something I want to—"

"Actually, I've got to go. I have another doctor's appointment in a few. Let's talk soon, okay? Love you!" she says. Before I can respond, I hear a click, and then the dial tone.

*Congratulations, Jules—mission accomplished,* I think. *You managed to avoid discussing Nathan with me yet again.*

# Sixteen

The holidays go off without a hitch. Dave and I take the train to his parents' house in Chappaqua and have a wonderful Hanukkah celebration with his family. We spend Christmas Day alone, exchanging gifts and preparing a delicious three-course dinner that takes longer than we anticipate because we stop cooking to christen the kitchen floor of the new apartment. That night, I do a hilarious-if-patchy video chat with Sarah, Ella, Marcus, my mom, and Phil, and even have a pleasant phone conversation with Julia, Grace, and Jim. When December 26th rolls around, I am surprised to find that the post-Christmas blues I usually get are missing. This year, all I feel is relief.

For reasons I'll never understand, much of the publishing world insists on keeping their offices open between Christmas and New Year's, even though there is little to no work that can or should get done then. Never one to buck the trend, *Svelte* pretends to be in full swing for that entire week, and those of us who have decided not to take vacation time duck into the office with our heads down just before lunch and sneak out a few hours later.

I, however, have decided to make the most of the six hours I'm chained to my desk. After poring through every book, online resource, and research journal I can find on young women and traumatic brain injury, I have decided that the next logical step is to write a story about the subject.

Truth be told, I'm beyond bored with weight loss. Each new story on fat-sapping superfoods or butt-blasting workouts or carbohydrate-counteracting supplements feels like a screw being slowly drilled into my skull. Even the straightforward food pieces, which I usually enjoy, are beginning to seem like the most mindless drudgery. If I don't tackle something vaguely stimulating soon I may have to do one Richard Simmons jazzercise video after another until my heart stops.

"Naomi, I want to write a story," I announce, sitting in the canvas director's chair across from her desk.

"Um, okay," she says, putting down the document she's been marking with a green pen. "You know we're always encouraging you guys to switch things up from time to time. What do you want to write about? Maybe an 'I tried it'? Or a celeb interview?"

"That's the thing," I say, sitting on my hands. I feel oddly nervous. "I don't want to do anything weight-loss related. I was thinking about doing a health piece."

"Great," she tells me. "We need to freshen up that section. You can only write about breast cancer and the swine flu so many times. What are you thinking?"

"I want to do a story about traumatic brain injury."

Naomi gives me an "I'm humoring you" look.

"Before you say no, it's actually surprisingly common," I tell her. "In fact, it's a leading cause of injury in women under forty and kills more young women than heart disease and most forms of cancer. So it's actually right on target for our readers."

"I see that you've been doing your research," Naomi says, and leans back in her chair. "Tell me more."

I take a deep breath. "Well, what I find really interesting is that a lot of women who experience brain injury aren't the same after their accident. Their personality changes. It can be devastating to them and their families."

"Like with Julia?" Naomi asks.

I nod. "She's doing well, though, so I'm hoping she'll be one of the people who recovers." I wish I felt as confident as I sound. Some of the research on personality change was so hard to read that I actually had to put it down and come back to it later; I may have been searching for answers, but I wasn't necessarily prepared for what I would find. Still, I am convinced that this would make a great article, and it could definitely be the challenge I need to light a fire under my well-padded butt. And I need—I *crave*—a project that will consume me. Because maybe that will help me forget how lonely I am. Maybe that will silence the broken record in my mind that's stuck on the ballad of Julia, Nathan, and me.

"Well, you're right that it's interesting," Naomi tells me. "We don't want to make this about Julia, but if you could find other brain injury survivors to interview, I think that could make the story really strong. All backed by lots of statistics and studies, of course," she adds.

"Does that mean it's a go?" I ask excitedly.

"I think so." Naomi turns to her computer and pulls up the editorial calendar on her screen. "Yep. We have room for it in the June issue. So that gives you"—she pauses and clicks on the calendar again—"until the middle of March to get the first draft in. Is that enough time?"

"Plenty," I assure her. "Thank you. I just really wanted to work on something different."

"No need to explain that to me." Naomi laughs, and puts her feet, clad in bright green Crocs, on her desk. "I almost applied for a job at *Boating Today* last month."

"You did not."

"No, I didn't," she admits. "But I thought about it. Trust me, I know how hard it can be constantly doing the same stories over and over." She points her pen at me. "When it gets to be too much, you let me know what I can do. We want to keep you happy."

"I finally have a real project for you to work on," I say over the wall of Ashley's cubicle later that afternoon.

Ashley looks up from her computer, making no effort to conceal that she's on Facebook. In the spirit of the season, I ignore my inner Scrooge and let it slide. After all, she was remarkably competent at completing the paperwork I gave her last week.

"Really?" Her eyes sparkle with interest.

"Really. What do you know about brain health?"

"Well, I took several psychology classes when I was at university in New Haven," she says, using thinly veiled code for "I went to Yale." She adds, "Although I majored in classical literature, so I'm not sure how helpful I'll be on that front. But if you need an editor, I'm sure I could help you polish your article."

I stifle a snort. "I don't think we're going to start you on editing just yet. I need research help—someone to line up experts, sort through studies, really get their hands dirty." An extremely satisfying image of Ashley's pearly pink nails coated with grime flashes through my mind. "Are you game?"

"Of course," she responds, her baby blues suddenly flat and bored. For a second I wonder if I'm making a mistake, but I remind myself that with nearly a dozen different projects coming up over the next several weeks, it's in everyone's best interest for me to be a team player, even if my impulse is to go it alone.

"I'm glad. I think this will be really rewarding for you, and if you do a good job, I'll even talk to Naomi about letting you write a sidebar," I tell her. "That's actually how I got my first clip."

"Oh, I have dozens of clips from my column at the Yale Daily News," she informs me proudly. So much for Ivy League innuendo.

"But a clip from a national magazine couldn't hurt your portfolio, could it?" I ask, not sounding nearly as caustic as I'm feeling.

"No," she concedes, flipping her blond hair over her shoulder.

"Great," I tell her. "Let's see how things go after you tackle the research portion of the story."

Her perkiness resurfaces. "Terrific! I can't wait to get started."

Prolific Yale prodigy though she may be, I decide it's in my best interest to spell everything out for Ashley. With that in mind, I type up a detailed assignment e-mail, instructing her to hold off on the sidebar until she gathers the rest of the material and I've had a chance to think about the topic. Almost as an afterthought, I add a separate paragraph at the end:

> I know you're juggling work for other editors, but I do expect this story to be a priority; it's a very important project for me. If you fall behind or have trouble with the research or experts, let me know right away.

She e-mails back immediately:

> I wouldn't dream of doing anything else.

# Seventeen

I can't believe how nice this place is," Sarah says to me. We're sitting on the couch at Dave's new apartment. Correction: *our* apartment, as I am almost entirely moved in, although the majority of my boxes remain unpacked.

"And I still can't believe you're actually here!" I respond, referring to the fact that she called me last week to let me know she and Marcus decided to fly to New York for a last-minute weekend getaway. In the nine years I've been living here, Sarah has come to visit exactly twice. Her first trip, which was a few months after I moved to the city, went poorly, to say the least: I gave her the wrong directions to my apartment, she ended up in a scary section of the Bronx, and was so rattled by the experience that she didn't come to New York again until two years ago for a mandatory work conference. On that visit, she refused to leave the Times Square vicinity. The only time I saw her was for dinner at Ruby Tuesday, where we were seated next to a group of teenage German tourists who were so loud we could barely hear ourselves chew, let alone talk to each other.

"The travel package was such a good deal, and when Marcus's sister said she could watch Ella, we were sold. Plus, now that you and Dave are getting serious, we figured we should probably give him a good grilling," she says, looking pointedly at the kitchen where Dave and Marcus are chatting.

"I don't think we're *that* serious," I tell her, and glance over at Dave, who has somehow managed to make jeans and a polo look like the hottest thing I've ever seen on a man.

Sarah pokes me in the side. "Um, news flash, sis. Living together is usually considered serious."

"Spoken like a true Midwesterner," I tell her. "In New York, living together is practically a business deal. Besides, cohabitation is something you holy rollers frown upon, no?"

"Well, premarital sex is also out of the question, and you know how that turned out," Sarah says, referring to the fact that she was pregnant with Ella when she and Marcus got married.

"Then there's no point in telling you I'm contagious—you've already got the heathen fever."

"You know it."

"So . . . how are things with you and Marcus?" I ask in a low voice, so he can't hear me.

Sarah tucks one foot under her thigh and shifts to face me. "Better, actually," she says. "A lot better. I didn't talk to him about the bimbo, but I did tell him that I need more attention, and he's really stepped it up."

"That's good," I tell her, and look at Marcus, who is gesturing animatedly as he bickers with Dave about Johnny Damon and the fate of the Red Sox. "But don't you think you should say something about her?"

"Why would I?" Sarah asks, frowning. "I feel like he'll just be paranoid and act uncomfortable around Tina—that's her name— which will be weird for everyone. We're in a small group with her and her husband now."

"Small group?"

"It's a Bible-study-type thing," she explains. "It means that in addition to seeing her at church, I now see her every Thursday night, too."

"Um, sis?" I say. "You know I love you, but did it ever occur to you to switch to another group? One without Tina the Temptress?"

"You always were the smart one in this family," she says, pretending to look pensive, and we both giggle.

"So, there's something I need to tell you," Sarah tells me later that evening while we're clearing the makeshift card table we ate dinner on.

"What?" I ask, slightly alarmed by the tone of her voice.

"Calm down—it's nothing huge. It's just that I ran into . . ."

"Julia?"

"Let me finish, motormouth." Then she whispers, "*Nathan.*"

"Shut up! How do you remember what he even looks like?" I whisper back, glancing at Dave and Marcus, who are practically comatose on the couch watching television.

"I didn't at first. I mean, keep in mind that I only saw him a handful of times while you guys were dating," she says, and motions for me to follow her into the bedroom, where Dave and Marcus are out of earshot. "I ran into him while I was doing errands last week. He thought I was you for a minute—he called your name when he saw me."

"*No.*"

"Yes. He realized right away that I wasn't you—"

"Obviously, as you're thinner and prettier—"

"Please. Anyway, I asked if he meant Marissa Rogers, and when he said yes, I said I was your sister and introduced myself. Reintroduced myself, technically."

"What happened?" I ask eagerly, unable to disguise my excitement. Ancient history or not, some stupid little part of me wants to know that the book he gave me wasn't just a goodwill gesture. That, as ridiculous as I recognize this wish to be, he's still attracted to me . . . and not Julia.

"Well, he wanted to know how you were doing."

"And?"

"I said you were great. That you were working as an editor and living in New York, which he apparently already knew, and that you were dating a really terrific guy. He said he was happy to hear it, and asked if you were engaged." This makes my heart skip a beat, but I try to look normal, and Sarah continues. "I told him you weren't, but that it was only a matter of time," she says protectively. As she recounts the encounter, it dawns on me that sometime over the past few months, my sister has gone from being a disinterested party in my life to being my friend. It's an unexpected but welcome change.

"Did he say anything about us seeing each other in November? Or about Julia?"

"That's the weird thing," says Sarah. "Not that the entire scene wasn't weird. But given what you told me about the last time you saw him, I couldn't help but pry a little."

"We're obviously from the same gene pool." I laugh.

"Just doing my sisterly duty," Sarah says, and salutes me. "So I told him that you were holding up especially well given Julia's accident. Then I said, 'You know Julia, right? I think Marissa said you guys talk?'"

"Nooo."

"You're very welcome. So he says, 'Oh, yeah, Julia. I heard she's doing a lot better.' Like he's getting his news from someone other than her! I think he figured I'd end up telling you about it and wanted to make it seem like they weren't in contact. He clearly has no idea that I know the whole sordid ordeal."

"Wow. What does he have to hide?" I wonder out loud. Maybe my instincts weren't entirely off—maybe there *is* something going on between them after all. "Well, regardless, thank you for telling me," I tell Sarah, and give her a hug.

She laughs and hugs me back. "Don't thank me. I didn't want to say anything—as far as I'm concerned, this guy is *not* someone you should be your wasting mental energy on. He's not good for your relationship with Dave, or for your relationship with Julia, for that matter. But I realized that I'd want to know if I were you. So there you have it."

"There I have it." I nod. "The question is, what do I do with it? I feel like I'm not going to have any peace until I know what's going on with Nathan and Julia."

"Are you sure you really want the truth?" Sarah asks.

"Pretty sure."

"Get your answers, then forget the whole thing."

Not an hour after I wave good-bye to Sarah and Marcus, I get a FedEx delivery from Julia. As I rip open the cardboard, I smile wistfully; I'm glad my sister and I are growing closer, but her visit made me realize just how much I've missed Julia lately.

The second the box's contents fall onto my lap, my nostalgia is replaced with a feeling of dread, and I wish to God I'd left the package on the stoop.

Atop three framed photographs, I find a greeting card with a syrupy photo of a kitten sleeping in a basket, with a brief note from Julia scribbled inside:

*Marissa,*

*I was looking through my old stuff in Mom and Dad's basement and found these. Of course, I had to send them to you! Look at how young and happy we were. I wish we could go back in time, before the accident. Sorry to sound depressing but it's true. I miss you tons, my dear.*

*xoxo, Julia*

If I hadn't already seen the pictures, Julia's letter would have had me in tears. Not a day goes by that I don't wish we could rewind time and change what happened on that fated September evening. But as I stare down at the faded three-by-five images in their white wooden frames, there is no question that things will never, ever be the same again.

The first photograph is harmless enough: It's Julia and me, arm in arm, just after our high school graduation. She looks shockingly similar to the way she would at thirty, which is to say, glowing and beautiful. Me, not so much—but I'm happy to see that at I look far better in the fourth decade of my life than I did in the second. Regardless, Julia's right: The happiness on our faces is unmistakable.

The second picture is similar. Taken the summer between our freshman and sophomore years of college, Julia and I are washing her car in Jim and Grace's driveway. Our T-shirts and shorts drenched, we're laughing hysterically and threatening to turn the hose on whoever snapped the photo.

The third picture, however, sends my stomach lurching. It's Julia, Nathan, and me, at the bar the night that started it all. I

remember Julia, who loved to chronicle our outings, had her cam-
era with her, although I don't remember the photo being taken, nor
who took it. As in the two other shots, Julia is happy, and Nathan
is giving his best dimpled grin. I'm attempting to smile, but there's
an unmistakably sad, almost haunting, uncertainty in my eyes.
How could Julia have missed the fact that I look miserable? And
even if she didn't notice, why would she think it was okay to send
me this photo after seeing how upset I was when she orchestrated
the Nathan meet-and-greet?

I look at the photos one last time before throwing them back in
the box Julia mailed them in and stashing the whole mess in my
closet. I don't like the third photo one bit, but I hate what it stands
for even more. Julia used to tell me what was on her mind, no matter what. Now she seems unable to communicate with me unless
it's through passive-aggressive messages. Well, I decide resolutely,
I am not going to engage in her twisted games. She's going to have
to start operating under *my* rules.

I sit on my bed and dial Julia's cell.

"It's Marissa."

"Oh, hi," she says, out of breath.

"You have a minute?"

"Of course," she says, panting into the phone. "Sorry, I just finished with a ballet class."

"Really? I thought you couldn't dance? That's good, though," I
tell her, reminding myself not to let Julia veer the conversation so
far off track that I can't bring it back around to the photos.

"Yes. Too bad it made me want to drown myself in the river,"
she says flatly and then, as though an afterthought, forces a laugh.

"Whoa, not so fast, Ophelia. What's the deal?"

"I can't remember anything."

"Oh."

We sit in silence for a minute, which should be comforting—although we're known for our marathon chats, Julia is one of the few people with whom I can easily spend time with without speaking—but in this case, it just underscores the tension that I'm feeling.

Finally, she clears her throat and continues. "It's bad enough that they won't let me do any leaps because of my head," she says. "Then I get to class and I can't even remember stuff that a toddler should know. Like, positions were a challenge."

"I'm really sorry," I tell her. "Is this the first time you've danced since the accident?"

"Second."

"Well, it's going to take some time, no?" I say, recalling a study I came across last week. It said it could take a brain injury sufferer more than a dozen times of recalling something to have it finally click. Then again, given what I read about false memory, I wonder if the recalled memory is actually the real one—or if it's just something the person eventually relearns. I file this question away as possible fodder for my story.

"Screw time," says Julia angrily, her high pitch making her sound like a pubescent boy trying to act tough. "I'm trying to live my life right now. Not tomorrow. Not next week."

"I know," I tell her, and walk over to the window. It's raining lightly, and the grass in the backyard looks spongy and gray.

"No, you don't," she says, now sounding more tired than anything.

"You're right. I don't," I admit. "But I do know that this has got to be really difficult, and that makes me sad."

"I don't need your pity."

I swallow hard, thinking about how to respond. Then I say, "Julia, I don't *pity* you. But like you said in the card you just sent, it's impossible not to wish the accident hadn't happened. Particularly when it means that you have to go through things like not remembering how to dance."

"So you got my package?" she says, sounding slightly more upbeat than she did a second ago.

I take a deep breath. "Yes, I got it this afternoon. I really appreciate you sending me something—that meant a lot to me. But, Jules, I have to ask: What the heck were you thinking, giving me a photo of us with Nathan? I know you know that things went badly in November. And you *still* haven't answered my question about what exactly is going on between the two of you. Am I supposed to take that picture as a sign that you're dating?"

Julia sighs audibly. "I told you, I'd never do anything to hurt you."

*Is that why you made me give up what might have been the love of my life?* I wonder, but say nothing.

After a minute, Julia continues. "Mar, Nathan's just a friend who helps me out sometimes."

"Helps you out? How's that?"

"Well, he's been giving me apartment leads, and sometimes he makes me a meal if I stop by the restaurant."

Now it's my turn to sigh. I think about how Nathan used to whip up four-course meals for me in his tiny rental kitchen; food was always his idea of romance. Which means that my instincts about the two of them may be right, even if they haven't actually started a relationship yet.

"That still doesn't explain why you got in touch with him in the first place," I tell Julia. "Or did he get in touch with you?"

Silence.

"Julia?"

"Marissa, I'm lonely. You're not here for me. I don't have any friends left in Ann Arbor. What am I supposed to do?"

"Jules, I'm lonely, too. And you know I'm doing all I can to support you. I'm sorry I can't be in Michigan right now, but I'm going to visit as much as I can."

"It's not the same anymore," she sniffs. "You and I, we were a team. And now I'm all alone."

Brain injury or not, Julia still remembers exactly how to push all of my buttons. I don't want to feel guilty—I didn't shove her in front of the cab, nor did I decide that she needed to move back to Ann Arbor—but I do all the same. Because she's right. She is all alone, in the middle of the Midwest, while I'm in New York living out the dream life that we'd conjured up together so many years ago.

"Okay," I concede. "I'm sorry. Just please, please, no more Nathan references, okay?"

"Okay!" she says, obviously thrilled that I'm not going to push the issue any further.

And once again, I let it go.

# Eighteen

For exactly fifty-seven hours each week, I am not working, sleeping, or commuting. I take this precious, fleeting free time very seriously. So I'd be lying if I said I enjoyed spending a sunny weekend in February attending Take the Lead training. However, I promised Naomi I would help her, so I plastered a smile on my face and committed to mastering the fine art of communicating with nine- to eleven-year-old girls. Two full days of ice-breakers, seminars, group exercises, and educational videos later, I was deemed coach-worthy.

The minute I step in front of the dozen eager, quizzical faces staring at me from their semicircle, I wish to God coaching would have lasted three times as long. I am wholly and completely unprepared to help these little humans reach their full potential. In fact, I'm sure that the only guidance I should be offering them is how to get to the bathroom.

"Don't be nervous," Naomi whispers, then claps several times to get everyone's attention. "Hi, girls! I'm really happy to see all of you. I'm Coach Naomi, this is Coach Alanna," she says, nodding at the lanky brunette I just met a few minutes ago. "Those of you who were here last season might be surprised to see that we have a new third coach. Please welcome Coach Marissa."

"Hi, Coach Marissa," they say, their voices echoing off the walls of the gym where we will be meeting each Tuesday afternoon for the next four months.

"Hi, girls," I say, as the butterflies in my stomach reveal themselves to be flesh-eating caterpillars.

A string bean wearing a SpongeBob T-shirt raises her hand. I glance at her name tag, smile, and say, "Yes, Lisa?" as I was instructed to do in training.

"*Where* is Coach Beverly?" she demands.

"Coach Beverly moved to Los Angeles for her job," says Alanna, addressing Lisa in a slow, childish voice. I look over at Naomi, who seems nonplussed by the baby whisperer's patronizing tone. "Coach Marissa was nice enough to take her place. Now, why don't each of you introduce yourselves, and tell us one thing that most people probably don't know about you?"

As we go around the circle, I learn that Caitlin, a third grader who is the smallest of the bunch, wants to be a singer one day. "Like Lady Gaga," she informs us. Margarita, who is painfully shy, can barely mumble her name, but Naomi somehow gets her to share that her grandmother, whom she describes as her favorite person, is coming to visit from Mexico next week. Lisa tells us that, shockingly, she likes to watch *SpongeBob* after she gets home from school. And Josie, who is very pretty and appears to be well aware of it, informs us that her new brother cries too much. "I wish he would go back into my mother's *vagina* where he came from," she says and looks at the other girls, who laugh hysterically, although I'm certain the majority of them have no idea what she's talking about.

"That one is trouble," Naomi tells me under her breath. "She was the ringleader last year. Do your best to ignore her when she talks like that, unless she's picking on anyone or swearing."

As we go around the circle, a chubby girl in glasses sitting at the end of the semicircle is bouncing up and down on her knees and appears to be having a hard time containing herself. At one point, she sits on her hands as though to keep herself from waving to get everyone's attention.

Finally, it's her turn. "I'm Estrella," she says enthusiastically, and slowly smiles at each girl as though they're judges and this is her one shot to be the next American Idol. Josie rolls her eyes, but if Estrella notices, she doesn't let on. "The one thing you may not know about me is that my name means 'star,'" she says slowly and articulately.

"Yeah, *sabemos*," a girl named Charity says sarcastically.

Naomi looks at Charity, but addresses the group. "Ladies, let's give Estrella the same courtesy she gave you all when you were talking, and not interrupt her." The girls settle down immediately, calmed by Naomi's quiet authority, and suddenly I see why she was named Take the Lead's coach of the year last season.

When we finish with introductions, Naomi, Alanna, and I take turns reading a lesson plan about the importance of appreciating individuality and personal strengths. To drive the point home, we instruct the girls to do a warm-up exercise that entails running from one end of the basketball court to the other, then back again. Upon return, each girl is supposed to yell out something they like about themselves before passing a baton to the next girl in line, who then takes her turn. "Try to say things that aren't about how you look. For example, I'm nice to my classmates, or I'm good at math," Naomi tells them. Then she turns to me and smiles. "Coach Marissa, why don't you start?"

I open my eyes wide as though to say, *It's my first day. Give me a break!* But Naomi just keeps smiling and motions for me to go to the red streamer we have placed on the ground as a makeshift start and finish line.

"Okay," I mutter under my breath, then remind myself that whether I feel up to the task or not, I've signed on to be a role model. Which means that I will have to wait until after practice to murder Naomi.

I jog down to the wall, slap the yellow drywall, and turn back. I'm sweating profusely, not only because the gym is about a zillion degrees, but also because the girls—having never seen a woman's boobs hit her chin before—are staring at me with their mouths open. Needless to say, I am relieved when I finally reach the red streamer. *Whew.*

"Coach Marissa, what's your favorite individual attribute?" says Alanna deliberately, as though I am dense (which I apparently am; I just forgot the entire purpose of the activity).

I freeze. "Uh"—*Think fast. I have nice hair. No, that's physical. What else . . .*

"I'm a hard worker," I spit out.

"Good one!" enthuses Naomi. "Now pass the baton!"

I look at the front of the line, and there is Estrella, beaming as though she were about to shake hands with Barack Obama himself. She reaches for the baton I'm holding, then leans in and says sagely, "Everyone's nervous their first day, Coach Marissa. Don't worry. You did *great.*"

"Thanks, Estrella," I say. *I just got schooled by a fifth grader,* I think in amazement as the four-foot-nothing fireball jogs down the court, arms akimbo, stomach heaving up and down.

"Ha-ha, there goes thunder thighs!" says Josie, just loud enough that everyone, including Estrella, hears her.

"Josie, that's not okay," Naomi says pointedly. "If you want to be a part of Take the Lead, you'll need to respect everyone here. Including Estrella."

"Sorry," says Josie, not sounding the least bit contrite.

After the longest two hundred yards in history, Estrella finally reaches the finish line. "I am extremely intelligent!" she proclaims proudly once she catches her breath.

She hands the baton to Josie and adds, "Not *everyone* can say that."

It's impossible to tell whether or not her dig is intentional. But as I watch Josie jog away, so graceful she could balance a book on top of her head, I find myself secretly rooting for odd, unflappable Estrella.

# Nineteen

In the middle of the worst recession in more than three decades, Dave's law firm has decided to throw a blowout party. "It's supposed to be a morale booster," he explains sheepishly as he hands me an embossed five-by-seven card that's nicer than any wedding invitation I've ever received. "They waited until after the holidays to save money."

"*Printed* invites?" I say, unable to contain my incredulity. "Why not just write the details on hundred dollar bills and call it a day? I mean, they could at least look like they're trying to cut back."

"You know that lawyers tend to prosper during economic downturns."

"Not *that* much."

"What can I do?" he says, throwing his hands up in the air in mock exasperation. "Barring a major catastrophe, I have to go."

"Don't tempt fate," I retort, and tack the invite to the fridge with a Gaudí magnet Julia brought me from Spain a few years ago.

"Does this mean I have to go, too?" I ask. I don't want to be difficult, but I can't help but resent the fact that one of the few date nights we'll have this month is for his work—otherwise known as the place where he spends more than two-thirds of his life.

"Will you? Everyone's bringing their significant others and I really don't want to go without you." He walks over to rub my shoulders, knowing I'll agree to do almost anything if there's a massage involved.

I sigh. "I suppose."

"Thank you, baby," he says, and kisses my neck. "Maybe you'll meet someone fun?"

"Maybe."

Surveying the array of Muffies and Buffies milling around in silk cocktail dresses that each cost more than my entire wardrobe, I decide that there is definitely no one "fun" here for me to meet. Luckily, Dave's coworker Pete has shown up. Pete is catty and callous and normally the type of person I can't stand, but I'm convinced that his bitchiness is the result of deep denial over his latent homosexuality, so I give him a pass. And Pete likes me, which makes him more likable. It's one big dysfunctional circle of friendship.

Pete, decked out in a tailored suit, pink shirt, and fuchsia power tie, ambles over to where Dave and I are standing. "Marissa! You're looking . . . good," he says, kissing both of my cheeks hello and then giving me a deliberate up-and-down.

"You've gained weight yourself," I shoot back, not offended in the least. I'm wearing my favorite strapless black dress and have had my hair blown out into a sloppy, teased bob ("Like *Valley of the Dolls*!" Rubia said excitedly when I told her what I was going for). I feel sexy and confident, in spite—or perhaps because of—the Stepford wives I'm surrounded by.

"You know I'm kidding," Pete says. "You look like you just rolled out of bed. *Delicious.* Apparently domesticity agrees with you." He raises his eyebrows approvingly at Dave.

"Apparently." I laugh.

Dave starts chatting with a partner, so Pete and I make our way over to a waiter passing hors d'oeuvres.

"Gotta hand it to the firm," he says to me, his mouth full of a bacon-wrapped date. "They do know how to throw a party."

"Please don't get me started."

"Well, your highbrow ethics sure aren't stopping you from feasting on the riches," Pete says as I grab a mini crab cake from another waiter's tray.

"Aren't you supposed to be chatting up your coworkers?"

"I'd rather mingle with the plebeians." He smirks.

We head to the bar, and Pete fills me in on the latest at Wyman, Stewart, and Piechowsky. Among other banal exploits, I learn that Phillip Wyman himself was recently caught in flagrante delicto with Jeffrey Stewart Jr.'s legal secretary. Pete points out Wyman, who has a firm arm around an attractive older woman. "His wife, of course," he says under his breath. "The entire firm knows, but she's none the wiser."

I dab at the corners out my mouth with a linen napkin and discover errant cocktail sauce on my bottom lip, making me wonder how long I've been walking around like that. As I blot a second time, Pete lets out a long whistle. "Fresh meat."

"Where?" I ask warily. I am used to Pete's cattle calls, which are reserved for the young, the gorgeous, the cosmetically enhanced— that is to say, women who would never, ever go for a guy with thinning hair and a pot belly unless he was worth at least a few mil (which Pete is not). This furthers my belief that Pete is not unlike a gay male fashion designer: His interest in the female form is strictly aesthetic.

"Ten o'clock," he says, turning me around so I can see the sacrificial calf in question.

"Oh, no. Now I'm *really* going home," I mutter, and spin around so my face isn't visible to the tall blonde that Pete is leering at.

Of all the gin joints in all the towns, *why* does Ashley have to be here?

I explain to a baffled Pete who Ashley is, and that I'd rather impale myself on my stiletto than make small talk with the assistant who I suspect believes she's better suited to be my boss. But just as I'm frantically trying to steer us toward a table in a dark corner, I find myself face-to-face with Malibu Barbie herself.

"Marissa? I thought that was you! What are *you* doing here?" Ashley asks, sounding simultaneously perky and perplexed.

"Oh, hi, Ashley," I say, as though I didn't notice her a minute ago. "I'm here with my boyfriend," I say, nodding in the direction of Dave. In a testament to the power of prayer, he looks up as I say this, and seeing the panic on my face, makes his way over to where we're standing.

I make the requisite introductions, and in turn, Ashley introduces me to her fiancé, Jason Benninger, who happens to work down the hall from Dave.

"Small world, huh, Benny?" Dave asks, taking a swig of his Amstel. "I can't believe you're engaged to Marissa's assistant."

"I'm an editorial assistant, not Marissa's assistant," corrects Ashley. To my delight, Dave raises his eyebrows at her as she says this.

"That's right, baby. You're going to rule the world one day," says Jason. He puts his arm around her and says to us, "Ashley and I were engaged a few months ago, when we were in Capri with my family."

Ashley holds out her ring for me to examine, as though I haven't already seen her flash the sparkling boulder four hundred times already.

"Pretty."

"Thank you," she says, and examines the ring herself with a pleased expression on her face.

"So anyway," I say, intending to leave the conversation at that.

Jason doesn't take the hint. "Marissa, Ashley tells me you guys are writing a story about traumatic brain injury together. Fascinating stuff."

*We're writing it together, are we?* "Did she?" I ask Jason.

Ashley smiles, and puts her hand on my arm. "I told Jason how great you've been, Marissa. Teaching me the ropes, giving me a chance to work with you on this big story. It's been such a great learning opportunity for me to comb through all those studies— thank you again," she says, appearing sincere.

I can't tell if it's the alcohol or Ashley's frequent flip-flopping, but I am thrown off guard by her gratitude. No sooner have I decided that I've misjudged her when she adds, "Obviously, working at *Svelte* wasn't exactly my first choice. It is a recession, after all, so I know that I couldn't just walk into *The New Yorker* or *Vogue* and get a job like I'd planned. But this story gives me hope that it's not going to be all cellulite cream and cookie diets. Brainless blather," she says, and gives me a knowing smile.

I blink and stare at her. "You know, I'm not even sure how to respond to that," I finally manage through gritted teeth.

Apparently, Ashley's bronzed skin is coated with Teflon because she smiles again and says, "Well, it's been fascinating, but Jason and I should probably go mingle."

I toss back the last of my champagne like it's a shot and slap the glass down on the table to my right. "*So* glad we've had a chance to talk, Ashley. See you at the office."

# Twenty

The following Tuesday afternoon, I am surprised to realize that I'm actually looking forward to coaching—particularly because it means I get to leave the office early. As Naomi and I ride the 6 train uptown to the Bronx together, where the girls' school is, I glance through my coaching folder and see that today's lesson is on bullying. I think of pretty, pushy Josie and make a quick wish that the lesson will hit home for her.

When we walk through the gymnasium door, the girls greet me as though I'm Hannah Montana in the flesh.

"Coach Marissa!" says Charity, and throws her arms around my waist.

"Are you going to run with us again today?" asks Lisa eagerly. "Coach Beverly never ran with us."

"She didn't?" I ask. I thought running was mandatory—otherwise I would have skipped the tedious laps I did with the girls last week.

"Nope," says Lisa, shaking her head. "Not one time." The disappointment in her voice makes it very clear to me that I will be running today, and every practice from here forth. Damn.

"Coach Marissa is *way* better than Coach Beverly," says a girl named Anna, whose tight black curls are pulled into five different ponytails.

"Totally!" agrees Margarita, bouncing up and down on her tip-toes.

I am not sure what to make of this development, and eye the girls suspiciously to see if they're pulling my leg. But unless I'm missing something, they're being sincere.

"They just had to get used to the idea of a new coach," Naomi tells me as we riffle through our bin of supplies to find materials for the lesson. "Now they'll want to be your best friend."

*Good, because I could use one right about now.* "Probably because I'm the freak-show adult who happens to be the same height as them."

"Actually, Piper is taller than you," Naomi points out with a wicked grin.

I wag my finger at her. "Now, Coach Naomi. Today's lesson is on bullying. You don't want to be a bully, do you?"

"Nooo hooo," she deadpans, then erupts into laughter.

For today's warm-up exercise, we give each girl either a pink or a green sticker, and put a rubber dodge ball in the middle of the gymnasium floor. "Anyone with a pink sticker is the person you want to keep the ball away from," Alanna instructs the girls. "Anyone with a green sticker should try to throw the ball to another green girl. If you're green and a pink girl gets the ball after you've had it, you have to go to the sidelines." Josie, Anna, and Renee are pinks; to my relief, Estrella is one of the nine greens.

I had assumed the girls, most of whom appear about a million times more in-the-know than I was at their age, would think the game was lame. Instead, they run around, laughing and completely delighted. Even the girls who get tagged seem to be having a good time.

After almost all of the greens have gone to the sidelines, Naomi, Alanna, and I grab a ball and ask the girls to watch us. I stand in the middle, and Naomi and Alanna stand on either side of me, saying "mean" things as they toss the ball back and forth over my head, trying to keep the ball from me.

"Don't give her the ball—I don't like her," says Alanna.

"Me, neither! She's a goody-goody who knows all the answers in class," says Naomi. I unsuccessfully try to block her pass to Alanna. "See!" says Naomi. "She stinks at sports."

This goes on for a few minutes, and then the three of us stop and join the girls in their circle.

"How was that different from the game you all played?" Naomi asks.

Estrella's hand shoots up.

"Yes, Estrella?"

"You guys were mean to Coach Marissa. We weren't mean to each other."

"That's right, Estrella," I tell her. "Girls, does anyone know what it's called when a person or group of people is deliberately mean to someone else, because they think it's funny, want to get something from them, or even for no clear reason at all?"

Only Estrella raises her hand, and I have to bite my lip to conceal a smile; she's nothing if not persistent.

"Anyone else want to take a guess this time?" Alanna asks. "Margarita? Jessica?" The girls shake their head no. "Okay, Estrella, what do you think?"

"Bullying!" she announces.

"That's right, Estrella," I say. "That's what today's lesson is about. Bullying."

Naomi tells the girls how she was bullied when she was younger—which, looking at how cool and confident she is now, is especially hard to imagine—and that she used to cry every day after school. "Does anyone here want to share a story of how they've been bullied before?"

Instantly, Estrella's hand is up. I look around the room and notice that Josie and Lisa are whispering nervously. "Girls," I say, and thankfully, they quiet down.

"Go ahead, Estrella," says Naomi after it's clear that no one else is going to step up to the plate.

"Last week, someone"—she narrows her eyes dramatically—"and I won't say who, but someone who is very popular, took my skirt during gym class so I had nothing to change into. I had to wear my gym shorts the rest of the day," she says, pointing at the blue canvas shorts she's wearing now.

"How did that make you feel?" Naomi asks, and I smile, realizing that her favorite therapy catchphrase is poached straight from Take the Lead lessons.

"It made me feel bad at first," says Estrella, looking at the group. "But then I went home and talked to my mom about it. She helped me see that whoever would do such a thing doesn't feel very good about herself." Estrella puts her fists on her hips and leans forward. "She has to be mean to other people to make herself feel better. It's very sad," she says, shaking her head.

Alanna, Naomi, and I glance at one another in surprise, and I'm almost tempted to clap by Estrella's stirring performance. Apparently the girls are impressed, too, because one after another opens up about a time when she, too, was bullied.

Anna is the last to speak. "I'm not sure if my thing counts as bullying," she says sheepishly.

"Go ahead and tell us. There's no wrong answer in group discussion," Naomi says kindly.

"Well," Anna says, pulling at one of her ponytails. "I have this cousin. She always gets me to do what she wants. Like, I'll want to go to the park and she'll say, 'No, we're going to get ice cream,' and I have to do what she says or she gets angry and stops talking to me. It makes me mad, but I don't ever say anything to her."

"I'd say that's bullying," Naomi tells her. "Bullying isn't only about calling names or physically hurting others. It's also about pushing people around and making them do what you want. That's not being a good friend, or a good sport."

"Oh," says Anna. Then she smiles. "So I was right."

"You were right," says Naomi, and several of the girls nod solemnly in agreement.

Later, as we run around the gym, I think about how fragile the girls are—even tough-acting Josie. After several laps, I find myself reminiscing about childhood. When I was the girls' age, three of my classmates—who continued to torment me through junior high school—used to pinch my stomach and call me "Shamu" if I didn't let them copy my homework. (To this day, I refuse to visit Sea World.) It made me dread going to school, but unlike Estrella's mother, my mom told me it was my own fault. "They'll only keep torturing you as long as you let them," she reprimanded me. Of course, standing up to them made it worse, hence my decision to go to a new city for high school.

A few Christmases ago, Julia and I were out at a bar in Ann Arbor when I ran into one of the girls who'd bullied me during junior high.

"Marissa?" Stacy asked, walking over to our table in a way that made me suspect she was several Miller Lites into the night. She was a good thirty pounds heavier than the last time I'd seen her, and her brown hair was now a badly dyed shade of blond that only made her curls look frizzier. Shallow as it may be, when I saw her, I was glad I was having an especially good hair day.

"Stacy?" I said, feeling off-kilter by this chance encounter with the primary source of my adolescent trauma. I half expected her to reach across the table and grab my midsection.

"Yeah! You remember! So good to see you!" she warbled, confirming my earlier suspicion that she was well marinated.

"Really?" I asked a bit snottily, leading Julia to raise an eyebrow at me.

Stacy inquired about what I'd been up to since junior high, so I told her, not without a hint of pride, that I was living in New York and was home for the holidays. In turn, she told me that she was a hostess at Chili's. "It's not fancy, but it pays the bills," she said, clearly embarrassed by this admission. I was contemplating whether or not to make a snide comment when Julia interjected. "I'm sure it's fun," she told Stacy. "After all, in this economy, a job's a job."

"Yeah," she said, looking drunkenly pensive. She looked at Julia, then back at me. "Well, I'll let you get back to talking. I just wanted to say hi."

After Stacy left, I scolded Julia. "You ruined my chance to get back at my childhood nightmare!"

I half expected Julia to suggest one of the elaborate practical jokes she was famous for. But she just shook her head, looking wistfully in Stacy's direction. "Nope," she told me. "That girl doesn't deserve it. Even this early in the game of life, it's clear that you've won."

Julia could be needy and, yes, even manipulative, but she was never deliberately unkind. Most times, as she had with Stacy, she went out of her way to make people feel good about themselves; that was part of her magnetism. As I recall that evening so many years ago, I can't help but wonder if that person—the one who boosted me and everyone else around her up—is still inside of her somewhere, and if so, when she'll reappear again.

# Twenty-one

I know that roughly between two and three p.m., body temper-
ature drops, circadian rhythms slow down, and the dreaded
midday slump takes hold. I also know that the best antidote for
afternoon sleepiness is not M&M's and coffee, but rather a dose
of sunlight and exercise administered in the form of a brisk walk.
I know this because I have written about it, in some incarnation,
no fewer than half a dozen times in the past five years. And still,
when I find myself staring at the back of my eyelids after lunch
instead of tackling my massive workload, I do the only thing that
I can manage: trek over to the vending machines in the kitchen
for a caffeine and chocolate one-two punch.

"I didn't take you for the candy type," says Ashley, coming up
behind me with Farrah, another editorial assistant, hot on her
heels. She opens the fridge, pulls out a lime green Tupperware
container, and peels back the top. "Want one?" she asks, and I see

that the Tupperware holds perfectly sliced green apple pieces, each smeared with just the thinnest layer of peanut butter. Of *course* Ms. twenty-five-inch-waist would be snacking on the perfect combination of protein, carbs, and fat.

"No thanks," I tell her, and insert a wilted dollar bill into the vending machine next to the fridge. I hit the number/letter code and my M&M's hit the bottom of the metal machine with a satisfying thud. I rip open the paper and pop a few in my mouth. Then I look at Ashley. "Nirvana." I sigh contentedly, then hold the bag out to her. "Want one?"

She holds up a flattened palm. "I only do dark chocolate."

"A shame," I say with a hint of pity, and head back to my office, feeling markedly more energized.

Lynne Pelham is the queen of five o'clock edit meetings, but their frequency does not make them any easier to handle. This particular January evening, she's summoned the entire editorial staff to the cavernous conference room across from her office to discuss the June issue. Typically, it's a cash cow, because around May, women begin to panic in anticipation of the impending bathing suit season. But although it is too early to know for sure, this June issue, Lynne informs us somberly, looks like it will be much thinner than usual— a good attribute for a woman, she notes, but *not* for a magazine.

"That's why I've brought you all here today," she says, clasping her vein-roped hands together.

She may be my superior, but Naomi can't help but act like she's a schoolgirl forced to sit through the most insipid class. *She means tonight,* she scribbles on her notepad where I can see it. I smirk. The windows in the conference room look over Bryant Park, and I can see that the streetlights are already on. *Should be home in time for Letterman,* I write back, and look away so it's not obvious that the two of us are trading notes.

Lynne continues. "We need some major wow factor infused into this issue. It's true that health magazines aren't taking a hit the same way the fashion and general interest titles are. But there's absolutely no doubt that aside from food advertising, which remains the sole reason why you're all sitting here instead of collecting checks at the unemployment office, ad pages are down. *Way* down. We. Are. Not. Doing. Well." She tosses her golden hair over her shoulder and straightens her spine, looking like a European princess who's just survived a trek through the Serengeti and lived to tell the tale.

"Lynne, tell us what you mean by 'wow,'" asks Roxanne, our executive editor. "Do you want pieces like we normally run, but repackaged? Or do you mean completely out-of-the-box like that hundred-word-essay series we did last September?"

"Both," Lynne answers ambiguously. She looks at Naomi. "Let's run through the current lineup. Tell me which stories you have scheduled and then we'll brainstorm for ways to make them more appealing to advertisers."

I swallow hard, nervous. Suddenly my brain trauma idea seems unbelievably stupid; I can't believe it ever got the go-ahead. There is no way it will make the cut.

Sure enough, when Naomi mentions it, Lynne barks, "Whose idea was that?"

"Mine," I manage to squeak.

Then Lynne surprises me. "Well done, Marissa. I like it. That's not our normal type of story, but we need to up the ante if we're going to win any Ellies at the American Society of Magazine Editors conference. And we all know those awards mean more advertising dollars. Ladies, I want more of what Marissa came up with. Think sharp, smart, and service-oriented. Think *The Atlantic,* but for women who don't want to get fat."

Naomi writes "!!!!" on her notepad and I can't even look at her because I know I'll lose it.

"*The Atlantic* for women who don't want to get fat!" she howls in my office an hour later.

"I know, I almost died," I tell her, wiping laughter-induced tears from the corners of my eyes. "And to think that my article has set the bar for our new standards of journalism." I hear footsteps outside my door. "Shhh," I tell her.

There's a knock, and before I can answer, Ashley lets herself in.

"We're in the middle of something," Naomi tells Ashley in her best coaching voice.

"Oh," says Ashley. "Sorry." All traces of the attitude she usually pulls on me are gone.

"That's okay," I say to her. "It's late, anyway, and I'm heading out. Can you swing by first thing in the morning?"

"Sure, absolutely," Ashley says almost meekly. When she closes the door behind her, I turn to Naomi. "Um, why is it that she suddenly acts like an angel when you're around?"

Naomi looks amused. "You ever watch the *Dog Whisperer?* Same techniques apply to humans, really. You just have to make it clear that you're the boss. Otherwise she'll walk all over you. It's not the most kosher thing to say, but it's true of anyone who you're supervising. Mammalian Behavior 101."

"Is that how you keep me in line?" I chide her.

"No, thank God. You're easy," Naomi says, flinging a pen at me. "Now bark!"

I laugh. "Well, I wish I could say the same about Ashley, but she seems hell-bent on undermining me at every turn," I tell her, and then fill her in on the scene at Dave's company party.

"I think you're overthinking it. She's probably just talking herself up to her fiancé and doesn't mean anything by it."

"I'm not so sure about that."

"I'm willing to bet that's at least a large part of her motivation," Naomi says to me. "But even if she's trying to reenact *All About Eve*, I'll tell you what my mother always tells me: Think about what you want out of the situation, not how you feel about it. You'll get better results that way."

"Interesting theory."

"Well, you want blondie to do a good job for you, right?"

"Obviously."

"Then, don't worry about how highly she thinks of herself. Just check her work. If she's doing what you ask her, great. If not, tell her what you need. And if that doesn't work, take her off the story."

"Easier said than done. It's not like we've got assistants to spare."

"True. But it's a good story, and it's not worth letting her mess it up. Just keep that in mind if you're not pleased with how things are going."

But the next morning, Ashley surprises me by showing up outside my office door with a bulging research folder, a detailed story memo, and, to seal the deal, two cappuccinos.

"Thought you might want some coffee while we go over everything," she says, handing me the second cup before she sits down next to my desk. I wasn't planning on running through the entire story with her this morning—I've got four articles to edit in the next two days—but the caffeine is more than welcome, so I let it slide.

"Okay, let's start by comparing research," I tell her, and pull up my notes on my computer. We spend the next hour poring over studies and statistics. I discover that with little instruction from me, Ashley has done an impressive job sorting through the medical jargon and pulling out the information that's actually relevant to my story, and I tell her so. "You mean it?" she asks me with a huge smile.

"I do," I say. "And I appreciate it. I think you're ready to take on that sidebar we talked about."

She practically squeals. "Yay! What do you think it should be about? Because I have some ideas."

"Hmm . . . that's a good question," I tell her. "Maybe a first-person interview with someone who's had a brain injury?" I tug on a stray lock of hair and think for a minute. "Actually, it should probably be more service-oriented. Something like, 'Signs you need to get to the hospital after hitting your head' or 'What to do if you think you've suffered TBI.' Why don't you e-mail me your ideas, then I'll compare them with mine and pick one?"

"Will do," she says confidently. "Marissa, I can't tell you how excited I am about this. It's been the most fun thing I've worked on since I started here."

"Me, too, Ashley," I tell her. "Me, too."

# Twenty-two

It's an unseasonably warm February day, but beyond the weather, nothing is out of the ordinary when I leave my office for lunch. Same crowded elevator ride to the first floor; same security guards checking ID in the lobby; same mob of tourists to push past in order to get to the deli on Forty-third Street where I usually go for salads. Yet, from the minute I leave my office, I cannot shake the unsettling feeling that I am being watched.

I'm so on edge that when someone taps me on the shoulder at Friendly's Grocer, I jump, even though it's just another customer letting me know that my MetroCard fell out of my wallet when I went to pay for lunch. And while I know I'm only making myself more conspicuous, I can't help but glance over my shoulder every few minutes to see if someone is trailing me. I am Grace Kelly in *Rear Window*, minus the glamour, flaxen locks, and murder plot.

Intuition is a funny thing. Most people assume that their "gut feelings" are sheer luck, or God giving them a nudge in a certain direction. In fact, studies show that it's the brain's way of adding past experience and external cues together at lightning speed— a spontaneous burst of logical thinking, so to speak. Intuition can make a person choose the right stock, or say yes to a date with a stranger who they end up marrying. But from a biological perspective, its primary purpose is to protect us from danger.

Which is why, although I am not entirely surprised to see Nathan—something deep in me already knew I would run into him today—the sight of him leaning against the granite slab of my building's entrance when I return from lunch sets off multiple alarms in my head.

My first instinct is to duck and walk the other direction. On top of the fact that I'm fairly certain nothing good can come of us talking, my hair looks like I'm auditioning to be Bride of Frankenstein, my shirt has a coffee-stained Rorschach blot on it, and I'm exhausted. But it's too late; he's already seen me.

My escapist urges must be obvious, because the first thing Nathan says is, "Wait! Don't go, Marissa." He holds up both hands, palms toward me as though he is surrendering. Clad in jeans, boots, and a well-worn brown suede coat, he is squinting in the sunlight, and I can see tiny golden flecks in the dark stubble shading his jaw.

"What are you doing here?" I ask, sounding sharper than I intend to. I soften my tone. "I mean, I wasn't exactly expecting you."

I look around to see if any of my colleagues have seen us. I'm not doing anything wrong, I know, and yet I'm as embarrassed as if I've been walking around with my skirt tucked into granny panties.

Then it hits me. Dangerous though he may be, I'm embarrassed because I'm secretly thrilled to see him, and not just because I may finally get some answers about his intentions with Julia.

"I know you weren't expecting me," Nathan says, breaking into a sheepish grin. I remember that he always used to smile when he was uncomfortable and am glad to see that he's as jittery as I am.

"You flew all the way to New York to track me down outside of work?" I ask, shifting the plastic bag holding my lunch from one arm to the other.

"No," he says quickly. "Well, not exactly. I'm in town for a wine and spirits convention. You know, for the restaurant."

"Oh."

"But, uh, obviously I wanted to see you, or I wouldn't be standing here." He looks at me and smiles again, sending a shot of electricity straight through my body. "So I Googled you to see if you were still working at the magazine, and decided it would probably be better to show up here than at your house."

"Probably," I say, because this is all I can manage to get out. The thought of Nathan showing up at my apartment—the apartment I share *with Dave*—is enough to give me a minor panic attack.

"Why didn't you call?" I ask him.

"Can I blame it on a sudden burst of spontaneity?" he jokes. "Because the truth is, I kind of figured you'd say no if I got in touch ahead of time."

"You're probably right," I confess.

We say nothing for a minute or two, just standing there staring at each other like idiots. I cannot get over how good he looks, even better than when I last saw him. An image of him lying on his futon in college flashes through my head, and I blush and turn away so he won't see my face. Again I think of Dave, and more blood rushes to my cheeks. What am I doing here? It doesn't matter if Nathan were Johnny Depp himself, waiting to whisk me off to his private island in the Caribbean. I am in a committed relationship, and regardless of whether it constitutes as cheating, I know for certain that the thoughts I'm having are not kosher.

And yet. Nathan showing up unannounced may be unnerving, but it's exactly the kind of crazy gesture I wish Dave would make once in a while. Steadfast, predictable Dave, whom I love . . . and whom I can't seem to stop comparing to Nathan. Nathan! A man I don't even know anymore. Still, the contact we have had is enough to signal that he's changed little since college. And so, unlike Dave, he isn't the type to spend his entire life chained to his desk, doesn't break out in hives if he skips a shave, and would undoubtedly head to Tahiti on a moment's notice like Dave and I always say we will (and never do). Who wouldn't be attracted to that?

"I'd better go," I tell him, and hoist my handbag back on my shoulder resolutely.

"You're always saying that," Nathan says wistfully. He reaches out and touches my arm. *Zing.*

"Have dinner with me tonight," he says, then laughs. It comes out deep and throaty and I think of Dave's light, breathy laughter. "That sounds like such a pickup line," he says. "Seriously, though. I'd really like to catch up, and I want a chance to explain some things to you. Please."

*Like this time, how you really are in love with my best friend? Not a chance,* I think.

But what comes out of my mouth is, "Where?"


The rest of the day is a total loss. I pick at my salad for nearly an hour before finally tossing it in the trash. I attempt to read a manuscript four times before realizing that I haven't processed a single word. I'm so distracted that I can't even bring myself to play Scrabulous. And although I'm dying to confess to Naomi, I don't dare do so, because I know exactly what she'll say.

To my relief, Dave e-mails to say he's going out to dinner with a client, negating the need for any explanation about what I'm doing with my evening. I contemplate running home to change but decide it'll look too much like I care (which I do, but I don't want to broadcast it). Instead, I dash over to Pauline, our beauty director, to beg for her help.

"I'm meeting an old friend for dinner tonight and I look like a mess. Can you work your magic?" I ask her.

Pauline looks up from the pile of eye shadows she's been sorting on her desk. "I've been hoping you'd ask me that sometime this century. Come on over." She motions for me to sit on the tall stool against the wall and starts pulling products out of the beauty closet.

A heaping dose of hair product and a generous application of makeup later, I look better. Actually, I look damn good, considering the sorry state I was in not fifteen minutes ago. "Can you please make me up every day?" I ask, checking my reflection in the mirror one more time. "I don't know what you did, but I need this"—I make a circle around my face—"more often."

Pauline grins and presses a lip gloss, cover-up stick, and some grooming cream in my hands. "Samples. Keep them and practice a few times at home before going out in public."

"I owe you."

"No, you don't," she says. "It was fun. And I have to say, it's not just the makeup. You look so much nicer now that your face isn't buried under all that hair."

I'm not sure if this is a true compliment, but I decide to take it. "Thanks, Pauline."

.   .   .

I'm half a block from the downtown bistro where I'm meeting Nathan when a minor panic attack strikes. What are we going to talk about? Am I going to freak out like I did at Beber? Do I look too made-up? What am I going to tell Dave? I am so fraught with anxiety that I'm practically gasping for air when I reach the restaurant. As I ask the hostess about a table, I feel a hand on the small of my back.

"Hey," says Nathan, leaning forward and touching his cheek to mine, not a real kiss but an intimate gesture all the same. He smells faintly of freshly cut wood, and his hair looks damp, leading me to believe he just showered. He's wearing a fresh blue shirt with the same jeans and boots he had on earlier.

"Hi," I say, and move slightly to the left so that I'm just beyond his reach. I can't risk feeling that jolt again.

"This way," the hostess says, leading us through the dining room. It's early enough that a few chic parents are parsing out steak frites to toddlers who look like they belong in a Benetton ad, but the restaurant is dimly lit. We're seated at a table in a particularly dark corner, which has the unfortunate effect of making this seem even more like a date.

The waiter appears and runs through the night's specials, then asks if we want to order wine.

"Bottle?" Nathan asks me.

"No, a glass is all I can handle. Have to be up and at 'em early tomorrow," I say in a chipper voice, although the real reason I don't want a bottle is because lowered inhibitions are the last thing I need right now.

We order drinks, and make small talk until the waiter returns to take our order: Niçoise salad for me, duck for Nathan.

"This restaurant is très chic for a Michigander," I joke, trying to lighten the mood.

"I'm in the city once or twice a year and I always try to eat at a French place," he says, unfolding his napkin and placing it in his lap. "I'm a sucker for the ambiance."

"Well, you've come a long way from World Cup."

"I guess I have," he says jovially. "And clearly, so have you. Big magazine job, living in New York . . ."

"Life is good," I admit. "But look at you, running the most popular new restaurant in Ann Arbor," I say, referring to the sign I saw hanging in the window at Beber. "You must have your hands full, no?"

"That's putting it mildly," he says, looking weary. "You know when you really dream about something for a long time, and it doesn't turn out to be quite as fantastic as you were hoping?"

"Yeah," I admit, thinking of my job.

"Well, that's what the restaurant is like. I love being there, but dealing with the staff and paperwork is enough to send me over the edge sometimes."

"But are you happy?"

"Are *you* happy?" he says, stretching out the word "happy" with his seductive drawl.

"I asked first," I say, and cross my arms over my chest.

"Ah, there's the Marissa I know and love," he retorts, and holds my eye longer than I'd like.

*You mean loved,* I think. *Past tense.* But I say nothing, and set about buttering my bread like my life depends on it.

Finally, I say, "This is really weird for me. Isn't it weird for you?"

"Not really. I wanted to see you, so here I am. Pretty straight-forward."

"*Why* did you want to see me?" I blurt, staring at my fork. "If you're here to ask me if it's okay for you to date Julia, then yes, it's fine. I mean, I'm not crazy about the idea, and you'd probably get a better idea of what you're getting into, given her head injury . . ."

I stop babbling for a second and look up. The way Nathan's gazing at me from across the table is enough to tell me that my fear about him and Julia is just as irrational as when I had it a decade ago. Still, the e-mails between them, Julia's constant mentions of him, the photos she sent—it all adds up to something decidedly unpleasant. It may not be true love, but Julia is undeniably beautiful, and now she sees Nathan regularly. What are the odds he's not at least a *little* tempted?

"Ah, I see that some things never change." He sighs. "There's nothing between Julia and me, and there never will be. She e-mailed me to tell me she was moving to Ann Arbor, and I e-mailed her back; it seemed like the right thing to do. I didn't know about the accident until she came in to Beber at the beginning of November. It was pretty obvious something was off with her."

"You think?" I say, unable to conceal my irritation.

"I'm not sure what to tell you," Nathan tells me wearily. "The accident left her a wreck, and she needed a friend."

I think back to what Julia said to me a few weeks ago: *"Marissa, I'm lonely. You're not here for me."*

He continues. "I make her a meal every once in a while, put her in touch with people she might be able to hang out with. It's not like we see each other all the time. Trust me: I am *not* the one you should be worried about. You know she's having an affair with a married man, right?" he says, pushing his plate away as though the thought of it has killed his appetite.

"I don't believe you," I say, but seeing the pained expression on his face, it's obvious that he's telling the truth.

"You didn't know?" he says, surprised. "Do you know about the shoplifting incident?"

"About the sunglasses? Yeah."

The waiter appears with our meals and we assure him that

everything looks fine. The minute he leaves, Nathan turns back to me. "It wasn't just sunglasses. She had half the store in her purse."

"No way." Julia could have bought anything she wanted in that store. Why would she steal? And what else has she been concealing from me?

"The only reason they let her off was because of her brain injury. Turns out it wasn't the first time that the cop assigned to her case had to deal with something like this, so he knew how messed up she was."

All of what he's just told me should be reassuring, if only in terms of their relationship. And yet, even if he's not interested in her, Julia seems entirely too obsessed with Nathan. "I'm still pretty sure she has a thing for you," I tell him.

"She's not interested in me," he says plainly. "I think she likes being around me because for whatever reason, I remind her of you. She recently told me her whole reason for getting in touch with me was to apologize. She said something vague about making amends for contributing to our breakup."

"She didn't contribute to it, she *caused* it," I spit out before I can check myself. "She was the one who wanted us to break up in the first place." *Verbal diarrhea much, Marissa?*

"So that whole line you fed me about us living in different places and having different goals was a crock?"

"Not exactly," I mumble. "It was true, but the real reason I broke up with you was because Julia asked me to."

"That's the one thing she didn't tell me," he says, leaning toward me over the table.

"Well, what's done is done," I say, as much for my own benefit as for his. "Things turned out for the best—I'm happy with my life now. I'm happy with my relationship with Dave," I add. "I don't see the point in rehashing our breakup when we shut that door a decade ago."

"Did we?" he asks, his hazel eyes searching my face. "Because you just told me it wasn't your choice. From where I stand, that means you never stopped caring. I know I didn't."

*Of course I never stopped caring. Otherwise I wouldn't be sitting here right now.* But as light-headed as I am right now, I'm alert enough to not utter this out loud. "Nathan, it's been eleven years," I say a little too forcefully, trying to cover the fact that my heart is in my throat. "We don't even know each other anymore, really."

"I know that we had something amazing. Something I've never been able to re-create with another person."

I don't respond. What Nathan and I had *was* amazing. He was my first love, the first person I slept with, and it was magical in a way that nothing else ever will be again. But what I have with Dave is amazing for different reasons. Can I really give that up, having no idea whether Nathan and I would work the same way at a totally different moment in time?

"I think you're idealizing what we had," I finally tell him.

"Marissa, trust me on this one," Nathan says, not deterred in the least. "I just went through yet another bad breakup. My fourth in five years. And you know what I finally realized? All this time, I haven't been satisfied because what I want is what you and I had. I want someone who can spend hours talking with me and not get bored. Who doesn't think it's stupid to have fun. Someone who *gets* me the way you got me."

I stare at him, trying to process what he's just said. It's no use; the best I can manage is a halfhearted response. "But, Nathan, I've changed. I'm sure you have, too. It would never work."

"Marissa, I'm looking at you right now, and I can tell from the look on your face that you're bluffing," he says quietly.

*Oh God,* I think.

*What if he's right?*

# Twenty-three

Dave's watching *SportsCenter* when I get home.

"Late night at the office?" he asks, turning down the volume. "I tried calling you."

"I left my phone off," I say, avoiding his question, and busy myself with hanging my coat and purse up so that I won't have to look at him. "I didn't check because I thought you'd be out with your clients."

"They had an early flight to San Fran, so we just had drinks." He gets up from the sofa and walks over to the kitchen island where I'm standing. He puts his arms around my waist and says in a low voice, "You look gorgeous tonight. Apparently working late agrees with you."

"Apparently," I reply vaguely, and rub my forehead. "Baby, I'm really sorry, but I have a terrible headache." It's true; my temples are throbbing. "Do you mind if I shower and hit the hay?"

"Of course not," he says, and kisses me lightly. "Want me to get you some water and Tylenol?"

"No, it's okay," I say. Although I deserve to be tarred and feathered, this headache will have to suffice as punishment for now.

After a quick shower, I slip into a pair of brown silk pajamas with cream lace edges that Dave bought me last Christmas. My limbs are heavy and I'm exhausted, but sleeping is impossible. I toss and turn, and the smooth fabric of my pajamas tangles around my limbs.

I can't stop thinking about Nathan. After our discussion about our past, he must have sensed my discomfort, because he quickly changed the subject; we spent the rest of the dinner talking about benign topics—my brain injury article, his restaurant convention, the respective merits of living in Michigan and New York. After we finished our entrees, I begged off dessert, and when we said our good-byes, I made a point to tell him Dave was waiting for me at home.

"I understand." Nathan nodded, putting his hands in his pockets. "I'm glad we had a chance to get together." This time, he didn't try to kiss my cheek, or even hug me. Instead, he just looked at me. "I'll talk to you soon," he finally said, and walked over to the street to hail a taxi.

As I squeeze my eyelids closed, trying to will myself to sleep, all I can see is the image of Nathan's face as he stood outside of the restaurant. It was not the look of a man who had moved on. It was the look of a man who was hopeful. Who thought he had a fighting chance. The knot in my stomach is a clear sign that deep down, I am worried that I'm the one who gave him that impression.

As Nathan sat there babbling about his dog and old friends of ours whom he's kept up with, my mind spun more and more

elaborate story lines about the life we might have had. We'd probably be married, living in a cute house near downtown Ann Arbor.
Maybe I'd be writing for magazines part-time when I wasn't caring for our gaggle of children, who would have my hair and their
father's dimples. We'd spend summers at our cottage up north,
and I'd chip in at the restaurant when it was short-staffed, wow-
ing customers with my killer martinis. It may not have been the
dream existence I'd conjured for myself with Julia when we were
teens, but it would have been good, I decided.

And although I know it's entirely ridiculous, I cannot shake the
feeling that all that time I was daydreaming, Nathan knew exactly
what was going through my head.


As a child, I desperately wanted a dog, but no amount of begging
could convince my mother that dogs weren't unclean creatures
who would destroy her house. Yet so strong was my desire that
when my friend Karen Topler's beagle had puppies, I immediately
told her I'd take one. I arrived at her house with my empty back-
pack, somehow managed to assure Karen's mother that my mom
had given her blessing, and carried the tiny, frenetic animal—whom
I had dubbed Henry—home, yelping and scratching in my bag.

My grand plan (which was admittedly harebrained, even for an
eleven-year-old) was to raise Henry in the small shed behind our
garage and keep him out of my mother's sight. When she discovered him—as I assumed she eventually would—he would be so
charming and well behaved that she'd immediately fall in love and
welcome him into our home.

Henry, who was all of a few months old, was not a fan of being
left alone behind the garage, and he let me know it by howling at
the top of his lungs. When it quickly became apparent that treats

and toys would not appease him, I had no choice but to take him up to my room before my mother came home from work. I decided that the most discreet place for him to spend the night was my closet, so I cleared out the shoes and discarded clothes on the ground. In their place, I bunched up an old towel for his bed and placed a bowl of water and a plate of baloney scraps next to it. I recalled Karen saying something about using newspaper to housebreak puppies, but I couldn't find any, so I decided some pages torn from an old coloring book would have to do. I swore Sarah—who shared a room with me and immediately heard Henry scratching at the closet door—to secrecy and crossed my fingers that it would all work out.

What I didn't anticipate was my own reaction. I felt so sick that I couldn't make a dent in my Stouffer's microwave lasagna, which I usually Hoovered off the plate. Despite my suspiciously absent appetite and the fact that I retreated to my room immediately after dinner instead of parking in front of the television as I usually did, my mother never suspected a thing.

In my room, I found Henry fast asleep. I decided to follow his lead, and got into bed even though it was still light out. I don't know how long I was there—it felt like years—but I felt worse and worse, going from anxious to clammy to feverish to so nauseous that I was certain I would vomit all over my peach and green bedspread.

Finally, I couldn't take it for another second. I found my mother in her bedroom, sitting in an armchair and gabbing on the phone to one of her friends. She looked annoyed to see me.

"What is it, Marissa?" she asked exasperatedly, still holding the receiver.

"I don't feel well," I said, clutching my stomach.

"Oh, all right," she said, although her tone was softened. She hung up the phone, then came over to feel my forehead. "You're burning up," she said, a concerned look coming over her face.

"We're going to have to get you some Tylenol and a cold wash-cloth." Her unexpected kindness spurred a torrent of my tears.

"My goodness, what is it?" she asked, peering at me. "Are you okay? Was Sarah being mean to you?"

"Noo," I managed to choke out between sobs. "There's . . . a . . . pu . . . pu . . . puppy in my room."

"Oh my good God," said my mother, looking at me as though she expected me to yell "April Fool's!" "Really, Marissa? *Really?* Where on earth did you get a puppy? And how long has it been there?"

And so I confessed the entire sordid affair to her. I felt so much better after telling her that I didn't argue when she told me I'd have to take Henry back to the Toplers' house the next day.


Turns out that keeping a dinner date with my ex a secret from Dave is not much different from keeping a puppy hidden from my mother. Because I have the exact same "I'm a horrible person who will surely rot in hell" feeling that I did twenty years ago. And so, after what seems like hours of torture in a plush, queen-size prison, I push back the crisp white sheets and climb out of bed.

Dave is sitting at the kitchen island typing on his computer. "Can't sleep?"

"Not a wink," I confess.

"You want a back rub?" he asks, pushing his wavy brown hair out of his eyes and giving me a look that serves only to remind me that this sweet, sensitive man is a deity that I, a mere mortal, do not even remotely deserve.

"I want you to throw me out on the stoop and call a locksmith," I tell him glumly. "I am the world's worst girlfriend and I think you should kick me to the curb."

"What on earth are you talking about?" he asks. He walks over to the fridge, takes out two beers, and hands me one. "Here, it'll help you relax."

"Thanks," I say, and even though I am not a fan of beer, I take a sip. The cool, bubbly liquid goes down easy, soothing my churning stomach.

My relief is short-lived. "I have to tell you something," I say to Dave, and pull at the label on the beer bottle nervously.

"As long as you didn't cheat on me, I think I can handle it," he jokes, and I have to stop myself from cringing.

We walk into the living room and sit facing each other on the sofa. I take a deep breath. "You know my ex from college?"

"The stoner?" asks Dave, referring to Evan, a great guy who happened to be completely uninterested in any physical contact other than cuddling after he hit the bong (which was no fewer than three times a day).

"No, the other one," I tell him. "Nathan."

"The guy from the coffee shop? Sort of," says Dave.

"I had dinner with him tonight," I practically whisper.

"Um, okay?" says Dave, obviously irritated. "Why didn't you tell me that earlier?"

"I don't know." This is the truth.

"Well, that's ridiculous." He looks at me and I see a light go on in his head. *I'll take good-for-nothing girlfriends for seven hundred, Alex.* "Wait—you don't still have a thing for this guy, do you?"

"No!" I say quickly. Although it's cool in the living room, I am sweating up a storm, and wipe my brow with the back of my hand.

"Then why are you hiding things from me? That's not our style, Marissa," Dave says.

Unsure of where to start, I pause for what feels like the single longest minute in history. "Well . . . he showed up outside my office today. He's in town for some work event. Asked if I wanted to have dinner." I cannot bring myself to say Nathan's name again, because every time I do, it feels like I'm releasing poison gas into my home.

"Wow. Well, that confirms he has a thing for you." Dave puts his beer down on the coffee table with a thud. "You could have at least done me the courtesy of letting me know you were going to see him. It's not like I'm the possessive type, but I don't like to be kept in the dark."

"I know, honey. I'm so sorry," I say, practically in tears. Dave looks at me with clear concern—and yes, even love—in spite of his anger. And suddenly, it dawns on me just how much I stand to lose by indulging in this stupid mind game.

"I haven't talked to him since college," I tell Dave. "But after the accident, Julia started bringing him up again—a lot—and it turns out she's been in touch with him since moving back. The thing is, she was the one who'd encouraged me to break up with him when I was in college."

"Encouraged you?" Dave says with raised eyebrows.

"She claimed that she was in love with him, too, and that it wasn't fair to our friendship for either of us to have him."

"Nice," he says sarcastically, and I realize with some degree of regret that my admission will go in Dave's mental list of Julia's mistakes. "No wonder you flinched when she mentioned him in the hospital." *So that didn't go over his head after all.*

"I thought that I was okay with it, but when I saw him today, I realized that I had a lot of questions about what was going on between them now, and that I needed answers."

"Marissa, I adore you, but what is it with you and volatile peo-ple?" Dave asks, making little spirals around his head to imply that both Nathan and Julia are crazy.

"What do you mean?"

"Well, let's see. You've got a best friend who, even prior to her brain injury, is amazingly adept at pulling your puppet strings."

"You think I'm Julia's puppet?" I ask, now truly crying.

"You know what I mean. Now it turns out that your ex is a quasi-stalker who thinks it's perfectly acceptable to park himself outside of your work until he 'bumps into you.' And somehow, these two tornado-like human beings have managed to intertwine and cause even more disaster in your head."

He's right, of course. For the first time, it's apparent to me just how similar Nathan and Julia really are: exciting, unpredictable, and prone to making everything far more complicated than it needs to be.

"I may be boring and stable, but damn it, I think I should take priority over them," Dave says. "I mean, I don't get it. Isn't our life together good, Marissa? Don't we have exactly the kind of relationship that you've always wanted?"

"Yes," I tell him, wiping my eyes with the corner of my sleeve. "You know that."

"So if you're really over this Nathan guy—and I'm going to take you at your word unless you give me another reason to doubt you—then stop trying to get answers about other people and start focusing on *us* for a change."

I apologize profusely and promise Dave over and over that I'll never jeopardize our relationship again. To his credit, he not only accepts my apologies, he comforts me until I stop crying. Kissing the top of my head, he tells me, "We've got our work cut out for us, but we're going to be okay."

*Just as long as I stop playing Choose Your Own Adventure with my life*, I think.

# Twenty-four

Researchers at the University of Arizona recently discovered that the average toilet bowl is seven times cleaner than the average kitchen counter. While this fact doesn't make me want to julienne red peppers in my bathroom, it has encouraged me to spend Thursday evening Lysoling every square inch of black and gray granite in our kitchen. I spray and scrub as though my life depends on it (which may actually be the case, as salmonella has been known to kill perfectly healthy women from time to time). But my frantic cleaning is really just an attempt to divert myself from the anxiety I'm feeling over Julia's arrival this evening.

She called last week to say that she wanted to come to New York, and that her doctors had given her the go-ahead to travel provided she stay with a friend or family member. "So . . . I booked a ticket for next weekend!" she squealed. "I'm finally coming to visit you!" The short notice wasn't ideal, but she'd seemed so disinterested in me since her shoplifting confession that I decided the uninvited visit was an improvement. Since learning that she and Nathan weren't dating after all, I felt guilty for doubting her, too, and wondered if I couldn't find a way to make it up to her while she was here.

At the same time, I fretted about how much could go wrong, even over the course of three short days. What if she pulled another Jekyll and Hyde—or worse?

Half an hour before I'm expecting her, Julia sends me a text message. "Plane early! I'm almost there."

I glance out the front window and sure enough, Julia's climbing out of a black town car in front of my house. I quickly wash my bacteria-encrusted hands and throw open the door to find her grinning like a maniac, her arms outstretched toward me and her oversize suitcase resting on the cement stoop next to her.

"Yay!" she yells in lieu of a greeting. "Best friends, reunited again! It's going to be just like old times." She walks in the apartment without bothering to grab her luggage.

I haul the fifty-pound bag behind her. "Just like old times."

Inside, Julia flings herself down on the sofa, causing her wispy chocolate hair to fan around her head like a mane. "Is it too early to raise some hell?" She giggles. "Let's have a drink."

Looking at her, I'm instantly transported back to our first year in New York after college. Everyone warned us not to move in together, saying that it would be the death of our friendship. We blithely ignored them and signed a lease for a tiny two-bedroom in a seedy section of Alphabet City. The apartment was dim and dingy, but Julia managed to infuse it with charm by repainting every square inch from the cupboards to the molding, strategically hanging mirrors to add light and placing vases of fresh-cut flowers in each room.

As it turned out, we had little opportunity to irritate each other. Our starter jobs kept us busier than we could have imagined, and the scant spare time Julia did have was taken up by her recreational ballet corps. And yet, every night before bed, we managed to squeeze in time to talk. Julia would serve us each a nightcap—to "preserve tradition," she'd pour even the cheapest beer into crystal goblets—and we'd sprawl on either end of the Ferrars' hand-me-down couch. "To living our dream," she'd say, clinking my glass with hers. "To living our dream," I'd repeat.

More often than not, we'd sit there for a good hour or more, recounting the day's events. If my horrendous boss at the alternative weekly where I was working berated me, Julia would give me just the right comeback to use. When she couldn't seem to master a ballet sequence, I'd help her visualize so she could nail it the next day. It was us against the world, and we truly (and perhaps naively) believed that there wasn't anything we couldn't figure out together. Two years later, when Julia moved into the apartment the Ferrars bought her and I settled into my new Park Slope studio, I was so unmoored that I slept with the TV on for weeks.

Tonight, however, there will be no pre-bed chatfest: The shot of whiskey Julia requests instantly triggers a migraine. She goes into the guest bedroom to lie down and ends up sleeping until the next morning, shattering any illusion either of us had about reliving the past.

Despite my assurances to Grace that I'll keep a close eye on Julia while she's visiting, I'm forced to leave her alone in my apartment when I head off to work the next day.

"These are *delicious*," Julia says. She is perched atop my counter, spooning Lucky Charms into her mouth from the oversize salad bowl she's poured them into. I can't remember ever having seen her consume that many carbohydrates in one sitting, and for some reason, this makes me happy. That is, until she announces, "Ever since Nathan started cooking for me I've had the biggest appetite. You really need to let him whip something up for you, Mar."

"Jules, I don't think that's the best idea," I say, speaking slowly as I search for the right words. "I saw him a few weeks ago—"

"I know," she says, her mouth full of food. "I was the one who told him he should try to have dinner with you while he was in town."

"You did what?" I ask incredulously.

"Marissa, if there's one thing I've realized over the past few months is that you've got to grab life by the horns and just go for it."

"Okay," I say, not really following her.

"You and Nathan are meant to be together," she says, waving her spoon in the air.

*So that's why you sent me his photo and have been dropping his name constantly. Well, you're about ten years too late, my friend.* "I really don't think so," I tell her, thinking back to the conversation I had with Dave after seeing Nathan. Since that night, Dave and I had been doing great—better than ever, really, although I don't say this out loud for fear of jinxing things.

I look Julia straight in the eyes. "You know I'm in a relationship with Dave. I love him."

"I know you love Dave," she says. "But that doesn't mean he's the one."

"He *is* the one," I say defensively. Best friend or not, she already meddled in one relationship of mine; I'll be damned if she's going to screw this one up for me, too.

"Whatever you say, Marissa," she tells me, but she is smiling like a cat who just swallowed a whole flock of canaries.

I glance at the clock. *Crap.* I'm really late. "Jules, I hate to cut this conversation off, but I really have to get to work."

"You can't play hooky?" Julia says, a hint of a whine in her voice.

"I wish I could, but I have too much work to tackle today to call off." Not wanting to sound like a stern parent instructing their teen to suck it up and deal, I add, "I'll sneak out a little early."

I expect Julia to continue to give me a hard time, but she just shrugs. "Okay." She grabs the cereal box next to her, and instead of filling her empty bowl, she sticks her hand directly in the box to fish for marshmallows. "I'll watch some talk shows and maybe go for a walk. I could use some exercise."

"That sounds good," I tell her, although the thought of her walking around my neighborhood, which is unfamiliar to her, worries me a little. "I should be home by five or so. If you need anything, call."


Around two, I make a coffee run to fuel up for the rest of the day. When I return through the lobby, I find Ashley standing next to Gladys's desk. Across from her, Julia is sprawled in a leather recliner, tissue paper–tufted shopping bags hanging from both arms.

Sensing my confusion, Gladys explains, "This young lady asked for you, and since I knew you ran out, I called Ashley to come greet her."

Julia jumps up to greet me. "Marissa! I got bored, so I went shopping, and then that got old, so I decided to come to your office."

"You remembered where it is?" I ask her. In the five years I've worked here, she's never once actually stepped foot inside the building where *Svelte* is housed, so I have no idea how she found her way today.

"Sure," she says. "Why wouldn't I?" *Because you can't remember the word "marker" or what a hard drive is*, I think, although I'm also sort of impressed.

"Listen, I better go," Ashley interjects. "Lots of work."

"Oh! That's too bad. It was so nice to finally meet you in person," Julia says. She jumps up and gives her a huge hug like they're old friends.

I look at Julia quizzically; I don't recall ever mentioning Ashley to her.

"You, too," says Ashley hurriedly. "Marissa's told me so many great things about you." This is a nicety, but it's also a blatant lie; I know for a fact that I've deliberately mentioned as little as possible about Julia to Ashley, even in relation to the brain injury story. I have no interest in sharing the details of my life with her when she's likely to use them as ammunition later down the line.

"Well, if you need me, you know how to reach me!" says Julia, waving at Ashley.

As I watch Ashley book it down the hall back to her cubicle, I get a strange sensation that something, somehow, isn't right.

# Twenty-five

I'm still tense when Saturday rolls around.

By all accounts, the day goes smoothly: Julia and I have lunch at a Thai restaurant near my house, then the two of us spend the mild and dazzlingly sunny afternoon roaming around Brooklyn. That night, we watch a Meg Ryan marathon on Oxygen, which is exactly the type of thing we used to do before Julia's accident. But I find myself downing the better part of a bottle of wine in order to dampen the nails-on-chalkboard pitch of Julia's voice.

Sunday morning, Dave, Julia, and I are sitting around the kitchen eating the slightly burned but otherwise delicious frittata that Julia insisted on cooking for us ("A friend taught me this recipe," she informed me with a wink, and I quickly changed the subject, knowing full well that said friend was Nathan).

"Do you think Sophie's lost weight?" Julia asks me quizzically, pushing a stray piece of tomato around her plate. "Because on Friday night, she looked *very* thin to me. Like, skeletal."

"I don't know, Jules. She's always been tiny."

"Huh. Well, I hope she doesn't have an eating disorder again," Julia says. She stabs the tomato with her fork and pops it in her mouth emphatically.

"What eating disorder?" I ask, skeptical. Given Julia's new-found love of hyperbole, and the fact that Sophie—a vegetarian and champion rock climber—has always been slim, I'm prone to think that this is a figment of Julia's imagination, influenced by her own history of incessant dieting. "Actually, you know what? I don't want to know."

"Seriously," says Dave, mouth half full of eggs. "Let's not pathologize poor Sophie when she isn't even here to defend herself. Isn't there something else we can talk about?"

This catches me off guard. While Julia may never have been able to charm him the way she does most men, he's always treated her sort of like a pesky younger sister. Something in him has shifted, though, and he's been downright chilly to Julia since she arrived.

"Sorry," she says, making an exaggeratedly sad face at Dave, who ignores her. "It's just that food makes me so much happier. In fact, it was Nathan who taught me that delicious meals can actually boost levels of good brain chemicals!" she says, eyes gleaming. "I can only imagine what it would do for Sophie."

Of *course* she had to mention his name. "Huh," I mumble noncommittally, not looking at Dave or Julia.

"Is that so?" says Dave, obviously less than thrilled to hear Nathan's name.

"Yep!" she enthuses.

Later, when she's in the bathroom, I whisper to Dave, "I'm sorry about that. Is she driving you up the wall?"

"No," he whispers back. "Yes. I just—I don't know. I don't feel like it does her any good not to call her out on her ridiculousness. I mean, how is she going to get any better if everyone acts like it's okay when she says things that are totally inappropriate, like inventing eating disorders out of thin air and name-checking your ex to see if it ruffles my feathers?"

"I know, honey. You're absolutely right. Let's just try to make it through this weekend, okay?" I ask.

"Okay," he concedes.

"Been meaning to tell you, it's quite the fancy place you have here," Julia tells me later that afternoon. She does a little twirl on the living room's hardwood floor, and I grimace thinking about all the sharp edges she could hit if she slipped; the worst thing that could happen to her right now, according to her neurologist, would be another bump to the head. "You and Don really did well for yourselves," she adds.

"Dave," I correct her. She'd been getting his name right for a while now, and I can't help but wonder if her sudden regression is a subconscious response to what he said about Sophie earlier.

"Crap, you're right," she says, scrunching up her face in disgust. "I don't know how that even happens. It's so frustrating."

"Sorry, Jules. That stinks," I tell her. "What does your doctor say?"

"Which one?" she asks, throwing her hands up in the air. "I'm still seeing, like, a zillion of them. And they all tell me something different. The neurologist says I'm doing great. The neuropsychologist says he can't tell how good my progress is at this point. The occupational therapist says that he thinks I'm not trying hard enough. It's enough to make me want to blow my brains out."

"Please tell me you're not contemplating killing yourself. I don't think I can handle it at this point."

Julia gives me a big hug. "Of course not. I know how lucky I am." She bites her lip and pauses. "Do you know how many people have told me stories about their brother/aunt/dog's cousin's babysitter who died or is lying in a hospital bed in a permanently vegetative state after having a brain injury like mine? I mean, really? Do I really need to hear that?" she says with exasperation. "I *know* I could have died. I may be a little nutty, but I do think about it."

Deciding to take advantage of Julia's candor, I casually ask, "So . . . are you dating anyone?" I don't mention the fact that I heard through a good-looking Michigan grapevine that she's seeing a married man.

"Oh. Yeah," she says, and blows at her bangs. "His name is Rich. I really, *really* like him. Maybe even love."

This catches me off guard. For most of her life, she discarded men like they were dirty clothes, and it was *moi* who ended up cleaning up afterward. "It's not you, it's her," I'd reassure her high school flavor of the month, regurgitating the stale speech that Julia begged me to use. "She's just not ready for a commitment," I'd add, leaving them dazed but less likely to stay obsessed with her.

When she announced her interest in Nathan, I was afraid he would fall hard for her—but I knew deep down that if that happened, he'd last all of three months before Julia tossed him out like the rest. Then I would be left pining for her sloppy seconds.

When we both landed in New York after graduation, she threw herself into work and dance, staying mostly single for several years before starting a relationship with Craig, a choreographer she met through the ballet. Craig was too pretentious for my taste—he was constantly name-dropping famous people he knew, and seemed to throw French phrases into every other sentence. Still, he loved Julia, and he knew how to handle her when she was acting clingy, which was more than I could say for any of her previous boy-friends.

Equally important, Craig and Julia's relationship made it pos-sible for Dave and me to be together. Julia usually freaked out on me when I was dating someone. "I'm not important to you anymore, Marissa," she'd complain, spending an epic brunch date telling me how I didn't have time for her, never recognizing the irony of the situation. But she started seeing Craig several months before Dave and I would meet at Nina's party, and for once seemed too preoccupied with him to complain about my new relationship. It wasn't until Julia and Craig broke up a year later that I learned she wasn't actually serious about him, either. "Eh, he was never the one," she said over one of many margaritas the night of their breakup. "But I thought it was better for me not to be alone when I realized that you and Dave were falling in love." Her generosity almost—*almost*—made me forget about what she'd done in col-lege, and I couldn't help but suspect that it was motivated, at least in part, by guilt.

"So what's wrong with Rich?" I say, trying to dig for informa-tion without being completely transparent. "Crazy ex-wife? Kids? Bad in bed?"

She takes the bait. "Crazy not-quite-ex-wife."

"Get out. Jules, I can't believe you'd do that."

"Not so fast," she squeaks. "Rich and his ex are legally separated. I've seen the papers myself. And he lives in his own apartment in downtown Plymouth. So it's the real deal. The divorce should be final in June. They don't have kids, and his wife made more money than him, so it's not as messy as it could be."

"Well, that's a relief," I tell her. "How come you haven't mentioned Rich to me, though?"

"You never asked," she says, as though it's the most obvious thing in the world. Which it kind of is. "Besides, I think he's long-term material. So we have time."

"I'd like that. Maybe next time I'm in town?"

Julia claps her hands. "I know! Maybe you, me, Rich, and Nathan can have dinner together!"

"You mean *Dave*?"

"No, Nathan," she says, looking at me as though *I'm* the one with the head injury.

"Jules, I have no intention of seeing Nathan again anytime this century. Not even if it involves having dinner with you and your new boy toy."

"Mar, why can't you just trust me on this one?"

"Julia," I say with as much force as I can muster without yelling. "I am not a puppet whose strings you can pull and suddenly I'll behave accordingly." Yes, I have stolen this line from Dave, but it does seem appropriate given the circumstances. "This is my life. It's not a game, and I'm not going to just pick up and leave my boyfriend because you think it's a good idea."

"Okay, Marissa," she says, sounding exhausted. For the first time this weekend, I notice how frail she looks, and that the deep circles under her eyes aren't just shadows from her long lashes. I instantly regret coming on so strong.

"I'm sorry, Jules. It's just that I have a good thing going here with Dave, and I'm not going to do anything to ruin it."

"I get it," she says, but the tone of her voice tells me that she doesn't.

.  .

Sunday evening, Julia rolls her packed suitcase into the living room and asks me to call the car service to take her to the airport.

"No problem," I say, trying not to make it too obvious that I'm relieved she isn't extending her stay. The tension between Dave and Julia hasn't dissipated, and all morning, Julia's filter has been malfunctioning, resulting in several flesh wounds to my thin skin (particularly her comment that I should replace my go-to black pants because they make my thighs "look like charred tree trunks").

At the same time, I feel like the fragile tenets of our friendship are finally on the mend, especially now that I understand what's going on between her and Nathan, and I'm reluctant to see her go. Julia must pick up on this, because she looks at me and says, "Oh! You're sad!" She rushes across the living room to embrace me. "I love that you're going to miss me. But don't you worry. I'm convinced that I can get you to move to Ann Arbor. Life would be so much better for you there."

"Ann Arbor, huh?" asks Dave from where he's sitting in the kitchen. He closes his laptop abruptly. "Something tells me my firm isn't going to like the sound of that."

Julia glances at him. Then she says, just barely under her breath, "Well, I didn't say anything about you coming with her."

Dave, who has obviously heard Julia, chooses to ignore the comment. Instead he says, "Julia, please leave the spare keys you used on the table in the vestibule. We don't have another set." His voice is measured, but his brown eyes are flashing an anger that I've rarely seen.

I hold my breath and pray that Julia doesn't further antagonize him. But she's either oblivious to his anger or putting on a damn good show. *"Bien sûr!"* she chirps in agreement.

Minutes later, the car honks out front. "Jules, you ready?" I ask her.

"Ready as I'll ever be." She grabs her coat and purse from our coatrack, then breaks into song. *"Thanks for the memory!"* she trills. *"Of things I can't forget! Of journeys on a jet!"* She is still singing when she walks through the front door without saying good-bye.

# Twenty-six

There are many perks to being a diet editor: free food, all the complimentary gym sessions you'd ever (and perhaps never) want, occasional face time with buff celebrities who are desperate to be on your cover, which at the very least makes for great water cooler gossip. Less enticing are the long hours, the endless quest to find something—anything!—new to write about and, of course, the conferences. Oh, the conferences. This spring, Lynne has sentenced me to a nutrition conference in New Jersey, which means I have no choice but miss Take the Lead practice.

I emerge from four straight days of fluorescent-lit conference rooms and tasteless-but-healthy catering armed with an extensive knowledge of the benefits of soybeans and a grumbling hunger that only a cheeseburger can silence. Although I'm loath to return to work, I'm surprised to discover that I can't wait to get back to coaching; it feels like I have not seen the girls in months.

"Hey, guys," I say to Layla, Margarita, and Josie, who have run across the gym to greet me. "I missed you!"

"We missed you, too, Coach Marissa," says Caitlin. "You're not going to quit coaching, are you?"

"Of course not," I tell her. "I'll be here all year."

"Yay!" says Margarita, and hugs me.

"Thanks, Margarita," I say, hugging her back. "That's really sweet of you."

One after another, all twelve girls come up to embrace me. Renee and Charity squeeze me tight, while Josie and Nancy awkwardly circle their skinny arms around my waist and Caitlin pats me on the back. Before I know what's happening, I feel the tears welling up; it's overwhelming to be on the receiving end of such adoration. I blink them away and resolve to buy stock in Kleenex the minute I get home.

Appropriately, today's lesson is about kindness. Alanna, Naomi, and I act out several scenarios and ask the group to give examples of kindness for each one. In the first, Alanna pretends that she is really hungry but discovers she's forgotten her lunch. It's a no-brainer for the girls, who offer a little bit of their own imaginary lunches to help her out. For the second scenario, Naomi pretends to be the slowest runner in her grade, and that her classmates never pick her for their relay team. It takes the girls a little longer this time, but Anna finally volunteers that she would pick Naomi for her team anyway, and Renee says that she wouldn't make fun of Naomi's slowness. "Great job, girls!" Naomi beams. "You are very smart. But let's see if you can figure this last situation out. It's a tricky one."

For the "tricky" scenario, I pretend to lose my mother's purse, which contains a lot of money. "I'm such a dummy," I say in exasperation, slapping myself on the forehead. "My mom is going to be *so* angry with me. And now I definitely won't get the Razor scooter that she had promised me. I'm the worst person in the world."

"Now, girls, if we were going to be kind to Coach Marissa, we'd help her look for the purse. But I'm curious: How can she be kind to *herself*?" Naomi asks them. The girls look positively stumped; even Estrella sits quietly with a puzzled look on her face.

Suddenly, Josie's eyes light up. She tentatively raises her hand.

"Yes, Josie?" I ask her. "How do you think I can be kind to myself?"

"By not calling yourself names like dummy?" she asks. "Or not thinking that you're a bad person 'cause you made a mistake?"

"Exactly!" I tell her.

"That's very good!" agrees Alanna, and Josie, who appears to be shedding more of her mean-girl skin each week, beams.

During warm-up, Naomi reminds the girls that today is the first long run of the season—two miles. Although I have a beatific smile plastered on my face, inside I'm cringing as much as the girls are right now. Because all I can think of is the first time *I* was in their shoes.

There are few things more humiliating to an eleven-year-old than her gym teacher pinching the fleshy fat of her upper arm between cold metal calipers and then announcing, loudly and with disdain, her body fat percentage to the entire gym class. (In fact, I'm fairly certain that whoever came up with this practice as a way to promote healthy habits also decided nuclear weapons were an effective way to keep the peace.) But at that point in my life, there was one thing that was actually *worse* than the fat-finding mission: the two-mile torture trot that was de rigueur for fifth-grade Ypsilanti public school students.

It didn't start out a disaster. I was at the back, with other less-than-athletically inclined kids, but not alone. Somewhere around a half mile, though, I got a stitch in my side. Two hundred yards later, the stitch became a shooting pain, and I doubled over on the dirt path where we were running. "Keep going, Rogers!" my gym teacher hollered. "No quitting!" Panicked at the thought of having to continue, my throat constricted and I thought for sure I would pass out. "At least walk," my gym teacher admonished me after seeing that I was turning purple. "Don't just stand there like a lump."

And so I trekked along by myself, pretending that I was one of the Cherokees I had just learned about during our Trail of Tears history lesson, because somehow this made the laps more bearable. Occasionally I would break into a jog, determined not to be a quitter, only to fold over hyperventilating again. After eight torturous laps, it was finally—finally!—over. Coming in dead last, at a school record of fifty-three minutes and twelve seconds, tears streaming down my face as my impatient classmates jeered and heckled me, I stumbled across the finish line.

But today it's my job to pretend that I love running.

"The two-mile run is the *worst*," groans Anna, who did the program last year and considers herself the senior expert on all things Take the Lead. "It lasts forever and then you're all sweaty afterward."

"It won't be that bad," I say in a chipper voice.

"And you get dizzy from going around the gym a million times!" says Josie, another Take the Lead veteran.

"Actually, I thought we'd head out to the track, considering it's such a nice day out," says Alanna. "Just six laps around equals a mile."

"So we have to do twelve laps?!" asks Lisa in disbelief. "I didn't sign up for that!" she hollers, and the other girls laugh nervously.

"We can do it, girls!" I enthuse. Truth be told, I'm the one who needs the encouragement: I may know that I *can* do this, but that doesn't mean I *want* to.

"Now, you guys, remember that Take the Lead *is* a running program," adds Naomi. "This run can be very fun, especially if you spend the time focusing on what a major accomplishment it is to run two miles. And don't forget, you can walk if you need to. The goal is to finish, not to get there the fastest."

*The goal is to finish,* I tell myself as I start jogging around the well-worn asphalt track that surrounds the soccer field. The first lap is easy; the second is doable. By the third, my knees ache and I feel like I have been running for an eternity.

Just as I'm rounding the bend, I realize that Estrella is a good quarter mile behind the rest of the girls. Trudging along at a snail's pace and looking as though she's seconds away from passing out, she might as well be a flashback to my fifth-grade self, and my heart aches for her.

I slow down so that I'm almost walking, and let Josie, Margarita, and the rest pass me. Finally, Estrella comes up alongside me, her chicken-wing jog looking more like a dance aerobics move than a means of getting from point A to point B.

"Coach Marissa," she says, heaving and ho-ing, "don't give up now! You can do it."

I let out a little laugh; and here I thought I would cheer *her* on. Obviously, I've learned nothing over the past few months of coaching.

"Thanks, Estrella," I say. "How are you doing today? Tough run?"

"Nah," she tells me. "I'm just pacing myself." She tugs her hiked-up white polo shirt back down over her belly and glances sideways at me. "What about you? Running's hard, huh?"

"You know, I'm getting used to it," I tell her. "More than I thought I would. I wasn't a very fast runner when I was younger."

"But, Coach Marissa," Estrella protests. "Remember today's lesson? Being a fast runner doesn't matter. It's how you feel about yourself that counts," she recites proudly. "And how you feel when you run. Like me!" She stops and puts her hands on her hips while she catches her breath. After a few seconds, she continues. "I feel good about myself. Especially when I finish, even though it isn't easy."

"You're absolutely right, Estrella," I tell her, nearly dumbfounded by this little beacon of light, who I've once again misjudged. "I just wish that I would have known what you know when I was your age."

For all their complaining earlier, the girls trudge along with looks of sheer determination on their faces. Some of them take a break to walk, or go to the sideline to grab water, but not a single one mentions quitting. As for Estrella, despite the fact that she barely seems to be breathing, she somehow manages to serve as the unofficial Take the Lead cheerleader. "Five more laps!" she calls. "Four more laps!" And so on.

As for me, I'm genuinely shocked to discover that sometime after the first mile, I've fallen into a comfortable rhythm and am no longer tempted to impale myself on the flagpole. Sure, my flimsy Old Navy T-shirt is drenched and my thighs are chafed from rubbing against each other, but the shorter runs I've been doing with the girls for the past two months appear to have paid off. In fact, by the time I make my way around the track for the last time, I am feeling like a rock star. A sweaty, huffing, red-faced rock star, but a rock star all the same. Who knew this could be enjoyable?

When Naomi and I catch up to each other during the cool-down lap, she gives me a knowing smile. "Lookin' pretty good, Rogers," she says, wiping her forehead with the back of her hand. "You've got runner's high, don't you?"

"Not quite," I scoff, even though I can practically feel a surge of serotonin flowing through my brain, making me feel simultaneously relaxed and ready to take on the world.

"Whatever," says Naomi. "You talk a good game, but I wouldn't be surprised to see you crossing the finish line at the New York City Marathon next year."

"We'll see about that," I tell her. Two miles is one thing. Twenty-six is entirely another.

After practice, Naomi asks me to grab a drink with her and Alanna. "Life is short," she informs me when I tell her I should get back to the office. "And as your boss, I am ordering you to relax. Just this one time."

"All right. Work can wait," I tell her. After all, I can't exactly complain about being lonely if I'm choosing face time with my computer over human contact.

We take the train down to the Upper East Side, where Alanna lives. She directs us to a nondescript pub that's appropriately empty for a Tuesday afternoon. Still, we forgo a booth and grab three empty stools at the corner of the bar.

"Okay, now that it's just us, I have to know: What's the deal with Estrella?" I ask them. "I can't make up my mind whether she's totally annoying or the most inspiring tween I've ever met."

Alanna giggles. "That just about sums her up. She's best described as a force of nature."

"I've just never seen someone so bumbling be so . . ."

"Overconfident?" Naomi volunteers. "If only we all had that problem. I'm telling you, it may make her unpopular in school, but one day that little chica is going to be running the country. She isn't just sassy—she's smart, too. Did you hear her explain to everyone what self-efficacy is?"

"How could I not?" I say, rolling my eyes, although I was undeniably impressed at the time; even I had to look up the exact definition when I was prepping for today's lesson.

"Anyway," Alanna says to me, "it will make sense when you meet her mother."

I picture an awkward woman identical to Estrella. "Is she just like her daughter?"

Naomi lets out a laugh and shakes her head. "You'll see."

We talk for more than two hours, during which time the bar crowds with former frat boys in ties and girls in sleek power suits. I know Alanna fits right in with their lot, and yet over the past few weeks, I've grown to truly like her; she's revealed herself to be far wittier and more intelligent than her coaching skills initially implied. At one point, as I listen to Alanna laugh at a story Naomi's telling, it occurs to me that six months ago, I wouldn't have bothered to try to get to know her. After all, I didn't need anyone—I had Julia. Today, it's a different story. Besides Alanna, Naomi, and I having grown closer, Sarah's become a confidant, and even Dave and I have reached a new level in our relationship. If there's one silver lining to Julia's accident, I realize, it's that I actually have room in my life for other people now.

# Twenty-seven

A new day, a new near-catastrophe at *Svelte*. When I sit down to my desk Wednesday morning, I learn that today's crisis involves one of my stories, which is about how snack packs make you fat (true: I've never been able to eat fewer than three mini-bags of Oreos in one sitting).

*Do these women ever sleep?* I wonder as I click through a string of frantic e-mails between Lynne, Roxanne, and Naomi dated 6:40, 7:02, and 7:15 a.m. The problem, I discover, is that although there are several studies verifying that once you pop a 100-calorie bag open, you can't stop—apparently the calories are so low they lead people to believe that they can just keep eating—said research stands to offend several of our snack-pack-shilling advertisers.

Thankfully, as I scroll through the e-mails, I see that by 8:41, Roxanne has decided we can solve the problem by adding a line specifying that this is really only a problem for women with weak willpower (ouch). I delete the entire chain of messages and begin to make my way through the other 128 e-mails in my inbox, which primarily consist of publicists promoting their clients' latest products and near-identical pictures of Snowball that Julia sends daily.

My Outlook is down to a respectable twenty-four unread messages when a new e-mail pops up at the top of the list.

With my hand clutching the mouse tight enough to give me carpal tunnel, I hover my cursor over it for a few seconds before finally clicking.

> To: mrogers@sveltemag.com
> From: nbell79@gmail.com
> Subject: hey . . .
>
> M-
>
> It's been a few months and I haven't heard from you. I figure I have nothing to lose, so . . . seeing you in New York really got me thinking. I guess I didn't realize just how much I missed you until you were back in my life again. Call me sometime? And let me know when you'll be in town next. I promise to show you our version of French food.
>
> -N

I groan. Just when I was *sure* that the past several months of Nathan-free existence had been exactly what I needed to fully commit to Dave. And yet like a bad penny that keeps turning up, I can't seem to get him out of my head—or my life. I quickly type up what I hope is a discouraging response:

> To: nbell79@gmail.com
> From: mrogers@sveltemag.com
> Subject: Re: hey . . .

Hi, Nathan. It was nice to catch up. I'm not planning on being in Michigan again soon, but I'll let you know if that changes.

Marissa

Without so much as giving it a second read, I grimace and quickly hit "return."

Two minutes later, I get a reply.

To: mrogers@sveltemag.com
From: nbell79@gmail.com
Subject: Re: Re: hey . . .

And here I thought you were going to ignore me forever. I'm happy to come back to New York. You just say the word and I'm there. Until then—thinking of you.

-N

Damn it. Damn, damn, damnity damn damn it. The minute I read Nathan's e-mail I realize I took a wrong turn when I e-mailed him back. Although his forwardness makes me uneasy, it also results in that most intoxicating of feelings: the feeling of being wanted. Wanted by a man who is wily and charming and whose beguiling smile and twinkling eyes make me feel like I'm twenty again and floating on a cloud of lust. The sensation running through my body right now is the kind that derails a relationship, that sends it crashing and then disappears as you deal with the bloody, disastrous aftermath.

I think of Dave and how well things have been going since the night I saw Nathan, and yet again, reality sinks in. Try as I might to convince myself otherwise, I can't have it both ways: There is no room in my life for two men. I can't entertain thoughts of returning to Nathan or continue to fantasize about life with him if I'm going to make my relationship with Dave work. Which means savoring his tempting, come-hither messages is not an option. With new resolve, I swiftly delete both e-mails.

"Marissa? Is this a bad time?" Ashley's voice snaps me back to the present. She is standing at my door, her forehead wrinkled with worry.

"No, no, come on in," I say, motioning for her to come into my office. I quickly check my reflection in a mirrored compact, half expecting to find drool on my chin. "What's up?"

"Um . . ." Ashley sits gingerly on the edge of my spare chair. For once, the Ice Queen appears to be melting. I'd love to revel in the moment, but unfortunately, her bad news is about to be delivered to me. Just what I need after a month of frustration, not to mention this morning's e-mail surprise.

She hands me a single piece of paper. "This is the sidebar. I'm nervous to show it to you, but I'm really hoping you'll like it."

"You already wrote it?" I ask. "I thought we hadn't agreed on a topic yet?"

"I got inspired, so . . ."

"Okay, I'll give it a quick read," I tell her.

The minute I glance at the headline, my stomach sinks.

### "Brain Injury Gave Me a Chance to Fix the Past: A Q&A with Julia Ferrar"

So this is why Julia knew who Ashley was. Just as I'd suspected, something wasn't right.

The story is actually worse than I'm expecting. Although it begins benignly, I spot my name in the middle of the page. And it only goes downhill from there.

Julia: My injury may have made me have trouble speaking and remembering things, but it's also given me amazing clarity. I feel like I have a second chance to make amends.

Ashley: Can you give me an example?

Julia: Well, I asked my best friend Marissa [a senior editor at *Svelte*] to break up with her boyfriend a long time ago. I realized that this was so wrong of me, and now I'm trying to reunite them. Marissa is seeing someone else, but I actually think she and her ex will end up together!

*Take three deep breaths before speaking, I command myself. In . . . out . . .*

I get to two before I run out of patience. "You cannot honestly think I can run this."

"Why, because you're mentioned in it? Doesn't that make for a better, more interesting article? It's like the story behind the story," says Ashley with a hint of pride. She adds, "Julia thought it was a great idea, and that you would be thrilled when I surprised you."

I give her a sharp look. "Do you realize that you're talking about someone with major head trauma? Julia now thinks it's a good idea to tell people they're ugly and to sleep with married men, too. Just because she gave it the green light does not mean that you should have." I know I've just broken my own rule by revealing Julia's personal life, but the sting of her doing that exact thing to me is too fresh for me to stop myself. It has the intended effect: Ashley's face is contorted in a most un-pretty way and she appears to be having what I can only categorize as a freak-out.

I continue, barely resisting the temptation to wag my finger at her. "The bigger issue is that this is completely inappropriate from a journalistic standpoint. Inserting my personal life into the story gives it an instant bias."

"And you're saying you *don't* have a personal interest in this piece?" she says, her voice just above a whisper.

"Even if I do, I don't want my story to overtake the focus, which is to warn our readers about the dangers of brain injury."

"If you think about it, it's not really your story. It's Julia's," Ashley responds. "Besides, you said that a first-person story would be great."

"Actually, I nixed that idea and asked you to do a service-oriented sidebar. *Remember*?"

She ignores the question and plows on. "Lynne is always saying that she wants more real-life dramas. I thought this would be perfect. In fact, I'm pretty sure that she'll love it when I show it to her."

"Oh, I'm pretty sure you're not going to have the opportunity to ask her," I retort, and tear the paper in half for emphasis. It's childish—not to mention pointless, as there's an electronic version on our server somewhere—but I'm so steamed that I can't see straight, let alone act like an adult.

"Fine." She stands up. "I wish I wouldn't have bothered to go through all that trouble."

"You are off this story," I say. "In fact, you are off all of my stories for the time being."

Ashley stares at me with eyes so empty I'm sure that if I put my ear up to hers, I'd hear the sea. But I'm the dumb one, I realize miserably. I was charmed by her "I'm a great worker" act, when the truth is, I never should have asked her to help me with this story if I wasn't planning to double-check every single step she took.

Honestly, though, what I'm really upset about is Julia's betrayal. We've never been perfect—what friendship is without flaws?—but before her injury, she never would have blithely revealed my personal life to others. Now our relationship hasn't just deteriorated; it's actually become a liability for my career, not to mention my relationship with Dave.

Ashley leaves in a huff. I pace back and forth, but given the eight feet I can cover, there's really no calming down in this tiny office. After checking my calendar to make sure that I'm not expected at any meetings, I grab my coat and purse and head for the elevator.

As I push through the revolving glass doors and step onto Sixth Avenue, I'm immediately swallowed up by the crowd, which somehow relaxes me. I deftly weave through the hordes of people strolling and window-shopping and having cigarettes on the sidewalk. I walk so fast that I'm practically jogging, and before I know it, I'm standing at the south end of Central Park. After a quick glance at my cell phone confirms that I haven't been gone from my office long enough to be conspicuous, I decide to do a quick loop around the small pond.

By the time I reach the arched bridge overlooking the water, my blood has almost stopped boiling.

"Nice day, isn't it?"

I spin around to discover that the voice is coming from an older woman who is leaning on her elbows against the bridge wall. Jaded New Yorker that I am, I usually avoid eye contact and exchanging more than two words with anyone I don't know, but this woman looks harmless. Intriguing, even.

"It is," I agree. "Especially after what feels like the longest winter I've ever lived through."

"Well, my dear, be glad you lived through it," she tells me, and for a second, I get a weird sensation that I'm seeing a ghost. I look at her again, and realize with relief that there is nothing undead about her flushed cheeks and the map of wrinkles plotted across her face.

"Oh, I'm sorry, my dear." The old woman laughs. "I don't mean to upset you. It's just that today is my wedding anniversary and I'm missing my George something terrible."

"No, I'm the one who's sorry," I tell her, and dig my hands deep into the lint-filled pockets of my trench coat. "About your husband, I mean."

"Me, too," she says with a wistful smile. "You want to know something crazy? The entire forty years we were married, he drove me nuts. George had a very important job, you see, and so my entire existence revolved around meeting this dignitary or that senator. I always felt like I was living my life for him, rather than for myself."

"Huh," I say, surprised at how forthcoming she's being, given that I'm a complete stranger. Or maybe, I realize, that's exactly why she's so frank. "But you miss him now?" I say, as much a statement as a question, because the look on her face tells me she does.

"So much," she says, and looks out at the pond, where a few large white swans are floating in place. "They mate for life," the woman tells me, and it takes me a minute to realize that she is talking about the swans. "That's why they take a very long time to find a partner. Unlike me—I'll never find a replacement for George—they usually look for another love if their first dies or is unkind to them."

"Unkind?" I ask.

"Oh, yes," she says. "Swans are very intelligent, and their memories are as long as an elephant's. They never forget who has crossed them." Her eyes twinkle. "That's why they tend to be so damn mean."

"No kidding."

"Indeed. Swans will actually try to drown each other if they're angry enough. People admire their beauty and their devotion, but they're certainly not the animal whose social patterns we'd be wise to emulate. Unlike humans, they're unable to learn the art of forgetting."

This comment renders me speechless. Julia may be hell-bent on making a mess of my life, but at least she has a legitimate excuse for holding on to the one memory I'm desperate for her to forget. Meanwhile, I've been accumulating layers upon layers of anger toward her—not just since the accident, I realize, but for the past decade. Maybe, I decide, I'm the one who needs to figure out how to let go.

"Fascinating," I finally tell the woman.

"Isn't it? As you might have guessed, I'm a bit of a bird fanatic," she responds. "Anyway, I've kept you too long. But it was very nice to chat with you. I hope you have a lovely day, my dear."

"Same here," I tell her. I'm almost down the bridge when I turn back to her. She's exactly where I left her, leaning against the bridge and staring at the water. "Happy anniversary," I call out.

"In many ways, it is," she responds, and turns back to the water.

# Twenty-eight

The rest of the week flies by so fast that I don't have time to give much thought to Ashley's article, let alone stew over Julia's loose lips. Before I know it, it's Friday night and Dave and I are on the Metro-North to Chappaqua to see his parents. As the train whizzes along, Dave stares out the window, pretending to be fascinated by the scenery, but in the glass reflection, I see that he's smiling. It's obvious that he's up to something, but exactly what has yet to be revealed.

"What is it?" he asks, eyes opening innocently when I give him yet another suspicious look.

"Come on. Even your clothes scream guilt," I scoff, referring to the fact that he's wearing a button-down and gray wool pants instead of the usual jeans and T-shirt he lives in when he's not at work. Meanwhile, I've (just barely) squeezed into my favorite stretchy black dress—which, under the train's glaring lights, I now discover is covered with fuzz and looks as though I bought it at Goodwill. I say a silent prayer that whatever Dave has in store, it does not involve anything fancy, because this dress is the nicest thing I brought to wear for the weekend.

"You're as bad a liar as I am," I tell him, but he continues to play dumb. "Okay," I say. "Just know that I *will* figure out what it is sooner than later."

"Well, Nancy Drew, you'll figure out that there's nothing to be figured out," he says cryptically, and offers me some of the cheddar Chex Mix he's been snacking on.

I shake my head. "I'm back on the wagon."

"You'll only be on the wagon until you get a whiff of my mom's coconut cake," Dave informs me. "Then I guarantee that you'll throw yourself off the side as fast as you possibly can."

"Thanks for the motivation. You're a real pal," I tell him. He kisses me lightly on the lips, then makes a show of having more Chex, which results in neon orange crumbs falling on his freshly pressed shirt. "Serves you right," I say with a smirk, but he just keeps grinning.

When we get off the train, Dave's father, Len, is leaning against the door of his navy blue Volvo wagon in the parking lot. Built like a bullet, Len is short but sinewy from his twice-a-week squash game and daily six-mile runs. Dave is taller than his father, and from the pictures I've seen, more handsome than he ever was, but there's no doubt that Len is a crystal ball of Dave's future self. It's a comforting thought, because there are far worse ways to age.

Tonight, Len looks calm and normal, making me wonder if my imagination has been on overdrive—or conversely, if he simply has no idea what Dave has in store. He greets me warmly, as though I'm his relative and not just his son's girlfriend. "Marissa!

Joyel and I are so happy that you're here for the weekend." Then he gives Dave a hug. "Hey, champ. Good to see you," he says.

"Hey, Dad," Dave says, hugging him back, and although I know I shouldn't, I have a momentary twinge of envy because they have a closeness I don't have with either of my parents, and never will. There are some things you just can't create out of thin air, and that kind of affection is one of them.

After we load our bags into the station wagon, Dave and Len spend the five-minute drive debating the statutes pertaining to a case Len, who is also a lawyer, is currently trying in court. My understanding of the law is so dim that they might as well be discussing quantum physics, and so I find myself zoning out while they banter back and forth.

Even though I deleted Nathan's e-mails, I kept thinking about them all week, and wondering if I did the right thing by not responding. In the end, I stuck to my original plan. It felt like a failure of sorts, because if I was trying to be the new, assertive Marissa, I would undoubtedly send *some* sort of a "no really, leave me alone" message, even if it was curt and poorly executed. And yet something in me said: Let silence be your answer.

Before I can get too verklempt, the Volvo pulls into the Bergmans' gravel driveway. "Here we are!" says Len cheerfully. "Home sweet home." And it is. In an otherwise pitch-black night, the lanterns on the porch of the expansive slate gray ranch beckon us to enter, and above, the stars are bright and plentiful. It's hard to believe that we're less than an hour outside of the city.

"It's good to be here, Dad," says Dave, opening the front door. As he does, the most amazing savory-yet-sweet smell wafts over me. "Guess you're right about my diet, huh?" I say to him, my mouth watering.

"I'm not one to say I told you so"—he grins— "but I did tell you so." I swat him playfully.

"What did I hear about diet?" says Joyel, coming to greet us at the door. Although Dave most resembles Len, he and Joyel have the exact same smile—bashful and welcoming. She embraces me, and then says, "Marissa, I should warn you: That word is completely verboten in this house. It's my duty as your surrogate Jewish mother to make sure you are stuffed like a Christmas pig."

"Is that kosher?" Len jokes, and Dave groans. "Here we go. The Punch and Judy show," he says. Their mood is infectious, and I find my earlier jitters evaporating.

But no sooner have I relaxed when Joyel says, "Marissa, come with me into the living room. We have a little surprise for you."

"Okay," I say, hoping that I sound at least a little more enthusiastic than I feel. *Marissa Rogers, guess what's behind door number two?* I robotically follow her into the next room, afraid to even wonder what they have in store.

It is not a what, but a who, that I find waiting for me.

"Mom? Phil? What are you doing here?" I feel momentarily panicked, until I realize that my mother and stepfather, who are sitting on the Bergmans' leather sofa sipping red wine, are clearly not here because of an emergency. They appear to be deep in conversation, and they wait a second too long before looking up at me.

"Well, hey there, Marissa," says Phil jovially, hoisting himself out of the deep, low sofa. He extends a hand to my mother, who gracefully pulls herself into a standing position and glides over to where Dave and I are standing. I can tell immediately that she's in what Julia used to refer to as "Susan mode," where she pretends to be charming and witty and carefree. That is to say, not herself.

Clutching my upper arms, my mother leans forward so that our cheeks meet, but our torsos don't touch. "Marissa, honey," she says in a normal voice. "Can you believe we're here?" Then, as she air-kisses my cheek, she whispers, "What on earth are you wearing?"

"Great to see you, too, Mom," I say through clenched teeth.

Dave embraces my mother, then turns to me, beaming. "I thought it was about time our parents met, so I arranged for your mom and Phil to come in for the weekend and stay with my folks."

"So you're staying here? At the Bergmans'? Really?!" I give Dave a look that says *I am so going to murder you.*

"Of course! I wouldn't dream of putting them up in a hotel, not that there's even a good one to be had around here. And Susan and I have been getting along famously all afternoon!" says Joyel, putting an arm around my mother, who giggles. I am certain that this is a sign of the impending apocalypse, but I just smile as though it's the best news I've heard all week.

"We really do appreciate you having us," says Phil a little awkwardly, which makes me feel better. If he and Len were suddenly thick as thieves, I'd have to grab my bag and find a sympathetic yuppie to give me a ride back to the city.

"Dave! This is so not okay!" I whisper as the parents make their way into the dining room.

"I thought it was important for them to meet," he says, looking wounded. "And I didn't want you to say no without thinking it through. I figured that once you saw your mom, you'd realize it wasn't such a bad idea . . ."

"After three years together, you should know me better than this! I hate surprises. *Especially* surprises involving my mother." There are about seven trillion things she could say or do to make this weekend a disaster. And damn it, I like the Bergmans and they like me. The last thing I need is for my mother to ruin that.

"Marissa," Dave says gently. "Family is important to me. And although you have a hard time admitting it, I know it's important to you, too. Your mother may not be perfect, but she's yours, and I want my parents to at least have a chance to get to know her."

"Hmph." I sulk, still convinced he could have handled our little reunion better. "If this goes badly, I'm blaming it on you."

"Deal," he says, and puts his hand on my back to guide me through the arched door of the dining room together. "I love *youuuu*," he says in a silly voice, and I can't help but smile. "Now let's go make nice."

For dinner, Joyel has put together a light spread of cheese, cured meat, hummus, fruit, and homemade bread. After we're seated, Len pours us each a glass of wine, and raises his to signal a toast. "To family," he says, looking across the thick mahogany table at each of us. "And to the future."

"Cheers," I say, but instead of clinking glasses with me, Dave leans over toward my ear. "Our future," he says so that only I can hear. "Our family." Then he kisses me softly, and brings the edge of his wineglass to mine.

"Our future," I whisper back, and my words hang in the air, a promise to him.

# Twenty-nine

The next morning, I wake up a new woman. It's a beautiful day, I slept well, and most important, my mother behaved herself last night. In fact, she was downright docile throughout dinner, and even insisted on helping with the dishes afterward instead of begging off on account of her French tips like she usually does.

"Good morning, gorgeous," says Dave, slipping into the guest bathroom while I'm brushing my teeth.

"Hey, you," I say through a mouthful of toothpaste suds. By the time I've spit and rinsed, Dave's in the shower. "Come join me," he says, poking his head out from behind the damask shower curtain.

"Shhh," I say, trying to get him to lower his voice. "Your parents are right down the hall."

"First of all," he says, grabbing the edge of my pajama pants, "Mom is in the kitchen making coffee. And Dad has definitely been up for two hours, if not more."

"Like father, like son." I laugh, swatting his wet hand away from my silk pants. "I'm surprised you weren't awake at the crack of dawn to go running with him."

"I wouldn't dare. You were so warm and cozy this morning," Dave says, grabbing my pants again, this time pulling them down. "Come on," he says. "Get in."

"Sounds like someone's begging," I tease, then strip down and step in the tub.

"So what are we going to do the rest of the weekend?" I ask Dave as he soaps up my back.

"Well, after breakfast, I thought we'd take your parents on the scenic tour of Chappaqua, and then do a little shopping. And maybe pizza for dinner?"

"Sounds perfect."

I rinse off one last time and hop out of the shower. Dave gets out behind me, and wraps a thick white towel around my torso and shoulders before I have a chance to do it myself.

"You are too good to me," I tell him, rubbing the soft cotton on my skin. "Although you *do* still owe me for this whole surprise get-together." Truth be told, I'm no longer annoyed about my mother being here. In fact, I feel so relaxed that I could probably fall asleep on the spot. There's just something about the Bergmans' house. It's similar to being at the Ferrars', but better. I always felt at home at Julia's, but could never quite shake the sensation that one wrong move and I'd break something irreplaceable. At Dave's parents' place, I know I could spill red wine on their sofa and they'd laugh about it and flip the cushion over. The only thing I regret is that I can never expect Dave to be equally comfortable at my mom and Phil's place, particularly given that I myself feel like an impostor when I'm there.

"I like it here," I tell Dave, combing out my hair (a much easier task now that there's not two full feet of tangles to pull through).

"I do, too," he says. "I never felt like I had to escape. The way most kids in the suburbs do." He pulls my hair back and stands behind me, so that we are both facing the mirror. Talking to my reflection, he says, "This would be a good place for us to live one day. You know, when we have kids."

"Kids, huh?" I say with a grin. "I think I can handle that. Not right now, obviously. Susan doesn't approve of babies out of wedlock and whatnot. Look at how she freaked out on Sarah when Marcus knocked her up."

"Oh, I'm not Marcus, sweetie," Dave says deviously. "I will tell Susan where she can put her opinion, and how."

"I'm looking forward to seeing that," I tell him, slipping into the heavy terry guest robe that Joyel hung on the door for me. "Now, let's go get ready before they wonder why we're suspiciously absent."

Sure enough, everyone's sitting around the kitchen table drinking coffee when we finally make our way to the kitchen.

"Ugh, I'm sorry. Have you guys been waiting for ages?" I apologize. My mother raises her eyebrows as though to say, *Obviously,* but Joyel brushes my concern aside. "Of course not. Len barely brought breakfast in a minute ago," she tells me, pointing to an enormous brown paper bag filled with the most delicious-smelling bagels I've ever had the misfortune of encountering.

"What, Mom, now that you have an empty nest you won't make me waffles anymore?" Dave jokes.

"I think I recall a specific request for Angy's bagels," Joyel shoots back. "But I'd be happy to eat them all myself if you'd like."

As they banter back and forth, I notice my mother peering out from behind her *New York Post* like Margaret Mead observing Samoans in their native habitat for the first time. I'm tempted to tell her, "Yes, Mother, this is how happy families interact." Instead,

I pull the bagels out of their bag and place them on the vintage tray that Joyel hands me. At the bottom of the bagel bag, I discover Len has purchased not one or two but three different types of cream cheese. "Half a tub for each person?" I ask, eyebrows raised, and he laughs. "Something like that."

"Oh, I'm sure that Marissa will take care of at least one of those on her own," my mother pipes up, and Len turns to see if she's serious. She gives him a smile that I know to be about as authentic as a designer handbag from Chinatown. "Kidding, of course!" she twitters.

*Please God, don't let her get started,* I plead silently, placing the tray on the table like nothing's wrong. Apparently I'm due a favor from the Big Guy, because my mother doesn't make another even remotely snarky comment through breakfast. Equally impressive, she polishes off an entire bagel, which cost her more Weight Watchers points than she's normally willing to part with at one meal.

Sticking to Dave's proposed schedule, the six of us drive around Chappaqua in two different cars: Dave and I with Len; Joyel with my mom and Phil. We stop at a market holding a tasting for several Hudson Valley wines, and hit up Joyel's favorite boutique before driving around to see some of the mansions in the area. Then we head home to relax for a few hours.

Dinner is at Chappy's, Dave's favorite pizza joint. "You'd never know it was run by French Canadians, right?" he jokes to Phil, referring to the fact that the red-checked tablecloths, wood-burning oven, and wall of wine give the restaurant an old-school Italian feel.

"If the pizza's good, I don't care if a herd of goats owns the operation," Phil says good-naturedly.

Dave slaps him on the back. "Then you've come to the right place. I have yet to find better pizza anywhere, even in Brooklyn."

"Not so loud," Len whispers jokingly. "That kind of comment could get us shot if the wrong person hears." He turns to me. "If I were you, I wouldn't sit near him tonight. Could be dangerous if he keeps up those fightin' words."

I laugh; their ridiculousness is contagious. "I think I can handle it, Len."

Dave suggests that we order two large pizzas, and takes a poll to find out what toppings to order. When he gets to my mother, she says, "Oh, I'm not going to have pizza, dear. That bagel just about did it for me this morning."

"Really? Not even a little tiny slice?" Dave asks, mildly perplexed. "It's really ridiculously good. No one should visit without trying it."

"Really," my mother insists. She looks at me. "I'm going to order a chicken Caesar. Marissa and I can split it."

"That's okay, Mom," I tell her. "We're going to get a big green salad with the pizza. That should be fine for me."

"Marissa, don't you think you should go easy on the carbs? Especially after the bagels and wine?" my mother says shrilly. The minute she closes her mouth, she flushes with embarrassment, as though she just realized I'm not the only one at the table.

No one utters a word—not even Phil, who is used to smoothing over my mother's gaffs. I sit on my hands, frozen, the band of my jeans digging into my love handles. It's a cruel reminder that—although she shouldn't have said it—my mother is right.

Just when the silence becomes unbearable, a waiter swoops over to us. Like the rest of the servers at Chappy's, he is loud and showy, with a molasses-thick New York accent, and harasses us about our order until he gets a few smiles. It's a welcome interruption, but still raw with humiliation, I feel like I may burst into tears at any minute. The minute the waiter disappears, I excuse myself to the restroom.

Leaning over the white basin of the sink, I splash cool water on my face, careful to avoid my eyes so my mascara doesn't run. Then I reapply my foundation, concealing the dark circles under my eyes and the tiny capillaries under my nostrils that always turn bright red when I'm upset. I sweep a little blush on my cheeks, take a deep breath, and push my way through the swinging door. It hits my mother with an unexpected but satisfying *thwack*.

"I'm just going to the bathroom quickly," she says huffily, backing away from the door.

"Uh, okay. Apology accepted," I say, although I sound more exhausted than confrontational.

My mother gives me a withering look. "Please, Marissa, no drama today."

I glare at her. "Please, *Mom*, tell me you're kidding. No drama from me? I'm not the one criticizing my daughter's meal choices in a crowded restaurant. As if I'm twelve and it's never occurred to me how many calories are in a fucking slice of pizza! I am a diet editor, for fuck's sake!"

"Language, Marissa," she chides.

"Fuck fuck fuck fuck!" I practically scream. The word is foreign to me, but it elicits the desired response from my mother, who looks both offended and mortified. She glances around to see if anyone has heard me, and needless to say, at least half the restaurant has, which makes me feel even more triumphant. This is fun. Well, almost.

A waitress, on her way to the kitchen, stops to ask us if everything's all right.

"Peachy," I tell her, and turn to face my mother. "Now, Mom, if you'll excuse me, I'm going to go back to the table. And when you get there—"

"Marissa, enough. Just stop," my mother says.

"No, Mom," I hiss, and step closer to her. She looks afraid of me but doesn't move, so I continue. "I will *not* stop. And you will *not* shut me up yet again because you prefer starting fights to participating in them. *Now, as I was saying*, when you get back to the table, let's pretend that we actually like each other and that you aren't disappointed in my every move so that the Bergmans don't think we're complete freaks. Then you can go on your merry way back to Michigan tomorrow and call me next century for all I care."

My mother stares, her mouth hanging open in disbelief. I decide to make the most of my captive audience. "And by the way, Mom, I'd prefer if you hold your comments about my dietary habits until your plane ride back. I'm sure Phil would be fascinated to know how I'm ruining myself with simple carbs. But I, for one, couldn't care less."

The look on my mother's face morphs from shock to staged sadness. "I just don't know why you hate me so much," she warbles, dabbing at her eye with the corner of her sleeve.

"Save it, Susan. The only one who hates you is you," I say, surprising myself with this insight. Then, before she has a chance to respond, I spin on my heels and head back to the table.

Dave and his parents do their best to salvage dinner, but the mood is off, and I barely make a dent in my pizza. When we get home, my mother goes immediately to her room and Phil mumbles something about her having a headache before following her. Dave, having already profusely apologized to me ("I had no idea she could be *that* bad," he whispered in the parking lot, mortified), heads to the bathroom to clean up for the night, as does Len. But when I say good night to Joyel, she puts a hand on my shoulder to stop me. Cocking her head to one side, she smiles kindly. "You know, I think a drink is in order. What do you think?"

"I won't say no," I tell her, although what I'm actually thinking is that if she ends up being my mother-in-law one day, it will definitely be the universe's way of righting all the wrong things my mother has done to me over the years.

"Well, that was an interesting evening, wasn't it?" Joyel says, pouring equal parts vodka and tonic in tumblers. She deftly slices a lime and drops a wedge in each of the fizzling concoctions, then tries one. "Perfect," she declares, sighing. Then her eyes meet mine, and I see that they are filled with sympathy, but not pity. "How are you doing?"

"Well, I've certainly had better days," I say. "I'm really sorry to have dragged you all into this drama. And here you thought you probably were going to have an uneventful meet-the-parents weekend."

"Dear, you didn't drag anyone into anything. That was you being dragged."

"My mom's not entirely in the wrong," I say, looking down at my distended torso.

"You're kidding, right?" asks Joyel, somewhat incredulously.

"Sure," I tell her, clearly dead serious.

"Oh my goodness. Obviously, this is all off the record. You know I like your mother a lot, and I'm not trying to bash her. It's just that sometimes you've got to tune that stuff out. I mean, trust me, my mother sent me to a fat farm every summer for all of junior high and high school because I was ten pounds overweight. Ten pounds! Can you imagine?"

I shake my head, because I can't. Even now, in her early sixties, Joyel is lean and fit. "And you weren't worried that you'd raise Sascha to have a complex?" I ask, referring to Dave's sister. "Because honestly, that's what gets me the most. I don't want to pass on this kind of crazy fat phobia if I have a daughter." In fact, it occurs to me—although I don't say it out loud—that my mother's paranoia undoubtedly has more than a little to do with why I ended up being a diet editor.

"Honey, I think you should be more worried about yourself than about your future children," Joyel tells me with a wistful smile. "Because trust me, it's the weight of someone else's expectations that's the hardest to lose."

# Thirty

On Monday, I call Sarah on my lunch hour for a post-Chappaqua briefing.

The phone rings several times. I'm about to hang up when she picks up.

"Sorry," she says, out of breath. "Had to run to get the phone. Was on the elliptical."

"Must be nice," I tell her, because working out in my own personal gym in the middle of the afternoon sounds almost as luxurious as having a cabana boy feed me bonbons while I lounge at the side of the pool.

She snorts. "Sure. I *love* spending forty-five precious, kid-free minutes sweating my butt off while watching Oprah discuss how women should exercise for a full hour a day."

"We should also give ten percent of our salary to support the children, right?" I respond, laughing. "Anyway, should I call you back?"

"Nope. But don't mind my heaving and ho-ing. I'm going to put you on speakerphone and get back on the machine while we talk. So how was it?" she asks, referring to the weekend.

"Let's just say it wasn't *The Brady Bunch* reunion."

"I had a feeling that was the case. I picked Mom and Phil up from the airport yesterday. They tried to act normal and said the Bergmans were, quote, lovely people. I still got the distinct impression that it didn't go well."

"It didn't start out too bad, but Mom doesn't have the warm fuzzies for me right now." I recount our face-off at the restaurant.

"Oh, Mother." Sarah sighs. "I have to say, Dave's parents sound like saints. Now I know where he gets his temperament from. Can you imagine if the situation were reversed?"

"I *know.* The crazy thing is, Len and Joyel didn't act the slightest bit fazed by Mom's atrocious behavior, although Joyel went out of her way to be nice to me after it happened."

"That's because she loves you, dummy," says Sarah. "You're perfect daughter-in-law material. That is what this whole meet-the-parents thing was about, wasn't it?"

"Nooo," I respond, glad that no one's in my office to see me blushing.

"Yesss!" she shoots back. "I know you're turning red over there."

"Brat."

"You can call me names all you want, but I know the truth: *Marissa's in loo-ve, Marissa's in loooo-ve,*" she teases. "On a happy note, I'm assuming this means Nathan's off the roster, no?"

"Um . . ." I quickly bring her up to speed on *As the Nathan Turns,* including our dinner and his e-mails.

"Marissa!" Sarah scolds. In the background, I hear the whooshing of the elliptical pedals slow and then stop. "I can't believe you didn't tell me you had dinner with him! What happened to moving on?"

I'm not sure what I was hoping to get out of our conversation, but Sarah's comment rubs me the wrong way. "Never mind. I'm sorry I even mentioned it."

"Oh, come on, don't be like that. I should be able to ask you why without you flipping out."

I don't respond.

"Marissa," Sarah says gently. "You know I love you. So much. You're my blood." It is a funny, almost antiquated thing to say, but it's touching, and a reminder of just how far Sarah and I have come over the past several months. "I just want you to be happy," she tells me. "I'm pretty sure that sabotaging your relationship with Dave is not the best way to accomplish that."

"I'm sorry. I know you're right," I concede. "It's just such a touchy topic for me right now, because I *know* I need to get Nathan out of my life, but it's like my best intentions aren't enough—he keeps lingering, anyway. There's nothing good that can come of it at this point, and I hate myself for even striking up this weird quasi-friendship with him again in the first place."

"You want my honest opinion?" Sarah asks.

"Can I say no? Because I suspect you're going to give it to me anyway."

"You know I am." She laughs. "I think you've been letting too many things happen to you. Like, Nathan shows up in New York and wants to go to dinner? Sure! He thinks it's a good idea to keep talking to you? Why not?! Sit and watch Julia undermine your relationship with Dave, and give her a free pass because she's not one hundred percent right in the head? Okay! You see what I mean? I just think you might want to think about being in the driver's seat for a change," she says, echoing what we discussed last November. "*Especially* given that we're talking about your future with Dave. You're so lucky. Don't give that up for something—some*one*—that doesn't matter."

*"You're so lucky."* Sarah's words remind me of something Julia once said. In an instant, I am eighteen again, lying on a plastic raft in a red bikini that cuts into my hips, with Julia floating next to me.

"God, I can't believe this is it," she said, her face pointed up at the sun. "All that pomp and circumstance and I feel the exact same way I did before I got my diploma. It's sort of like losing your virginity. Like, what's all the fuss about?"

I nodded in agreement, even though I had yet to be deflowered and Julia knew it. We'd just graduated the previous day, and were in the middle of what she called our "official post-grad rehash" at her pool. My, ahem, tan had long since become the same color as my bathing suit, but I couldn't bring myself to get out of the water. As though if I just lay there a little longer, I could stop time.

I turned to look at Julia, who had somehow managed to avoid frying and had instead turned an enviable shade of caramel. "I don't know," I told her. "Maybe I do feel a little different. Kinda sad. Things are never going to be the same again. You know?"

"They might be even better," she told me, dipping her hands into the pool to splash herself with the cool water.

"So you really meant what you said today?" I asked her, referring to the salutatorian speech she'd given at the ceremony. Speaking so passionately that some of my Kennedy classmates were moved to tears, Julia urged us to embrace the change we were about to face, even if we weren't ready for it. "Life will happen either way," she said. "The difference is how you handle it. You can grab the wave and ride, or be pulled under with the current."

"Of *course* I believe it," she told me, flipping over onto her stomach. Reaching over with her left hand, she pulled my raft close to hers, and lifted her sunglasses up. Then she gently pulled my glasses off the bridge of my nose, so we could see each other. "I know you're nervous," she said. "But good things are going to come your way. Just you wait."

"I only wish I was half as sure about that as you are," I said, smiling wistfully.

"Mar, the very first day I met you, I thought to myself, *That girl is charmed.*"

"Pshaw. Now you're the one trying to charm *me*. I'm not one of your silly boyfriends, you know," I told her.

"Have I ever lied to you?"

"No . . . not that I know of."

"Whatever. You know I haven't," she said, splashing me. "But seriously. You know why we're such a good pair?"

"Why?" I asked. "Because we both like strawberry wine coolers? And we wear the same size shoe?"

"Nope," she said. "We're lucky people. You can't have one lucky and one unlucky friend. It doesn't work."

"Correction: *You're* lucky," I said. "I'm not the one with mile-long legs, a full ride to college, and a pool in my backyard."

"Oh, Marissa," Julia said, sounding almost weary. "You're so lucky. And one day you'll realize it. But I think luck isn't nearly as important as what you decide to do with it."

Julia was right; I *am* lucky, I think as I spin back and forth in my office chair. I'm healthy. I have great friends. A beautiful home. A family who, although not faultless by any stretch of the imagination, I love. A boyfriend who loves me more than I probably deserve. So the only question that remains is the one Julia posed so many years ago: What am I going to make of my luck?

I'm suddenly struck with what I can only describe as a revelation. Every time Nathan reaches out to me, he—we—are making our story a little longer, a little more complex, a little more memorable. My urge to fix the past is strong, and it's made me hesitant to completely walk away. But now I'm beginning to understand that trying to tie our loose ends into a neat bow is the worst thing I can do.

"You know what, Sarah?" I say to my sister. "As of this second, I'm vowing to cease contact with Nathan. I'm not going to talk to him, e-mail him, or even speak about him anymore. I think it's the only way to get past this ridiculous mess. Will you hold me to that?"

"That sounds like a good plan," Sarah says. "And of course, I would be honored to be your enforcer. Just ask Ella: If there's one thing I'm good at, it's policing bad behavior."

"Excellent. Then we have a deal," I tell her, feeling as though I've just lifted a twenty-ton weight off my shoulders.

Although I feel relieved after my call with Sarah, there's one little thing that's still nagging me. I know I have to come clean—as in, completely, 100 percent spotless—with Dave.

As usual, he's working late, so when I get home, I decide to get dinner ready. I order Chinese takeout, but rather than tossing plates on the coffee table, where we usually eat while watching TV, I put place settings and a bottle of wine in the dining room and turn music on low.

"What's this all about?" Dave asks when he walks in the door. "Special occasion?"

"I just thought it might be good for us to talk for a change, instead of zoning out in front of the tube. And," I say, pouring him a little wine and handing him the glass, "there's something specific I want to discuss."

"Please tell me you're not leaving me," Dave says, loosening his tie with his free hand. "Because after the day I've had, I might just lose it."

"No, sweetie," I say. I wrap my arms around his waist. "Things have been so amazing between us lately. I hope we're always this good."

"Haven't things been great?" he says. The pleased look on his face gives me a tiny glimpse of what he must have looked like as a little boy, and my heart swells with love. How could I have ever doubted that he was the right one?

"It's just that I feel like there's something I need to explain about Nathan."

"Oh, brother. That guy again." He groans.

I swallow hard and take his hand. "It's not what you think. I was never going to cheat on you with him. But when he showed up again a few months ago, I did have a lot *what if?* thoughts. I was questioning everything that had happened between him and me—and even wondering what would have been if I hadn't listened to Julia all those years ago. I feel like the worst person in the world admitting that out loud, but it's something you need to know."

Dave looks at me long and hard. "Marissa, I don't like this guy, and I don't want him in your life. You know that. But you wouldn't be human if you didn't question your past. I think about Tanya sometimes, even though I'm pretty sure she's off boiling bunnies in some poor guy's kitchen," he says, referring to his ex. "What Julia did to you was not cool, and because that choice was taken from you, you were bound to ruminate over it. What I need to know"— he pauses, searching for words—"is whether your 'what ifs' made you realize that everything worked out the way it was supposed to. Or are you still searching for a second chance? Because bad day or not, I want to know that right now, rather than a year from now. Or worse, after a decade passes."

"I don't want that second chance," I say with conviction. For years after I broke up with Nathan, I secretly believed that we'd be together again one day, which is part of the reason why I've had such a hard time detaching from him this time around. But seeing Dave in front of me, it's perfectly clear that I don't want or need the opportunity to relive my past—especially when it means I'll be destroying my future in the process.

"I've been thinking a lot about what you said to me a few weeks ago," I tell Dave. "About my attraction to volatile people." I motion for him to sit down next to me at the table. "If there's anything that's become clear to me over the past six months, it's that I need *this*. Us," I tell him. "I want stability. I want a relationship that's solid and adult, and yes, even a little boring." As I say this, I think of the cozy house we'll have in Chappaqua one day; the little brown-eyed toddlers who will reward our steadiness and predictability with an unbelievable amount of love; the way that we'll grow old and gray together—and in that instant, I know that there's no other path for me than the one I'm on now.

"Boring? Greaaaat," Dave retorts, but squeezes my hand to let me know he's taking me seriously.

"Every time I've had to deal with Nathan, particularly regarding the situation with Julia, I've felt *horrible*. I mean, seriously ill," I tell him. "If that's not a clear sign that roller-coaster relationships don't agree with me anymore, I don't know what is. But you, Dave Bergman—you make me feel amazing. I am never, ever, going to give that up."

Dave kisses me, then whispers, "That, Marissa Rogers, is all I need to know."

# Thirty-one

The first thing I think when Lynne calls me to her office is, *I'm toast.* The magazine industry is a bloodbath right now; at a press event I attended earlier in the week, two nutrition editors from competing publications were missing, and I was informed by another colleague that they'd been canned because of budget cuts. It's true that *Svelte's* entire content centers around my subject, diet—and I know Lynne likes me well enough, if only because Naomi does. But shrewd supervisor that she is, I wouldn't put it past her to replace me with someone younger and even less expensive to employ. Someone like . . . Ashley.

The second thing I think is, *Maybe I'm not getting fired. Maybe Ashley gave Lynne her sidebar to read, and Lynne wants to run it.* The prospect is so unappealing that I almost hope that I'm getting pink-slipped.

Whatever my fate, I know the only thing I can do is face it like a professional. I pat my hair down and take a deep breath before knocking lightly on the frosted glass door to Lynne's office. "Hello?"

"Come in," Lynne barks. As I push the door open, I see that she's leaning back in her chair with her arms crossed over her chest, waiting for me.

*Gulp.* I sit gingerly on the edge of the stiff metal chair opposite my boss.

She looks at me for what feels like an eternity. Finally, she says with a sigh, "I wanted to tell you myself, because I think you're doing a great job for us, and I don't want you to get the wrong idea. It's just that in this economy, sometimes I have to make choices for all of us that aren't easy to swallow."

*Whew,* I think. It's not Ashley's Q&A with Julia. Then it dawns on me that what Lynne just said is longhand for: *Sayonara, Marissa.*

"Could you clarify?" I ask, because I can't manage to choke out "Am I fired?"

"I'm killing the brain trauma story for June," she says bluntly.

"Oh." I sit for a second, processing this information. Okay, so I have a job. That's good. But . . . "I thought you loved that story," I whimper, trying a little too hard not to sound pissed. "You wrote on the last draft that it was my best work yet and that you couldn't wait to see how many awards it won."

"Doesn't test well," Lynne says sharply, the veins in her neck bulging. "That twenty-person panel we did in Minnesota last week showed that our readers want more weight-loss articles. They like tips, recipes, skinny celebrities. They're simply not interested in health unless it relates to shedding pounds. But lucky for you, that's ninety percent of what you do, which means your job is safe."

*Twenty people?* I want to scream. *You're getting rid of an article you deemed brilliant and told the rest of the staff to emulate because*

*twenty random women from one area of the United States didn't
like it and would prefer to read secrets of successful anorexics?*

But I just say, "I understand."

"I knew you would, Marissa," she tells me. "I'm fully aware that
this piece meant a lot to you, given what your friend went through.
But if you want to get ahead in magazines, which I know you
do, then it all comes down to the bottom line. Now, I can count
on you to fill that hole in the lineup with a big celeb weight-loss
story, right? Because we have only a month to get new copy in."
She slaps her bony hand on the top of her desk for emphasis, and
her platinum-and-diamond-studded wedding band clinks loudly
against the glass.

"Of course," I tell her. *Right after I'm done jumping off the Brooklyn Bridge.*

Having recently watched a friend go through a near-death experience, suicide isn't actually all that appealing. Quitting my job, on
the other hand—suddenly that sounds like just the thing.

When I get back to my desk, I find myself thinking about last
week's Take the Lead lesson, which was about coping.

"Why is it a good idea to talk to someone about your feelings or
go for a jog around the block instead of yelling at the person you're
upset with?" I asked the girls, glancing down at my TTL binder to
make sure I was relaying the information correctly.

Of course, Estrella's hand shot straight up. But so did Josie's
and Anna's and Margarita's. I pointed at Margarita. "What do you
think?"

"Because it won't actually make you feel better?" she said tim-
idly.

"That's right!" I told her. "You might actually feel *worse* afterward, because not only will your original bad feelings not go away,
but if you cope by starting a fight or smoking cigarettes or eating

lots of junk food, those unhealthy behaviors will eventually cause even more problems for you."

Okay, so it may have been worded like an ABC after-school special, but I can't deny that the lesson was right. I'd love to tell Lynne my thoughts on her twenty-person panel. But not only am I too timid to do so, I also know it won't solve anything. So I opt to take a walk instead.

I trudge around the block, but once I'm back in front of the *Svelte* building, I head north instead of going inside. Ten blocks later, my feet don't want to stop. I check my cell phone and see that our weekly edit meeting is in less than ten minutes, which means that unless I make like a Kenyan marathoner, I'm not going to make it back in time. But for once, I decide that my mental health takes precedence over my career.

Without slowing down, I hit the first number on my speed dial. Julia picks up immediately. "Hi, Marissa! What's wrong?"

I draw in my breath sharply. Julia and I always used to say that we were like twins: When one of us was hurt or upset, the other person often sensed it immediately, even if we were miles apart. Since the accident, though, it's like we've been on separate planets, and the distance was too far for us to connect signals.

"How did you know something was wrong?" I ask her.

"Jesus, my skull wasn't completely crushed," she says flippantly. "I just had a feeling something was up. Besides, you never call me in the middle of the day anymore."

"True," I admit. "I just got some bad news and I wanted to chat."

"What happened?"

"Lynne isn't going to run my brain injury story," I barely choke out, unable to conceal how upset I am. "The readers want weight loss, not health. And the story won't attract advertisers, because neurologists don't need to advertise in *Svelte*."

"That sucks, Mar," she says. "But you've had stories killed before, right?"

"Not like this. This one meant more to me. It was my chance to prove that I can do something other than weight loss. I feel . . . stuck."

"Mar, can I ask you something?" I half expect her to inquire about the fate of her Q&A, but instead, she says, "Why don't you unstick yourself? Just because you've been working at *Svelte* since forever doesn't mean you have to keep at it. Go get a new job. God knows you have enough going for you to be considered an attractive candidate at a million other places."

This catches me off guard. Julia may have wanted to be a dancer, but her professional instincts were always so sharp that she would have made a killer career counselor. And indeed, when I couldn't figure out how to get a position in magazines, it was her advice to take an entry-level journalism job at a newspaper and "network the hell out of your nights at events where magazine people will be" that ultimately landed me my gig at *Svelte*. The fact that Julia's career savvy has remained intact, even as her social skills remain questionable, gives me a small ray of hope.

"It's not exactly a good time to be searching for a job, given the economic collapse and whatnot," I say.

"Have you actually looked for anything in the past six months?" she asks.

"No," I confess. "It's been so long since I've job-hunted that I wouldn't even know where to start."

"Correct me if I'm wrong, but you used to talk about becoming a big-shot editor all the time, right? Maybe this is another case of my brain drain, but I haven't heard you mention becoming an editor-in-chief in, like, neons," Julia says, and I don't have it in me to tell her that I think she meant "eons." Besides, she's otherwise spot-on. I used to dream of running my own magazine—maybe even *Svelte*—one day. Now the thought of doing so makes me want to jab a hot poker into my thigh. It's not that I think my job is completely without value. Couched between the "Lose five inches in four weeks!" and "Get fit without trying!" claims, the magazine contains legitimate information that helps women live healthier, better lives. But I want to leave work at the end of the day feeling inspired and absolutely certain that I've done more good than harm.

"Oh, Jules." I sigh. "As always, excellent advice. I'm going to start looking to see what's out there."

"That's all I ask," she says, and I swear I can feel her smiling on the other line.

# Thirty-two

I've decided to devote Saturday to winning the war on dirt. Wielding our Dyson against the dust bunnies hidden in what appears to be every corner and crevice in our apartment, I zoom from room to room, sucking up anything that's not glued to the ground. By the time I make my way to the living room, I've decided there's no way that I can deal with the filth that would come with a dog. Too bad, as I've been contemplating getting one as a way to ward off my loneliness.

"Whoa there, tiger," Dave says, coming through the front door. "Don't use that thing on me." His T-shirt, spotted with sweat, clings to his flat stomach. I want to hate him for being motivated enough to exercise every day, but I'm the one who gets to enjoy the fruit of his labor. Fruit that I'd like to take a bite of right now, come to think of it. Although I was concerned that my confession about

Nathan would drive a wedge between us, blatant honesty seems to have had the opposite effect: Dave and I have spent the past couple of weeks in honeymoon mode.

"Rarr," I growl. "Why don't you bring that sweaty body of yours over here?"

"You are an animal." He winks. He tosses the pile of mail he's been holding on the coffee table and saunters toward me.

Just as he's about to move in for the kill, I spot a letter splayed among the other envelopes and magazines Dave just threw down. I don't need to look at the return address; the bubbly, sloppy script tells me exactly who it's from.

"Did you see that my mom sent me something?" I ask Dave, my lust already evaporated.

"No . . . but it can wait, right?" he says playfully, tugging on my sweater to pull me toward him.

"You know I'm not going to be able to focus until I know what it says," I apologize. "But I promise to make it up to you later." I tear impatiently at the envelope, ripping it and a corner of the rose-colored stationery tucked inside. Without sitting down, my eyes race over the words my mother has filled the page with.

*Dearest Marissa,*

*I love you very much.*

*I'm sorry I hurt you when we were at the Bergmans'. At the time, I thought I was doing you a favor, but after talking with Phil about what happened, I realize now that I shouldn't have said anything about what you choose to eat, especially not in front of Dave's family, but not alone, either. I hope that the Bergmans don't think I'm a terrible person, but more important, I hope you don't hate me.*

*Worrying about food is so normal for me that I seldom stop*

*to consider that you wouldn't want to hear it or that it could*
*sound like criticism. I'm beginning to see that my "suggestions"*
*aren't always welcome or helpful. I know it's hard for you and*
*Sarah to understand this, but I sometimes forget that you're both*
*grown women who are capable of making your own decisions—*
*decisions that are yours to make, whether I agree with them or*
*not. Although I can't promise to do the right thing every time,*
*I've vowed that from now on I'll try to bite my tongue, especially*
*when it comes to weight and food issues.*

*I'm really proud of you, and I am amazed that you've grown*
*up to be such a smart, beautiful, successful woman. You have*
*such an amazing life ahead of you, and I hope you'll continue to*
*make me a part of it.*

*Love always,*

*Mom*

Without a word, I pass the letter to Dave. When he's done reading it, he glances up at me. "Um, wow."

"What do you think?" I ask wearily. My mother's admission
doesn't make me feel nearly as triumphant as I would have
thought. Instead, it makes me very, very tired.

"I'm kind of shocked she apologized," Dave tells me.

"I know. It's the first time I can ever remember her doing that,"
I tell him, plopping down on the sofa. "I guess she really felt bad.
As well she should. I suppose I should call her . . ." I lean back in
the overstuffed cushions and cover my eyes with a throw pillow.
My head feels like a boulder on my twig of a neck, and I realize
that I'm not just tired; I'm beyond exhausted. Before I can spend
another second thinking about my mother, I'm fast asleep.

. . .

When I wake, I have no idea where I am or what time it is. I rub my eyes and look around at the dim living room and slowly, the earlier part of the day starts to come back to me. I glance at the illuminated red numbers on the microwave: 5:07. I've been asleep for more than three hours.

"Hey, Van Winkle," Dave calls from the dining room table, where his fingers are tapping away with lightning speed on his laptop.

"You didn't go into the office?" I ask, knowing that he'd planned on spending at least a few hours there.

"Nope," he says. "Didn't want to completely abandon you. Besides, I was able to get some stuff done here. Sascha and John called to see if we wanted to go to dinner. I was thinking that if you're up for it, we could meet them somewhere in the neighborhood."

Still groggy, I walk over to the kitchen sink and run my hands under cold water, then press them to my face. "Dinner sounds great," I tell Dave. "Just promise me you won't bring up the situation with my mother."

"I promise," says Dave. He closes his laptop and comes over to where I'm standing at the sink. He gives me a big bear hug, then kisses me on the forehead. "Now you promise me that you'll call her before the end of the weekend to accept her apology."

"Hmph." I pout.

"The lady doth protest too much," Dave says. "You know you'll feel better if you do."

"Whatever," I retort, and motion for him to follow me into the bedroom. "Let's talk about something more fun. Like how you think I'm an animal."

I don't call my mom that night, or the next morning. Speaking with her would put a damper on an otherwise perfect weekend, I tell myself. The reality, of course, is that my procrastination casts a shadow over me, making it impossible for me to enjoy what I'm doing. Even a shopping excursion to Bloomingdale's with Sophie on Sunday afternoon doesn't snap me out of my funk. As I try on enough shoes to make Imelda Marcos envious—settling for a sexy-yet-sensible pair of red snakeskin flats—I find myself wishing that I could compartmentalize everything the way Dave does, so I didn't have to schlep around my work, family, and friend drama all in one ridiculously heavy bag.

Sunday evening, desperate to avoid the inevitable, I decide to go for a long walk. I toss on my workout gear and my sneakers and head out the door just as the sun is starting to set. I trek along for two blocks, trying to get my blood pumping. But after several months of jogging with the Take the Lead girls, speed no longer seems possible when I have one heel on the ground at all times. Without thinking, I break into a jog, and my stride instantly becomes more comfortable.

I trek down my street, thanking God that it's dark out because I'm grinning like an idiot. Me, jogging—alone! On purpose, and not because I'm being chased by a robber or rapist! I can barely believe it. Even more astounding, I'm not in pain. On the contrary, I feel almost—gasp—*good*. Each time my feet pound the pavement, I leave a little more tension in my trail.

After a while, my thoughts return to the situation with my mother and her inability to deal with conflict. Like a faulty DNA sequence, I have inherited her ability to avoid confrontation, which is why I've been putting off calling her all weekend. Yet as I jog along, I start to think about how ridiculous I'm being. What's the worst thing that could happen if I called? We'd have an awkward conversation? We'd fight like we did at the restaurant in Chappaqua? Besides, if my mother—the original leopard—can change her spots and apologize, then I owe it to her, and to myself, to at least try something new.

When I get back to the apartment, I kick off my sneakers but don't shower. Instead, I head straight to the bedroom, where I grab the cordless phone from its dock on the desk. Without a second thought, I dial.

"Hello?"

I take a deep breath. Then I say what I don't want to say. I say the hardest words I've had to utter in a very long time.

"Mom? It's Marissa. It's okay. I forgive you."

# Thirty-three

Wednesday morning, I get a cryptic e-mail from Naomi.

> -Are you free around three-ish? Meet me at Starbucks—the
> one on 50th, not the one around the corner. Have some-
> thing I want to talk to you about.

Yep, I write back. What's up???

> -If I was going to tell you over e-mail I wouldn't have asked
> you to meet me. :)

I decide that there's nothing more cruel than telling someone you have something to tell them, then making them wait to find out what it is. Instead of focusing on the dozen different projects I need to finish by close of business on Friday, I find myself coming up with potential scenarios: Naomi is pregnant with sextuplets. Or she's quitting work to be Michelle Obama's new press secretary. Or she's accidentally discovered that Lynne's a serial killer who strangles her victims with a Thighmaster. The endless possibilities keep me from accomplishing anything all afternoon. Not that I can blame Naomi entirely for this; since my brain injury story was sent to the shredder, I have become astoundingly sluggish. It's not a version of myself that I'm fond of, but short of snorting lines in the bathroom, I'm not sure how to get moving again.

"Okay, you're torturing me," I tell Naomi when I spot her in line at Starbucks. "What's going on?"

"One sec. Two tall skinny caps, please," she tells the barista, then hands the cashier a ten. She collects her change, then motions for me to join her at a small circular table at the window that's opening up. "Hold down the fort and I'll go get the drinks."

"So?" I prod after she reaches the table.

"Time for a New York look," she orders, and we both spin our heads around a little too conspicuously to see if anyone we know is in the café. Negatory.

"Okay, so here's the deal," she says, leaning in conspiratorially. "I just found out this morning that Take the Lead needs a new national communications manager. And the position is here in the city. Decent salary with better hours and more vacation time than *Svelte*."

"And you're going to apply? That's great!" I enthuse.

Naomi gives me her signature "I'm humoring you" look. "Sweetie. I'm perfectly happy where I am. I'm talking about *you*. Trust me, it hasn't gone unnoticed that you're not thrilled with your job anymore."

"Oh, crap. I'm that obvious?" I mutter, mortified; my restlessness is definitely not something I've been trying to broadcast.

"Well, not to everyone. But come on, Marissa, we've been working together for almost six years now. If anyone knows that you've
lost your spark, it's me."

"Which means that Lynne probably knows, too," I say glumly.

"Lucky for you, I'm fairly certain she thinks you're in a funk
because the brain story was cut. But for future reference, skipping
meetings without warning isn't exactly a good way to hide the fact
that you're bored with work." She smiles, swirling her paper cup
so she can get the last of the foam. "So, thoughts? The job would
be perfect for you. In fact, I told that very thing to Rhonda," she
says, referring to the director, whom I met briefly during training.
"Be expecting an e-mail from her."

"You are incorrigible!" I reprimand her, but I'm secretly pleased.
The job sounds terrific, and I haven't found any other promising
leads. Then it hits me. "Why exactly did you think I was qualified
for this? I've never written a press release or issued a statement
in my life. And it's a running organization, for goodness' sake. I
barely just learned to jog."

"Is this the part where you tell me you're ugly and stupid, too?"
Naomi says with mock exasperation. "Because this is the part
where I tell you that I have you confused with my brilliant and
capable colleague Marissa."

I pick at the thick plastic lid covering my cup, avoiding Naomi's
gaze. "I know, I know," I eventually concede. "I'm too hard on
myself."

"That's putting it lightly. Seriously, though. You've been an editor for how long?"

"Eight years."

"And how many stories have you written and edited in that time?"

"About four million."

"Right. And I'm guessing you've received twice as many press releases, the majority so poorly written that you could do a better job while snorkeling in the bathtub. Plus, you're great with people."

"I am?" I ask with surprise. "And here I thought I was the villain in *The Devil Wears Old Navy*."

Naomi snorts. "Of course you are! And you're especially good at handling crazy, demanding lunatics. Maybe too good, come to think of it," she says, raising her eyebrows, and I can't help but wonder if she's referring to Julia. "Just tell me that you'll interview for it, okay?"

"Of course," I assure her, pushing in my chair. "Just promise me you'll prep me for the interview. I'm rusty."

"Deal," says Naomi. She links her arm in mine as we walk out of Starbucks. "Provided I get a free dinner once you land the job."

"Anywhere your heart desires, boss."


According to *The Wall Street Journal*, 35 percent of IT professionals admit to reading employee e-mails—and those are just the ones who fess up. Hopefully the *Svelte* techies have something better to do, because Rhonda Beshel e-mails me that same afternoon at my work e-mail. *Nice, Naomi. Thanks for giving her my Gmail address.*

Rhonda cuts right to the chase, and asks if I can come in for an interview tomorrow afternoon.

*Not a problem,* I write back, not even checking my calendar to see if I have anything else scheduled. *I'll see you at one o'clock. Looking forward to it!*

Naomi gives me a crash course in interview etiquette after work, and Dave does a trial run-through that evening. I spend Thursday morning Googling everything I can find on Take the Lead, and by the time I leave to meet Rhonda, I'm sure I'm ready to tackle anything she throws my way.

My confidence dissipates when I arrive at the Take the Lead office. Rhonda's lithe, perfectly polished assistant looks at me skeptically when I introduce myself. My blue sweater dress is all wrong, I decide; I should have worn a suit. And my lumps and bumps, ill-concealed under my dress, make it crystal clear that I am not a runner.

"Wait here," the assistant commands, pointing to an Ikea couch across from her desk that's identical to the one I owned before moving in with Dave. I sit with my bag on my lap, attempting to look composed. Taking one last step at prepping, I try to recall some of the brilliant answers I gave Dave yesterday when he was quizzing me, but find myself at a complete loss. *Crap. I'm going to be working at Svelte until 2045.*

Nearly twenty minutes later, I'm still waiting, and my nervousness has given way to extreme aggravation. Just as I contemplate taking off, Rhonda pops her head out of her office. "I am *so* sorry. We had an accident at one of the schools where the girls practice," she says, and I immediately soften at her genuine tone. "I hate waiting, so I feel terrible that I've left you out here all this time. Will you come in?"

Rhonda welcomes me with a firm handshake and a dimpled smile, seeming even more approachable than she did during training. Up close, I am surprised to see that she couldn't be more than a year or two older than me, which is simultaneously impressive and intimidating.

"Naomi speaks very highly of you, and she's one of our best coaches, so I take her word very seriously," she tells me, flipping through a steno pad where I see she's scribbled notes, presumably about the other people she's already interviewed. "And I saw from your résumé and LinkedIn profile that you have nearly a decade of writing and editing experience. That will come in handy—you'd be spending the majority of your day creating and revising materials for training and for the press."

"I haven't done communications work before," I say, but quickly catch myself. *Don't talk yourself down,* I think, remembering Naomi's instructions yesterday. I quickly add, "But I'm a skilled writer, and I know the Take the Lead material like the back of my hand now."

"That's excellent," Rhonda says, and makes a little check on her notepad. She leans back and puts her hands behind her head. "So tell me, how is your current group of girls?"

I tell her about Josie, who seems to have abandoned her bullying ways, and about Estrella's enthusiasm and unexpected self-confidence. Then I do something that definitely breaks protocol, and reveal that I'm fairly certain training has improved my life more than it has the girls'.

"That's half the point of volunteering," Rhonda says, laughing lightly. "It's no coincidence that people who volunteer live longer and are healthier and happier than people who don't. And the fact that you didn't start out a runner is actually to your advantage, in some ways. I see inspirational qualities in you, Marissa, and I have no doubt that your girls have noticed them, too."

"Thank you," I tell her, blushing. "I do feel like I've come a long way since February."

"I bet you have!" Rhonda says earnestly. "Not to sound too cheesy, but it really changes something in you. I know I've become a better person since I started coaching."

"You coach?" This surprises me; I figured she'd be so busy running the organization that she wouldn't actually have time to volunteer.

Rhonda nods. "I was never a runner. My sister talked me into coaching, and I liked it so much that I started working for TTL six months later. The rest, they say, is history," she says with a laugh. Then she leans across the desk. "Just wait until you finish your first race with the girls at your side. It's the most incredible experience."

"I can't wait," I say honestly.

We chat for another ten minutes before she glances at her watch. "Uh-oh. I have a meeting in just a few."

"No problem," I tell her. "It's been great speaking with you. I appreciate you taking the time to interview me."

"Listen, Marissa," she says, and frowns slightly. *Here's the part where she tells me I'm not the right fit for the job.* Rhonda continues. "I've interviewed a bunch of other candidates, and while some of them have amazing experience, none of them have actually coached before. And frankly, I prefer you to the rest."

"Really?" I say, flustered. I'm seconds away from having a Sally Field moment: *You like me! You really like me!*

"Yes," says Rhonda. "And I like to think of myself as a fairly decent judge of character. So if your references check out, which I'm sure they will, I'll e-mail you an offer letter within the next day or two with your salary and benefits information."

*There has got to be a catch,* I think. *Nothing in life is this easy.*

But then I remember my old friend karma, and the hell of a year I've had. Why shouldn't it be easy? Just this one thing?

"Rhonda, that sounds amazing." I beam. "I promise you that I will be the best communications director Take the Lead has ever had."

"That's exactly what Naomi said." Rhonda smiles. "It pays to have good friends, doesn't it?"


As promised, Rhonda e-mails the next day with a complete offer letter, including information about my salary, which will be five thousand more than I currently make. I immediately forward the e-mail to Naomi, Dave, and Julia with !!!!! in the subject line. Then I write Rhonda back to let her know that I gladly accept the offer, and will be thrilled to start in two weeks, which will give me enough time to finish up at *Svelte.*

Then reality strikes. This means I have to quit.

At my urging, Naomi collects her free dinner the same day Rhonda e-mails me.

"I'm so happy for you, Marissa," she tells me, sliding into the red leather booth at the burger joint she chose. She smiles as she says this, making her eyes crinkle up at the sides, and I think how much I'll miss working with her. Rhonda seems great, but she's no Naomi.

"I'm really thrilled," I tell her. "Just trying not to overthink the fact that I just chose to leave magazines. You know, the career I've been working toward for, oh, almost a decade now." In spite of my excitement about the fresh start I've just been given, I can't seem to get past a lingering feeling of sadness. Moving on from my childhood dream is yet another way that the plans Julia and I made together will never come to pass.

"Well, you can always return to *Svelte.* It's not like you'll be stuck at your new job," Naomi says, reminding me of Julia's comment: *Unstick yourself.* "Just tell me that this isn't all because of the brain injury story," she adds. "Because I feel horrible about that. I should have gone to bat for you more than I did. Lynne just seemed so hell-bent on replacing it with a splashy weight-loss piece."

"Not at all," I tell her, and it's the truth. "If anything, the story gave me a window to what has been going on in Julia's head, which has made it easier to cope with some of the stuff she's thrown my way."

"Well, that's good. Although I always thought you'd make one stellar editor-in-chief one day," Naomi says, looking like a proud mama hen.

"Never say never. I'd love to do the occasional freelance story after I get settled in at Take the Lead," I tell Naomi. "In the bigger scheme of things, though, something's changed for me. I can't put my finger on it, but moving up the editorial ladder doesn't excite me anymore. Maybe a year or two off will light my fire again and I'll want to jump back in. But right now, I'm ready for something different."

"It's going to be amazing for you. But you have to promise you'll still make time for me when I'm not your boss anymore."

"Are you kidding? First of all, I'm not quitting coaching, so you'll still see me every Tuesday. Second, I'm going to be around so much that you'll have to start screening your calls." I grin from across the booth. "But I do have a favor to ask. Because you haven't already done enough for me, landing me a new job."

"I'm here to serve," she says, mirroring my sarcasm.

"Can you tell me how to handle giving notice to Lynne? Because somehow, wrestling an angry, greased alligator sounds easy in comparison."


I knock on Lynne's door first thing the next morning. "Don't bother setting up an appointment, because she'll tell you she doesn't have time," Naomi instructed me. "And get right to the point."

"I've accepted a new job," I spit out the minute my butt touches the seat of Lynne's guest chair. The irony that I'm quitting less than a week after worrying that I was getting fired isn't lost on me, but I'm still sweating so much that I should have put panty liners under my armpits when I got dressed this morning.

"Cripes, Rogers," Lynne says. She eyes me as though she expects me to recant. When it's clear that I'm not going to, she lets out a sigh, her bony chest heaving visibly. "Who in the hell am I going to hire to replace you? Just tell me you're not going to *Fitness*, because I might have a coronary. Those skinny bitches are determined to bleed me dry."

"I'm not going to *Fitness*. I'm going to be the communications director at Take the Lead. It's an organization that teaches life skills to young girls by training them for a five-K race."

"That's very Mother Teresa of you. I hope it doesn't require a vow of poverty," she says, an amused look on her face.

"They're paying me well."

"Oh. If this is about money—"

"It isn't," I assure her. "And as I told Naomi, it isn't just about the brain story, either. I've been really happy at the magazine, and I truly appreciate the many opportunities I've been given." I pause, searching for the right words. "I'm just at a point in my life where I'm ready to try something new . . . even if taking a leap means I might fall."

She lets out a raspy laugh. "Marissa, mark my word; you're *not* going to fall. You may not like this new job, but you'll land on your feet."

"That's the nicest thing you've ever said to me," I say aloud without thinking.

"Well, now you know my management secret," Lynne says, somehow managing a wink in spite of her highly Botoxed brows. "Never let your employees get a big head, or they'll think they're too good to work for you." She looks at me and smiles. "Clearly, I'm going to have to rethink that strategy."

Later that afternoon, Lynne starts our weekly editorial meeting by announcing that I'm leaving. "I speak for everyone when I say that you'll be sorely missed, Marissa," she says to me from across the giant boardroom table.

"Thank you," I say. "I'm going to miss working here so much. Although I'm sure I'll still read the magazine every month to try to figure out how to finally lose the last ten pounds."

"Puhlease." Naomi laughs. "A year from now, we're going to see your mug on the cover of *Runner's World*."

"I don't think so," I say. I may not be sure of much right now, but I'm positive that competitive running is not in my future.

The meeting drags on, giving the several cups of coffee I drank earlier ample time to make their way into my bladder. When we finally adjourn, I run to the bathroom, seconds away from peeing myself. I exit the stall, only to find Ashley carefully applying lipstick in the mirror.

"I'm sad to hear you're leaving, Marissa," she says, meeting my eyes in the glass reflection. The harsh fluorescent vanity light washes her out and makes her look surprisingly plain, even with her ruby lips. "Of course, I'm looking forward to the challenge of helping fill your shoes," she adds, snapping the silver lid back on her lipstick tube. She spins around to face me. "I know we've had our differences, but I've worked my butt off for you. I hope you believe me when I say I'm really sorry about the Q&A with your friend. I thought you would be thrilled with it, but I realize now that it was a major misstep. You can bet I'll never do anything like that again."

"I'm glad to hear it," I tell her. "And apology accepted."

"Thank you," she says, visibly relieved. She takes a deep breath. "I know it's a lot to ask, but I'd really love it if you'd put in a good word for me with Naomi, so she'll keep me in mind if an associate position opens up." There's a hint of desperation in her voice, and it occurs to me that despite her fem-bot appearance, Ashley does care what people think about her. Still, given the lack of regard she's consistently shown for me, this sudden flash of humanity—however sincere—is too little, too late.

"Oh, Ashley," I say, matching her forced smile with my own genuine one, "I don't think that would be a good idea. But I wish the best of luck to you."

# Thirty-four

After fifteen weeks of training, race day is finally here. The girls arrive at school early Saturday morning, where Naomi, Alanna, and I greet them. A quick head count reveals that everyone except Anna, who's been battling the flu, has shown up. "Our best turnout ever! You guys are awesome!" Naomi cheers. Meanwhile, Alanna and I nurse our coffees and try to appear awake. Alanna turns to me and whispers, "A few years ago, we had only four girls. It was kind of a disaster. So this is a really, really good turnout. Rhonda is going to be thrilled."

We hand out breakfast bars and juice boxes, and after we're sure everyone's eaten, we usher the girls onto the bus waiting to drive us to Queens, where the race will take place.

The girls are uncharacteristically quiet on the ride over. "Are you guys tired?" I ask them.

"Um . . ." says Margarita, slouched low in the pleather bus bench.

"We're *nervous*," says Josie, with an authority that doesn't make her seem nervous in the least.

"I can understand that," I tell them. "This is my first time running a five-K race, too."

"Really?" says Charity, her eyes bulging. "I thought you coaches were, like, runners. You know. *Real* runners."

"Technically, we're all real runners—you and me and everyone else here," I tell her. "But other than gym class when I was younger, I didn't start running until I began practicing with you guys. I don't run races all the time like Coach Alanna does."

"So you're nervous, too," says Margarita, chewing on the straw from her juice box.

"A little," I tell her. "But excited. And remember, we just ran three miles last week at practice. That's the same distance we'll be running today. So I know for a fact that we'll be just fine."

"If you say so," says Josie skeptically, but I can see that she's holding back a grin.

We pull into the gravel parking lot, which is filled with buses and cars. Through the window, I see that girls and coaches and parents have swarmed the field. School flags, Take the Lead banners, and colorful tents blocking the bright April sun are propped up every few feet, making it look almost like a fair. At the base of the parking lot, I spot dozens of corporate sponsor stands offering free food, beverages, and goodie bags.

"This is *huge*," I say to Naomi.

"There are supposed to be almost nine hundred runners today, including the coaches and volunteers who run with the girls," she tells me. "But don't worry, everything's really well organized so the girls don't get overwhelmed."

"You mean so *I* don't get overwhelmed."

"You'll be fine. Although I advise visiting the spa tomorrow. You're going to need it."

We make our way over to a plot of grass that's set aside for the girls' school. There, we arrange blankets on the ground and put up the hand-painted Take the Lead sign we made at the last practice. Several of the girls' parents and siblings have arrived early, and Alanna, Naomi, and I introduce ourselves, making sure to tell each parent a little something about his or her daughter.

Just when I think I've spoken with everyone, a short, curvy woman in a kelly green sundress and high wedge heels saunters over to where I'm standing. Although not particularly beautiful, she's striking all the same, and oozes self-assurance.

"I'm Lorelei Reyes," she says, extending her hand to me. I smile and return her firm handshake, trying in vain to place her. Sensing my uncertainty, she adds with a laugh, "Oh! Sorry. I'm Estrella's mother." *So this is what Naomi and Alanna were referring to. No wonder Estrella is—well, so Estrella.* Even after having known her for all of thirty seconds, I can tell that Lorelei is one of those charismatic, super-confident people who couldn't care less what others think of her. She reminds me at once of Julia.

As if on cue, Estrella spots her. "Mama!" she yells, running over to where we're standing. She throws her arms around her waist and presses her head against her chest.

"Hello, my beauty," says Lorelei, kissing the top of Estrella's head. She turns to me. "Estrella has told me great things about you. I want to thank you for being such a terrific role model for my daughter." Leaning in, she says just loud enough that I can hear her, "You're her favorite coach, you know. I think she identifies with you."

Fifteen weeks ago, this comment probably would not have sat so well with me. But since then, my opinion of Estrella has done quite a turnaround. "Thank you," I say to Lorelei. "You have no idea what a compliment that is." I pat Estrella's arm. "I suppose I don't need to tell you that you've raised an amazing young woman."

"Aww, thanks, Coach Marissa!" Estrella says, unwrapping her arms from around her mother so she can hug me. "I like you, too. Are we going to run together today?"

"You know it, kid," I tell her. "I wouldn't miss it for the world."

The other coaches and I make sure each girl has her race number pinned to her shirt and has had a chance to go to the bathroom. Then, before I know it, Rhonda announces over a loudspeaker that there are just ten minutes until the race begins.

"Okay, girls!" claps Alanna. "Let's form a circle so we can get a good stretch in before we head over to the starting line."

The girls gather round, and Naomi asks each of them to lead a different stretch. As we wind down, I feel myself buzzing with anticipation, and some nervousness, too. I say a silent prayer that everything goes okay.

Holding hands so we won't get separated, we twist and wind through the masses until we reach the roped-in area behind the start line. Alanna leads us in a cheer, and tells the girls that the goal is to do their best. Then she reminds everyone to look for the parents and Welden teachers at the finish line. "They'll walk you back over to our designated area. And remember, if you need anything—Band-Aids, water, snacks—tell one of the volunteers along the way. They'll be wearing Take the Lead shirts, so you can't miss them." All traces of their earlier uncertainty long gone, the girls nod and yell, "Okay!" and "Yeah!" as they jump up and down with excitement.

The horn bleats and we're off.

As she promised, Estrella stays at my side, as do Charity and

Margarita—not an easy feat initially, as oodles of girls and coaches and volunteer "buddy runners" push past us. Although the crowd slows our pace, it's a blessing in disguise; a too-fast takeoff, I've learned, almost always leads to early burnout. "Let me know if you need a break," I tell our little group, and wave at Alanna as she jogs past with Layla and Josie, who are the two fastest girls at our school.

After a few minutes, the crowd thins, and the four of us are able to spread out. The racecourse takes us from the dirt path around the field onto the street, which has been partitioned off from traffic. We run past multifamily homes and churches and schools where bystanders watch, sometimes cheering, sometimes peering curiously at the hundreds of determined young girls trekking past them.

We've been jogging for what seems like years when we make our way to a line of volunteers holding out paper cups filled with water and Gatorade. "Yay, girls!" they holler, clapping and waving. "You can do it! You're almost at the one-mile marker!"

*That's it? Only one mile?* I think with a little disappointment, although I don't dare utter it out loud. Maybe it's the blazing hot sun or my jitters, but this mile has seemed so much longer than in practice.

"Only two miles to go! We are aaaamaaaaazing!" shouts Estrella, tossing her empty paper cup on the ground as the volunteers have instructed us to do. Her gusto instantly shoots down my disappointment. She's right, of course; two more miles is nothing. As I myself told the girls this morning, we've been covering that in practice for almost a month now.

"We can do it!" I cheer, and another group of girls running near us with their coach shouts at me, "Yes you can! Yes you can!" They put out their palms as they pass us and we high-five them.

As we make our way around a corner, I find myself easing into a comfortable stride, even though we're running slower than I would on my own. Every once in a while, Margarita picks up her pace and runs ahead of us, then walks for a few minutes until we catch up with her. "You can go ahead if you want to, Margarita," I tell her, but she shakes her head. "I want to finish with you guys," she says resolutely.

Before I know it, we come up on the second-mile marker.

"We're so close!" says Charity. Ever the joker, she adds, "I can see the finish line from across the field. Maybe we should cut across so we can get there before everyone else."

"We could," I say between breaths, "but we probably wouldn't feel as good about ourselves as if we actually finished the race, now, would we?"

"Probably not," she concedes.

Another loop around the field and I'm officially roasting. I wipe my brow with the edge of my T-shirt, and gladly accept a cup of water when we hit another volunteer stand.

"We can't give up now," says Estrella, splashing some of the water in her cup on her face.

"Nope," I agree with a smile. "We're so close."

"When we see the three-mile sign, let's run as fast as we can to the finish," Margarita tells us.

"That sounds good to me. Sound good to you, girls?" I ask, and they nod in agreement.

But just as the finish line and the crowd of cheering bystanders behind it come into sight, Estrella doubles over in pain.

"My side," she says, clutching at her waist. "It hurts. *Bad.*"

"Let's stop for a second," I tell her. "Margarita, Charity, you can go on ahead if you want. We'll meet you back at the Welden flag."

"No way, Coach Marissa," says Charity. "We've come this whole way together. We're waiting for Estrella."

"Yeah," says Margarita. "She's our friend. Friends don't leave friends behind."

*Damn skippy they don't.* "You girls are amazing," I tell them as I pat Estrella's back softly. Her face bright red, she huffs and puffs, and for a second I'm afraid she's about to start hyperventilating. But she slowly walks her hands up her thighs so that she's upright again. Letting out a big sigh, she says, "Okay. I'm ready. Let's do this thing."

I let out a little laugh. "Let's do it," I say. "We'll run fast if we feel like it, but either way, we're going to cross that finish line."

"Okay!" says Charity, doing a little skip. "Let's go!"

We start to jog again, so slowly that we're practically walking. Within minutes, though, we're back to the pace we were at before. Two hundred yards from the finish line, Margarita looks at Estrella. "How are you feeling?" she asks. "Ready to go fast?"

"I am," says Estrella, and although I swear I detect the slightest hint of pain on her face, she hikes up her arms as though she's about to sprint out of a starting block. "On your mark, get set, go!" she yells, and the girls start running as fast as they can toward the giant TAKE THE LEAD banner over the finish line.

I intend to stay just a few feet behind them, just in case, but Estrella hollers behind her, "Come *on*, Coach Marissa! Through the finish line with us!" I zoom ahead, and on either side of me, Estrella and Margarita grab my hands and lift them up as we cross the bright yellow line, to the cheers of the parents and teachers and other girls waiting.

It's a *Chariots of Fire* moment, but it touches something deep inside of me, and I find myself tearing up as the girls and I group-hug on the side of the track. Like Rhonda predicted, I feel incredible. Four months ago, I could barely run a mile. Now I've just finished 3.2 of them, in a none-too-shabby time of thirty-five minutes and eight seconds. More important, I've finally learned the true meaning of what I've been trying to teach the girls all these months: self-esteem.

# Thirty-five

S*velte* sends me off with a teary if anticlimactic good-bye party. After I've said my last farewell and have packed up two measly boxes with my personal belongings to ship to the Take the Lead offices, I do something I've never done before: skip the elevator and walk down all twenty-four flights of stairs to the lobby. Then I walk a block to the F stop, calves aching slightly, and hop on the subway. I expect to feel different somehow—after all, this is the last time for the foreseeable future that I'll do this exact commute, and moreover, I've literally just left a perfectly good job to do something that I'm still not convinced I'm qualified for—but as the train rumbles along the tracks, all I can think about is how I feel utterly untransformed. Somehow, though, this comforts me; I've done enough evolving recently to last the entire decade.

When I get home, Dave is waiting for me with a bottle of champagne. "I thought a celebration was in order, so I took off early," he says, pulling out the cork. Golden-white bubbles spill over the side of the bottle, but Dave just laughs. "It's good luck," he says, filling our glasses. He holds one out to me, and I clink it with his.

"To good luck," I say.

"And new beginnings," he says, meeting my eyes.

After we take a sip, Dave pulls me close. "Marissa, I love you," he says, touching his forehead to mine. *Who needs closure?* I think. *There's nothing better than this, right here and now.*

"And I love *you*," I say. "More than anything."

"Really?" he asks.

"Really," I tell him. "You're my life."

He pulls back so he can see me, and gently pushes my hair away from my face.

"Marry me," he whispers, his eyes searching my face.

This time, my instinct isn't to run. Because unlike when Nathan proposed so many years ago, I am not young and stupid and afraid of love. I am ready for commitment and its consequences.

I tilt my chin up and our lips meet. "Yes," I mouth before kissing him. "Yes, yes, yes, yes, and yes."

"That wasn't planned," he confesses later. We're sitting in the swinging bench on our patio finishing off the last of the champagne. It's one of the first warm evenings of the spring, and above us, a splattering of stars are peeking out from behind some lingering clouds. "I'm sorry I didn't have a ring ready. I looked at a few, but nothing seemed just right . . . and I thought I'd have at least a few more weeks to search."

"I don't care about a ring," I tell him. "That was perfect. I love that you did it because the moment was right, not because you had a whole elaborate thing set up."

"Well, now that we're doing true confessions, I didn't actually have *anything* planned. I was at a total loss for how to propose. But, damn, am I ever glad I did it anyway," he says, smiling at me.

"Mr. Bergman, are you losing your super-anal streak?" I tease.

"Future Mrs. Bergman, you'd better not be giving me a hard time. You yourself said that this turned out perfectly," he says. He kisses me again and I bite his bottom lip playfully. Then I look at him: his wavy brown hair, the hint of freckles across his high cheekbones, his deep-set eyes, which make him look thoughtful even when he's completely zoned out during a Saturday afternoon Xbox marathon. This is the man I'm choosing to spend the rest of my life with. It is an overwhelming but wonderful thought.

"Um, holy crap. We're getting married," I tell him.

"We're getting married," Dave says, his whole face lit up. "It's officially the end of our youth—although I'm sure several of our friends would say that we gave that up the minute we moved in together. That's how I knew I wanted to marry you, by the way."

"Why's that?"

"Because even though the past six months have been ridiculously hard, with everything that's been going on, they've been the best six months of my life. I love waking up to you every morning and curling up with you every night." He takes my hand and draws little circles around my ring finger. "So who are you going to tell first?"

My instinct is to say Julia. If this were a year ago, I would have texted her within minutes of Dave's proposal. But it's not, and while I love my friend, I don't want her to pop the blissful bubble I'm floating in with some comment about how Dave's not the one for me.

"I think I'm going to wait to tell everyone back home. We'll see them soon, anyway," I tell him, referring to the fact that we've agreed to spend the upcoming weekend in Michigan. "We can make our announcement then."

"Okay. But do you care if I call my parents tonight?" he asks, looking vaguely worried.

"Of course not!" I say, hugging him. "Let's call them together. I can't wait to tell your mom."

"And I can't wait to tell your mom," he tells me with a slightly evil grin on his face. "Just wait until we tell her that we're going to get you good and fat for the wedding."

# Thirty-six

plan; my subconscious laughs. Despite my intention to keep the engagement secret until Dave and I are with my whole family, the minute I see Sarah I blurt out, "We're engaged!"

"Oh my God, oh my God!" Sarah screams, bouncing up and down in the passenger seat of the Death Star. As usual, she has insisted on picking me up from the airport instead of letting Dave and me rent a car.

"*Ahem*," coughs Marcus from behind the wheel. "Language, Sarah."

"Whatever," she scoffs. "If ever there was a time to take the Lord's name in vain, Marcus, I think this is it." She leans over the armrest to give me a hug. "I am *so* excited for you. But tell me this doesn't mean I have to wear a Pepto-Bismol bridesmaid dress? Please?"

"Not to worry, my dear sister. Not only will there not be a trace of pastel at the ceremony, I'm not even sure that I want to have a bridal party. Although we really haven't worked out the details yet."

"Really? No bridal party?" Sarah says, looking slightly disappointed. Then her face brightens. "Who cares? You're getting hitched! Just wait until Ella finds out. Now you'll *officially* be Uncle Dave," she says to Dave.

"I could get used to that," he says bashfully, and I swear I detect the slightest flush across his cheeks.

Making our way down the highway, we pass field after field. In one green swath of land, I spot a deer and her two fawns in the distance, taking advantage of the last bit of light left in the evening. I feel a sentimental pang. I may have spent my childhood and adolescence dreaming about New York, but Michigan was home. Now, with my engagement, it's as though I've fully admitted that I won't be returning to the place that had so much to do with the person I became.

"I'm guessing Mom doesn't know?" Sarah asks.

"Uh-uh. I was going to tell you guys at dinner Saturday night. But apparently I'm not very good at keeping secrets."

"Well, I am *so* glad you told me!" she says, and I almost expect her to clap her hands and yell, "Go, team!" like she used to during her high school cheerleading days. "I bet I still have a stack of my *Brides* in the basement somewhere. I'll dig them up and we can start brainstorming for dresses."

"Looks like you and I will be spending all weekend shooting hoops," says Marcus, looking at Dave in the rearview mirror. "But seriously, congrats, dude."

"Thanks, dude," says Dave, and we all laugh.

. . .

It's already seven when we get to Sarah and Marcus's house, so we reluctantly wolf down pastrami sandwiches that deserve to be savored and retreat upstairs to unpack and get ready. "Are you sure you're prepared for this?" Dave asks, pulling a stack of neatly folded T-shirts and underwear out of his suitcase and placing them in the dresser in Sarah's guest bedroom. He's referring to the fact that we'll soon be heading over to Julia's for her housewarming party. I'm excited to see her and her new place, but I'm nervous, too, if only because I'm not sure how she'll react to the news that Dave and I are engaged.

"I'm ready," I tell Dave. "Ready as I'll ever be. Just swear you'll pry the vodka bottle from my hands if things get too bad."

"Not only will I do that, I'll hold your hair while you're praying to the porcelain goddess," Dave says, and kisses my shoulder.

"See? Now, that is exactly why I'm marrying you," I tell him. "Whoever says attorneys are good for nothing has clearly never met my barf buddy and future husband. Now, let's get out of here before I change my mind."

Julia's garden-level flat is nestled on a sleepy street just outside the center of town. As Dave and I pull up, I spot a small group mingling on her front lawn. "As usual, she hasn't had much trouble making friends," I tell Dave.

"I can't imagine Julia ever having trouble meeting people," he says, and I can't tell if it's a compliment.

"Go easy on her, okay?"

"M, I am always, always easy on her," says Dave, trailing behind me on the cement sidewalk that leads up to Julia's new place. "Come on. Let's stop stressing and go have a good time."

When we reach her, Julia is standing in the center of the grass, engrossed in conversation with a slimy-looking guy in a tight black T-shirt that shows off his bulging muscles, whom I assume is Rich. His hand rests possessively on her arm, and I resist the urge to swat it away.

"Marissa!" she squeaks when she sees me, handing her drink to Rich without looking to see if he's taken it from her. Fortunately, he's quick enough to grab the glass before it can crash to the ground.

"Jules." I embrace her, breathing in the familiar gardenia scent of her hair. "I can't believe it's been so long. You look amazing, as always." I say this in no small part because she's traded her favorite purple attire for a short silver dress from her preaccident days. She stands out among the sea of jeans and T-shirts, but she looks fantastic: Ann Arbor's very own Holly Golightly.

"As do you, skinny minny!" she says, surveying me as though it's the first time she's seen me up close in ages. I suppose I do look a little different. After finally calling it quits on my futile attempt to lose the twenty pounds I packed on over the past few years, the most curious thing happened: Ten of them fell right off. Even better, I've decided that the sleek runners' muscles I've recently acquired make me look better than I ever have—strong but still curvy.

Julia gestures to her left. "Marissa, Dave, this is Rich."

"So great to finally meet you," he says, extending his hand to me, and then Dave. "Julia talks about you *all* the time. I've even seen the complete Julia and Marissa photo collection. The early high school photos are priceless," he says, smiling, and in spite of myself, I find him markedly less loathsome than I did a minute ago.

"The high school photos? Ugh." I groan. "Some memories aren't meant to be revisited. Those bangs were—well, you saw them." I look at Rich again and realize that apart from his pending divorce,

I know absolutely nothing about him. "So where did you guys meet?" I ask.

"Jules didn't tell you?" He turns to her with a questioning look on his face. I'm usually the one to know everything about Julia, and here is some stranger, checking to see if it's okay to tell *me* something. It's an odd feeling, to say the least. "We met at group therapy," he says after Julia nods her approval. "For brain injury survivors. I was in Iraq three years ago when my Humvee was hit by an IED. I suffered major head trauma, although it was a good six months before I was actually diagnosed."

"But you . . ."

"Seem normal?" asks Rich. He chuckles, causing his crow's-feet to crinkle up, and I see that he's probably a decade older than I initially took him for. "Tell my ex that. It's been a tough couple of years, to say the least. I've had, uh—how to put this delicately? Temper problems."

*Great,* I think, but Rich says, "Don't worry, not temper problems of the domestic violence variety. But little, stupid things would set me off, especially before I started therapy. I ended up being discharged from the military, but it took me another eight months to find a civilian job because I wasn't ready for the real world. When I finally got hired at a consulting company, my neurologist had to meet with my colleagues so they understood the problems I was having." He shakes his head at the memory. "That was really what set my wife over the edge—thinking that I wouldn't be able to bring home my share of the bacon. So she started sleeping with my cousin. What a dick." He looks at us sheepishly. "Sorry. That's what I mean about the temper." *And the lack of filter,* I think.

Dave whistles at Rich's story. "Man. That is horrible."

"Yep. But the silver lining is Julia," says Rich, looking at her like he's not sure what she's doing in front of him. It's an expression

I've seen dozens of men give her, but this is different. In spite of his tough appearance, Rich seems almost provincial in comparison to the choreographers and artists and musicians she usually favors. And yet maybe he is exactly what Julia needs at this point in her life.

"Come on, I want to show you around," Julia says to me, and we leave Rich and Dave chatting on the lawn. "The apartment is barely set up, but you'll get the general idea." She yanks open the creaky screen door and we're hit with a wave of eau de cat urine. "Is that Snowball I detect?" I ask, trying not to scrunch up my nose.

"No, Snowball's completely litter trained, the little angel," she says, not insulted in the least. "The girls who used to live here had a bunch of animals and they really destroyed the place. Which is why I got such a good deal on it, I suppose. But don't worry, I've got air fresheners that should fix the stench by the end of the month."

We make our way to the kitchen, which is quaint if outdated, and reminds me a little of Dave's parents' place if it had been decorated in the seventies. Julia grabs a couple beers from the fridge door and hands me one. Then she leans against the yellow Formica countertop and takes a swig from her bottle. "It's not Buckingham Palace, obviously, but I do like it here," she says, looking around. "And I wouldn't let my parents pay a dime for it, which makes it even better. Dr. Gopal and I discussed it and decided that it would be a positive step for me to pay my own way as much as I'm able to." She bites her bottom lip, making her look like a child. I feel an urge to pat her back and tell her it will be okay, although I know that this is precisely what she does not want from me or anyone else. A wave of melancholy rises up in my chest when I think about how hard this must be for her. Not only has she given up her former life, but she also knows that everyone is hoping and waiting for her to return to the person she used to be.

"I'm impressed, Jules," I tell her. "Did Grace and Jim put up a fight when you told them no?"

"Grace wouldn't dare." Julia laughs with a hint of her old mischief. "She's terrified of me these days, poor thing."

"I think she's always been a little afraid of you," I tell her, thinking back to high school when Julia would run circles around her mother until she gave her what she wanted—a Ford pickup truck to replace her brand-new Audi sedan, permission to go to Cancún for spring break, her blessing on yet another doomed relationship.

"Listen, Mar, I should warn you . . ." she says suddenly, her eyes flashing with alarm. Before I can turn around to see why, a voice from behind me raises the hairs on the back of my neck.

"Hey, Marissa."

I stand, frozen, staring at Julia with disbelief. "Julia," I whisper sharply, "I thought we discussed this." I'm angrier at myself than I am at her; clearly, it was a mistake to assume that she would behave.

To her credit, she at least has the wherewithal to look embarrassed. "I was just going to say that I hope you don't mind that I invited Nathan. Speaking of the—the—" she says, floundering for the correct word.

"Devil?" Nathan volunteers. When it's clear that I will not or cannot seem to unplant my feet from where I'm standing, he walks in front of the fridge to face me. "Happy to see you, too," he drawls, grinning ear to ear.

*So much for my plans to never speak to Nathan again.* "Uh, yeah," I respond, sweating furiously and praying that Dave doesn't venture into the kitchen this very second. I'm visibly tongue-tied as I try to figure out how to react, but Nathan is his usual cool-cucumber self and fills in the gaps with ease.

"I was hoping to see you here. Especially after I never heard back from you," he says, digging his hands into his jeans pockets and giving me his best poor-little-me face. It may have worked the last time I saw him, but this time, it doesn't make my pulse race or send little flutters through my stomach.

No, this time it triggers a memory of an incident I haven't thought of once in the eleven years since it happened.

A month or so after Nathan and I started dating, I came down with a horrible flu. I couldn't get out of bed, even to take my final exams, and had to go to the emergency room at one point because my fever was so high. I holed up at Nathan's apartment and he watched over me, feeding me ice chips and little spoonfuls of soup, draping my forehead with damp washcloths, calling my doctor to find out how much cold medicine I could safely take.

Then, after seven harrowing days, I was fine. It could not be said that I looked as normal as I felt, however: My hair hung in clumps around my sallow face, and I had dropped so much weight that I could pull my jeans, fully zipped, down over my hips.

"Crap, I lost thirteen pounds," I said to Nathan, looking down with shock at the bathroom scale. Just to be certain, I stepped off of it and then on again, and the large black digits confirmed that I was officially thinner than I'd ever been since hitting puberty.

"Well, you're always saying you want to be skinnier," Nathan said, looking up at me from where he sat on the edge of his mint-green bathtub. "If you can keep the weight off now, you'll be set."

Although part of me was delighted in my newfound status as a waif, his words were still a slap in the face. It was the type of comment I'd expect from my mother, not my boyfriend. "So you're saying that I needed to lose weight?"

"No," he said defensively. "You're the one who's always obsessing about how thin you are or aren't. I just thought this would be something you'd be happy about.

"Come on, Marissa. I didn't mean anything by it," he said, laying on the charm. "Forget I ever said anything."

I didn't want to get in a fight with him, so I pretended to forget about it. And in time, I eventually did.

It's not as though I've just conjured up a memory of him tossing fresh dirt on a suspicious hole in the backyard in the middle of the night, or crawling out of bed with my sister. Which is too bad, because it would be so much easier if I were Tori Spelling and my life was a Lifetime movie. Then, at least, Nathan would clearly be the villain, and I, the heroine, would have bravely thrown him down a stairwell just before the police showed up. Then, with dignity and grace, I would have moved on.

But Nathan is not a monster. He's just a normal person with whom I happen to share a past. And it's not his fault that I've not only clung to that past, I've actually repainted it in the rosiest hue, when in fact it was messy and imperfect and far from ideal.

But what makes me feel especially horrible, I realize as I look back and forth between Julia and Nathan, is that I've given him the ultimate free pass while storing up resentment against her for one stupid thing that she did eleven years ago. This, in spite of the fact that Julia has been there for me for more than half my life. She is not perfect, I know. She can be needy and steals the spotlight without thinking about it. But she is the best friend I have ever had.

"I'm sorry," I tell Nathan, who continues to stare me down as though he's trying to master mind control. "I may have given you the wrong impression before, but I'm in love with Dave. My fiancé," I add. "We're engaged."

Julia lets out yet another squeal. "You're engaged! That's huge!" she says, giving me a hug, and my shoulders unclench in relief at her relatively drama-free reaction. From over her back, I see Nathan looking skeptically at my bare ring finger, but I don't bother explaining. After Julia finally stops squeezing me, I catch Dave's eye from across the apartment and wave for him to come over. I swallow hard, determined not to let my voice break. "There he is now," I say purposefully to Nathan.

"Hey, guys," he says to Julia and me. "I'm Dave," he introduces himself to Nathan.

"And I'm Nathan. You're one lucky guy, Dave," Nathan responds.

"I've been getting that a lot lately," Dave says, smiling slowly. "But I already knew it."

I look at the two of them in front of me and a wave of dizziness washes over me. It's not unlike the uncanny sensation I get occasionally after having one too many glasses of wine and then looking in the mirror: *Holy crap! That's you—that's really what you look like and this is your life!* Only this time, that little voice is saying, *Marissa Rogers, it's decision time! To your left, you have your past. And to your right, your future. Which man will you choose?*

*I made my choice years ago,* I remind myself. *And then I made it again three days ago when I said yes to Dave.* Because that's really what it comes down to. I've clung to the idea of Nathan because I felt like he was an option that was taken from me. But the truth is, while Julia may have pushed the issue, I ultimately made the choice myself. If I hadn't been so happy to constantly play second fiddle to Julia, to put our friendship above everything else—even my own happiness—then I could have stood up to her. Then maybe, just maybe, Nathan and I would be together today. But as I look at him, I suddenly understand that as painful as our past may be for me, our lives ultimately unfolded the exact way they were supposed to.

"I'm going to get going," says Nathan. "I'll see you around, Julia," he says, kissing her cheek good-bye. Then he looks at me for a second too long, as though he's trying to commit my face to memory. "Good-bye, Marissa," he says finally.

"Good-bye, Nathan," I tell him for the last time.

"Can I talk to you?" I ask Julia after Nathan has left.

"Um . . ." She stalls. "Right now?"

"Right now," I say firmly.

"Okay. Bedroom," she says, and motions me toward a door off the hallway.

The room is different from the one at her parents' house. Although the violet throw and pillows are in place, her purple knickknacks are gone, and the walls are painted a subtle cream color. "I like it," I tell her.

"Me, too. Although Rich is the one who told me no purple walls. He said it gave him a headache."

"Jules," I say, realizing I shouldn't derail the conversation discussing décor, "we need to talk about what just happened back there. About what's been happening in general." I shift on the bed so that we're both facing each other. "I thought you understood what I said before, and at this point, I don't know how I can make this any clearer: Nathan and I are *over.* We've been over for more than a decade now. I am going to marry Dave, and even though I can't ask you to like him, I need you to at least support me in this."

"I like Dave," she says. She is clenching a throw pillow and I notice that she's shaking slightly. *She's actually nervous to have this conversation with me*, I realize with surprise.

"I've always liked him, you know that," she tells me. "It's just that—well, my brain injury makes me really prone to fixations."

"I remember," I say, although I don't add that her purple passion is a constant reminder of that.

"Yeah, but it's not just things like colors," she says. "It's ideas and associations. When I saw you in the hospital, all I could think about was you and Nathan. It's like every time I saw your face all I could think about was how I made you break up with him in college."

"You didn't *make* me."

"Mar, I knew that you would choose me over him. I knew that you were so loyal to me that it wouldn't feel like a decision at all." She smiles wistfully. "Dr. Gopal has helped me understand that long before the accident, I had been burying the guilt I felt about doing that to you, and to him. You're the only true friend I've ever had, and I thought that Nathan would take that away."

"Julia, remember what you told me?" I blink back tears. "No man is ever going to come between us. Not Nathan, not Dave, and not anyone else. It doesn't have to be a choice."

"That's exactly what Dr. Gopal said," she confesses. "After the accident, I was able to really see how much I'd jeopardized our friendship, and I became obsessed with making things right. That's why I started e-mailing Nathan and trying to bring the two of you together. I even told Dave that you and Nathan were meant to be, which I realize now was unbelievably stupid."

"You told Dave that Nathan and I were supposed to be together?" *So that's why he had such an issue with her.*

"Yeah, when I came to visit. I cornered him when you were in the shower. Sorry," she says, looking sheepish. "I got a serious earful from Dr. Gopal about that one."

"It's okay," I tell her. I have some serious explaining to do to Dave about Julia's behavior toward him. Tomorrow, though. One thing at a time.

"Mar, the thing is, I still have those thoughts. They might never go away. I mean, I even invited Nathan here tonight when I knew I shouldn't have. But I'm getting better at ignoring my obsessions." She squeezes my hand again and locks her eyes with mine. "I want you to have the life that you want, even if I don't always know how to show it. Just promise you'll be patient with me, that you won't leave me. I don't know what I would do if we weren't friends."

"Jules, I am never going to leave you. We will always be friends," I tell her. As I say this, I know that it's the truth. Staying friends will mean that I have to let go of the misunderstandings, arguments, and hurtful comments again and again and again—maybe even forever, if Julia never fully heals. But it's a commitment that I'm willing to make.

I hold up my pinky, and Julia hooks it with her own.

"Always."

# Thirty-seven

From a distance, we look like one, big happy family enjoying a backyard barbecue on a Saturday afternoon. And I suppose we sort of are.

Which is not to say that things are going smoothly. Dave has managed to burn half his palm off trying to rescue a hamburger patty that escaped between the grill grates, Sarah and Marcus have already had two squabbles about God only knows what, and the ribs and burgers are cooked long before my mother and Phil decide to make an appearance. On top of this, Grace, Jim, and Julia, who are supposed to swing by, are MIA.

I pull my phone out of my purse, but before I can dial, Grace's number lights up on the screen. "I'm so sorry for the last-minute notice, but we have to cancel. Julia got a horrible migraine earlier on the way over to our place and it hasn't gone away," she apologizes.

Her voice drops to a whisper. "It was a bad morning, unfortunately. She also had screaming fit when Jim told her we were thinking of selling the house next year. It wasn't the best timing on our part, I suppose."

I'm surprised to hear about their house—they've lived there since before Julia was born—but more surprised about the news that Julia isn't doing well. "She seemed great last night," I tell her. "We had a really good talk."

"Oh, it's just the whole one step forward, two steps back thing. Anyway," Grace says, "in the grand scheme, Julia is doing excellently. Her neurologist says that she's progressing further and faster than he ever expected her to, given how bad her scans looked last September."

"She always has been an overachiever."

"That's true," she says, and I hear her mumble something in the background. "Marissa, darling, I have to run, but Julia did ask me to ask if you'd swing by her place tomorrow. She wanted to see you one last time before you head back to New York. Say around one?"

"I'll be there."

I toss the phone back in my bag and through Sarah's picture window, spot my mother and Phil pulling up in his burgundy Cadillac.

"How nice of them to show up before midnight," I say sarcastically as Sarah hands me a block of cheese and an industrial-size cheese grater.

"Some things never change," she sighs, tossing chopped cucumbers into the salad bowl on the counter. I take a bite of cheese I've just shredded and sigh even louder, and we both giggle.

Never one to help her cause, my mother walks through the front door with her head held high, making her best Jacqueline

Kennedy-at-the-funeral face. She embraces me awkwardly, but holds on longer than usual.

"Hey, Mom. Happy to see you," I tell her when she finally lets me go.

"Good to see you, too, Marissa," she says, and then looks at me almost suspiciously to see if I'm going to say anything snide. She should know me better than that, I think, but then it occurs to me that I've pulled quite a few wild cards on her recently and she probably has no idea what to expect anymore. I smile blandly, but it's apparently not reassuring enough, because she says, "Sarah, you have pinot grigio, right? I could really use a drink."

"Of course, Mom," says Sarah. She turns to me, her back to my mother, and makes a silent screaming expression.

"Just checking, dear. Just checking," my mother trills obliviously.

Experienced domestic dictator that she is, Sarah whistles to get everyone into the kitchen, and then parcels out various tasks. Dave and I have been directed to carry out an ice-filled copper tub filled with enough drinks to quench the entire U of M football team. Dave grabs the tub with his good hand and looks over his shoulder to make sure my mom and Phil are out of earshot. "I think we should tell them before we eat," he whispers. "The suspense is killing me."

"Really? Because I kind of think we should wait until a few days before the wedding to give my mom the news," I say.

"Too bad you didn't feel that way yesterday," he teases me.

"That's not fair." I kick his ankle with the edge of my sandal and he pretends to be in horrific pain.

"What's not fair?" asks my mother, coming up behind me with the salad bowl precariously in one hand, her glass of wine in the other. She puts both on the rustic wood table in the center of the backyard and flops down on a lawn chair.

"Nothing, Mom," I tell her.

"Dave, what secrets is my daughter keeping from me now?" she asks, fanning herself in spite of the fact that it's a perfect sixty-five degrees out.

"She's pregnant with an alien love child," says Sarah, Marcus and Ella trailing behind her with food in their arms.

"Now *that's* our ticket to fame and fortune," says Phil.

"Actually, now that we're all here . . ." says Dave. He holds my hand. "Marissa and I got engaged on Wednesday. We're getting married."

Ella squeals and jumps up, toppling her chair over. Not bothering to pick it up, she runs over and wraps her arms around my waist. "Auntie Marissa! You're going to be a bride! Can I go dress shopping with you? Pretty please?"

"Of course, cutie. We'll need to find you a flower girl dress, too."

"This is excellent news," says Phil, clapping Dave so hard on the back that Dave looks like he's about to choke. Then, for the first time ever, Phil hugs me. "Really happy for you guys. It seems like you're made for each other."

"Thanks, Phil," I say, blinking away tears.

My mother provides just the comic foil I need to keep me from crying. "Oh my goodness!" she cries, putting the back of her hand on her forehead dramatically. "My little girl is all grown up!" She's right, but it's not my engagement that's planted my feet firmly in adulthood. The past year has challenged me in ways that I never could have imagined, and yet I've surprised myself, increasingly able to take sharp turns like a pro. I look at Dave, who is beaming at me, and know that I'm more than ready to move on to the next chapter of my life.

"Susan, why don't you give a toast?" Phil suggests, reaching for the water glass in front of him.

"Sure," says my mother, although she doesn't look thrilled to have been volunteered for the task. She clears her throat and pauses for a second, searching for the right words.

I expect her to say something about how she doesn't understand how I was able to land a catch like Dave. Instead, she raises her wineglass and says, "Dave, as everyone in this family will attest, Marissa is a remarkable woman, and I have no doubt that she'll make an incredible wife, and a far better mother than I could ever be. Congratulations from all of us."

"Thank you, Mom," I say. "That means more than you know. Cheers."

"Cheers," my family responds, and we clink our glasses together.

The following day, I leave Dave to shoot hoops with Marcus and drive the Death Star to Julia's apartment by myself. When I get there, a purple Post-it note is tacked to the door.

*M—went back to my parents' house. Meet me there? xo, J*

I know Julia has a cell phone; is it so hard for her to call? But I quickly shake off my irritation and remind myself that the extra seven minutes it will take to drive from here to there is not a major inconvenience. After all, I don't how long it will be until my next trip to Michigan, and I want to at least say good-bye before I leave.

There's no answer when I knock on the door at the Ferrars', but the side entrance is open, so I let myself in. I wander into the kitchen, which smells like fresh bread, probably from one of Julia's baking sprees. "Hello?" I call out, but my voice is met with silence. As I walk down the hall, I hear a faint but frantic violin concerto coming from the far end of the house. Julia's not in her room when I peek my head in, so I follow the music to the old library-turned-dance studio. Of the hundreds of times I've been back at the Ferrars' since high school, I can't remember being in this room.

"Jules?" I call as I walk down the stairs into the sunken studio, which looks just as it did when I last saw it.

As I step in the room, I catch Julia in midleap, her legs in a perfect split several feet above the ground; her arms outstretched, swanlike. She lands expertly on the polished wood floor and pivots around to face me.

"Haven't you heard of knocking?" she says, eyes narrowing suspiciously. Then she smiles wickedly. "I'm kidding, Mar. But really, you don't want me to break an ankle."

"Jules, what are you doing?" I ask, shaken. "I thought you couldn't dance? Shouldn't your mom or someone be here—you know, just in case you bump your head or something?"

"Don't be ridiculous!" She laughs, and bends forward gracefully to tuck in the ribbon on her well-worn pointe shoe. "You *know* I know how to dance. Don't worry, I'm not going to hurt myself."

And with that, she returns to her position in front of the mirrored wall. She adjusts the knotted T-shirt covering her black leotard impatiently. Then, swiftly lifting her right knee, with her arms circled in front of her, she begins pirouetting in time to the music as though it were her only purpose in life.

Of all the body's organs, the brain is particularly delicate. It is also strong and stubborn and, of course, extremely intelligent. Because of this, it will desperately try to repair itself after injury. A devastated neuron may spontaneously attempt to regrow any healthy fibers that remain to compensate for the deficit the rest of its ravaged frame leaves behind. It's an imperfect, easily derailed process; it can cause surviving neurons to misfire and connect with healthy neurons in ways that researchers believe may contribute to pain, seizures, movement, and memory problems.

But often those surviving neurons hit their intended target. And that's why, even years later, many people who have suffered a traumatic brain injury continue to improve their memories—and with every year that goes by, become more and more like their former selves.

As I watch my best friend dancing, as beautiful as she's ever been, I whisper, *Thank you.* To God. To the universe. To Julia, for remembering the person she was.

. . .

# Resources on Traumatic Brain Injury

E ach year, an estimated 1.4 to 1.7 million people in the United States will suffer a brain injury. If you're one of them, or know someone who has experienced head trauma, here are resources that can help.

**The Brain Injury Association of America** offers information about brain injury research and legislation, as well as support for individuals living with brain injury.

1-703-761-0750

www.biausa.org

**The Family Caregiver Alliance** has a section on its Web site with reading recommendations and other support resources for family members of individuals with brain injury.

http://www.caregiver.org/caregiver/jsp/content_node.jsp?nodeid=579

**The National Institutes of Health's** Web site has a dedicated brain injury section that provides information and research, as well as links to ongoing clinical trials for individuals with brain injury.

http://www.ninds.nih.gov/disorders/tbi/tbi.htm

Call the **National Brain Injury Information Center** to connect with a brain injury specialist.

1-800-444-6443

**ReMIND/Bob Woodruff Foundation** provides resources and support to injured service members, veterans, and their families.

http://remind.org
info@ReMIND.org

**The Traumatic Brain Injury National Resource Center**'s Web site has answers to frequently asked questions about brain injury.

http://www.neuro.pmr.vcu.edu/faq/faq.asp?FAQ=21

**Think First National Injury Prevention Foundation** provides educational resources and holds events on preventing head injuries.

1-800-THINK-56
www.thinkfirst.org

# Acknowledgments

I often tell people that I won the literary lottery when my agent, Elisabeth Weed, offered to represent me—and it's true. This novel wouldn't exist if it weren't for her insight, enthusiasm and guidance.

A heartfelt thanks to Denise Roy, my brilliant editor at Dutton, with whom I share both a birthday and a sensibility. Seeing this story evolve under her direction has been humbling and incredibly gratifying, and I'm forever grateful that she took it on.

I'm indebted to Nadia Kashper, Christine Ball, Liza Cassity, and the rest of the Penguin team, as well as Stephanie Sun at Weed Literary and the Jenny Meyer Literary Agency, for their assistance throughout this crazy publishing process.

Thanks to Darci Smith, for cheering me on throughout the first draft; to my early readers, Laurel Lambert and Shannon Callahan, who assured me that *The Art of Forgetting* really was a tale worth telling; and to Bunny Wong, whom I miss dearly and whose wise words kept me writing even on the worst of days.

Thank you to my brunch partners and support system, Britt Carlson, Katie McHugh, Sara Reistad-Long, and Rachael Stiles; and to the writers who have inspired and assisted me along the way: Sarah Jio, Emma Johnson, Jael McHenry, Beth Hoffman, Maris Kreizman, Siobhan O'Connor, Sarah Pekkanen, J. Courtney Sullivan, Laura Vanderkam, Julie Weingarden Dubin, and Allison Winn Scotch.

For sharing their knowledge of brain injury, thank you to doctors Ausim Azizi, Amarish Dave, and Alain de Lotbiniere. And thank you to Girls on the Run (www.girlsontherun.org), an incredible organization I was fortunate enough to be a part of, and which inspired parts of this novel.

I'm so grateful to have the support of my family. Special thanks to my grandmother, Patricia Pietrzak, for encouraging my love of the written word (even if it meant slipping me V. C. Andrews' novels behind my mother's back); to Bill Pietrzak and Joyce Nelson for their constant support over the years; to my parents, Tip and Vanessa Noe; and to my sisters, Laurel Lambert and Janette Noe, who just happen to be my closest friends. And, of course, thank you to my children, who give me meaning.

Lastly, thank you to my husband, JP Pagán, who forever changed my life for the better when he walked into it ten years ago.

## ABOUT THE AUTHOR

Camille Noe Pagán's work has appeared in numerous national publications, including *Allure, Cooking Light, Glamour, SELF,* and *Women's Health*. A former magazine and online editor, she recently moved from Brooklyn, New York, to Ann Arbor, Michigan, where she lives with her husband and children. Visit her at www.camillenoepagan.com.